# Out of the Wilderness
## SeaMount Series
## Book 1

## Anita K. Greene

*Anita K. Greene*

# Dedication

To Mommy and Daddy,
For showing me the meaning of love
And encouraging me to use my gifts.
I love you.

*For I am about to do something new. See, I have already begun! Do you not see it? I will make a pathway through the wilderness. I will create rivers in the dry wasteland.*
*, Isaiah 43:19*

# Chapter 1

In the murky light of dawn, Grayson Kerr hunkered down in the rough, weedy fringe that separated the logging road from the forest. Suspicion crawled up his back like a hot rash.

Had the SeaMount Agency planted the mini van for him to find? Nothing about the last three days made much sense. A demented Boy Scout obsessed with treasure hunts must have created this wilderness survival trial. The haphazard trek from checkpoint to checkpoint was enough to make a man woods queer.

Gray burrowed a hand beneath the layer of dry grass stuffed between his long sleeve camouflage shirt and tee. The grass made him itch, but at this elevation the added insulation kept him warm. Soft stuffing from the seat of the van would be a welcome improvement, but only if this opportunity to upgrade his stash of survival gear from next to nothing to something, wasn't a lure into a new kind of perdition.

The tang of balsam scented the air. From high in the trees a faint chirp heralded the start of a new day. He unsheathed his knife. The early light softened the angles and edges of the fixed black blade. Hunched low he left the scrub's protection and moved to the front of the van. It had a Rhode Island license plate.

Three nights ago he'd gone to sleep at the SeaMount Agency headquartered in Rhode Island. He awoke the next morning beneath a pine tree in the middle of Nowhere, Maine with a serious case of brain fog. A crude map and instructions were pinned to the tree by the point of his own knife. He'd inspected his watch, knife and every stitch of clothing he wore and still couldn't figure out how SeaMount tracked him. He assumed they had eyes on him to extract him if he ran into trouble. Or worse, became truly lost. That would deep six his chance to work for them. Lost was not an option. He needed the job.

Sidling up on the driver's side, Gray peered into the dim interior. A woman reclined in the driver's seat. She was wrapped in a quilt and sound asleep. Her hair fell in gold ringlets about her attractive face. By the look of her jewelry and manicured fingernails, he'd found himself a real girly girl. What was a woman like her doing out here far from civilization? She should be home cozied up in a warm bed. Was she bait and the girly stuff window dressing? Did SeaMount even *have* female agents?

*You're about to find out, Kerr.* Gray tightened his grip on the knife keeping it low and out of sight. "Rise and shine, Blondie." He rapped on the window.

She jerked awake. Confusion flickered across her face. Her gaze landed on him. Mouth wide open and tonsils vibrating, she screamed. The confines of the van muted the volume of her voice, but couldn't mask the alarm on her face. Her hand came into view brandishing a heavy flashlight.

Pleased she didn't aim a gun at him, Gray focused on the back seat where shadowy movement produced thumps and more shrieks of panic.

A small pixie face framed in dark braids pressed against the window.

Gray muttered an expletive. A kid!

Two other faces popped into view. One with ears wired for sound, the other with hair so pale it appeared white in the gloomy interior of the van.

The Agency did things differently for sure, but even they wouldn't involve kids in an exercise like this. Which left only one other option. He'd stumbled on a nest of civilians.

"Go away." The woman shook the flashlight at him.

If he were smart he'd leave. But he'd never figured himself as overly bright. To get what he wanted he'd need to calm them down. Discreetly, he sheathed his knife. "Take it easy. You're safe." The panicked females made the van bounce like a desert patrol vehicle on rough terrain. Gray rubbed a hand across his face. Flakes of swamp mud fell from his three days growth of beard to his dirty shirt lumpy with grass. Not an appearance to inspire trust. He could easily take what he wanted from them. A hard knot formed in his gut. Never before had he preyed on those weaker than him. He didn't like it that the thought enticed him now. More evidence stacked against him for how far he'd slipped towards the darkness lurking inside him.

As a soldier for hire he'd fought stepping across the line separating the good guys from the bad. Six months ago at the hands of an Army medic skilled in treating more than just the body, he'd converted to Christianity. A lot of things can change in six months. To his surprise a man's heart was one of them.

It was that change that brought him here to the north woods pushing through a timed trial, hoping for a job with SeaMount and the chance to find absolution from the darkness that had become a part of him. Time to leave and reconsider his options while his better self had the upper hand. Frightening women and children wasn't what good guys did.

With a cursory wave he turned back towards the forest.

The metallic roll of the van door opening sliced through the muted wilderness hum.

Knee deep in weeds, Gray whirled around. The pixie ran at him full tilt. Her braids bounced on thin shoulders as her arms pumped hard at her sides.

The driver's door opened. A blood-curdling scream set the hair on his arms upright.

The woman jumped from the vehicle and ran after the little girl. "Andi. Come back here. Andi!" He recognized the terror etched on the woman's face. Too many war zones had burned the gut wrenching fear-filled grimace into his memory.

The pixie took a header and landed at his feet.

Leaning over, Gray helped the youngster up, her arm thin and fragile in his hand. "You okay?"

"Please." Her slight lisp was the result of no front teeth. "You...can't...leave us." Her brown eyes, open and honest, pleaded with him. The anxiety threading through her small voice tightened a burning ball in his gut.

"Oomph." His left side caught the brunt of a body

slam. His teeth clacked. Pushing the child away, he went down. Scrub twigs poked his back. Dead leaves crackled beneath his weight. A stone jabbed his hip.

A warm woman sprawled across him.

Not one of those skinny waifs a man might break if he got overenthusiastic with his loving. This one was a real woman. All soft curves and smelling sweet.

Blondie's manicured nails dug into his scalp, cutting the pleasant moment short.

"Hey!" He grabbed her wrist to ease the pain.

Her breath caressed his cheek in hot bursts as she sobbed and fought him. Dodging her other hand, a flurry of movement beyond her shoulder stopped Gray mid motion.

A tiny princess, sparkling tiara askew on her pale hair, peered down at him. He blinked at the vision wondering if he'd hit his head when he fell.

The flat of a hand connected with his cheek in a stinging smack. "Enough!" With a roar, he flipped Blondie to her back. With the bulk of his body he held her to the ground.

\*\*\*

The man's hard weight forced the breath from Sophie's lungs as he pressed her into the scratchy weeds. She gasped for air, chest aching, as she twisted and scraped the heel of her sandal the length of his leg. His hot breath seared her neck.

Sophie's vision tunneled to the frightening face staring down at her. Her girls! She had to protect them, God help her.

Heart ready to burst from her chest, muscles burning, she pummeled him with her fists. Lumps in his shirt made her blows ineffective. She clawed at his hideous face. A chunk fell off in her hand. Revulsion rocketed through her then turned to surprise as the piece crumbled to dust.

He caught her hands in iron fists. She struggled to pull free. Eyes as gray and cold as pond ice raked over her face. His grip tightened.

With a crushing jolt more weight bore down on Sophie as her daughters fell atop the man in a writhing pig pile. His head jerked up in surprise. Arms flailing, legs scrambling, and hair flying like flags of war, they screamed and pulled at his clothing.

He bared his teeth and with a harsh grunt surged up and off of Sophie. She lurched to her feet dragging great gulps of air into her aching lungs.

Her girls held on to him.

Would he take off with her daughters clinging to him? The impending custody battle with their grandparents paled in comparison to losing her girls to this madman.

Sophie grabbed a handful of lavender cloth and yanked. Lissa dropped off landing in the weeds on her backside, one ear bud still intact. The man shook and Hanna fell to the ground, her princess gown tangled about her knees.

Arms wrapped snug around his neck, Andi stuck.

"Andi. Let go!"

Andi tightened her hold. One braid had lost its elastic and come unraveled.

He grasped the arms threatening to cut off his breath.

Sophie's heart lurched. She charged and tore at his hands. "Don't hurt her. Don't you *dare* hurt her!"

He stilled. Behind the mud on his face, his eyes

filled with despair. He blinked and the anguish disappeared, replaced by steel.

"Mommy, he's got to stay with us." Andi's chin, smudged with dirt where she'd bumped against the man's filthy neck, rested on a wide muscular shoulder.

"Just let go, honey."

"But we prayed for him last night. Remember?"

His eyes widened with surprise but he said nothing.

"We don't know this man, Andi. He's a stranger. You know the rules about strangers." Every instinct urged Sophie to wrestle her daughter away from him.

"He's our angel, Mommy."

The slack-jawed shock on his face would have been comical had Sophie felt like laughing. And a theological discussion with Andi about angels would have to wait.

"Andi. Get. Down. Now."

Indecision flitted across her middle daughter's face. "But we asked God for an angel to keep us safe." Her hands loosened and she slid off. Sneakers hitting the ground she grabbed for his woven fabric belt.

Watchful of the girls, he spoke. "If you're waiting on an angel, you're not waiting on me." His voice, soft and deep, was at odds with his scruffy clothes and the hard eyes that turned to zero in on Sophie. "You're a long way from civilization."

Andi tugged on his belt. "We're lost and our cell phone doesn't work out here."

Sophie's heart hammered in her chest. "Andi, hush."

He swore.

She clamped her lips shut. *Pick your battles,*

7

*Sophie*. Taking him to task for using bad language in front of the girls could wait.

"Do you have a plan to get out of here?"

Her dignity in the pits, Sophie tried for some semblance of control even if it was only an illusion. She smoothed a hand over her hair and a leaf fell out. She straightened her blouse.

His gaze followed her every move.

"Maybe if I knew where we were." She clasped her hands together to keep them from fluttering like nervous butterflies.

"No." Lissa bolted to her mother's side dragging Hanna with her. Her gaze bounced between the adults.

Eyes on her 'angel' Andi said, "Mommy's not very good with directions."

Sophie's face burned. She wished her daughters weren't so eager to share her shortcomings with a complete stranger.

"Show me your directions."

She crossed her arms taking refuge in belligerence. "I don't have any. I thought I'd remember the way."

"Do you have a GPS?"

She shook her head. Unlike the Acura her late husband Tommy had driven, her van didn't come with a navigation system.

"A map?"

"Yes."

His relieved expression changed to incredulity when Andi piped up. "She can't read it."

Those gray eyes focused on Sophie. "Have you even tried?"

Swiping a hank of hair from her eyes, Sophie

ignored the question. They could be sitting smack on top of Mount Katahdin and she wouldn't be able to find their place on the map. "A map won't help. The van is out of gas."

He muttered under his breath and scraped a hand over his face. Dirt sifted to his shirt. "Where are you going?"

She sent another prayer for protection winging heavenward. "Bride Lake."

He glanced at the van before his gaze raked over the girls then shot back to her. "Saw an old sign for the place."

"You did?" Fragments of fear floated away in a wash of relief. "Can we walk there?"

He concealed his surprise behind narrowed eyes. "No way."

"Why not?"

His gaze went straight to Sophie's strappy sandals.

She huffed and jammed her hands on her hips. "We have sneakers."

"What about food and water? I saw the sign three days back."

The fight in Sophie ebbed. "Bottles of water and snacks."

He looked at each girl in turn. "You won't go far on that."

As a child, Sophie had heard the stories about hunters lost in the forest and never found. Years away from the North Woods had dimmed her memory of the unforgiving nature of the wilderness. Getting lost had been her first mistake. Another bad choice could compound her problems and cause the death of someone she loved. She pressed a hand to her stomach.

Time to bury her pride. "What do you suggest we do?"

From behind the chunks of dirt on his face, his gaze rested on each of them as though taking their measure. The muscle in his neck pulsed. He shifted his attention to the van.

Time slipped into neutral and idled to the quiet sough of the wind. Even the girls remained motionless as though tagged in a game of Freeze.

The harsh chatter of a whisky jack shattered the quiet.

"I suppose I could guide you."

His enthusiasm was underwhelming. Could she trust him? Did she have a choice?

"If I escort you to the lake you'll do exactly as I say."

Sophie hesitated. Trying to walk out alone could bring disaster. Praying she'd made the right choice she extended her hand, "I'm Sophie Moore."

"Gray Kerr." He enveloped her hand in the warmth and strength of his then turned and surveyed the girls. "You'll follow orders?"

Eyes glued to the play list on her mp3 player, Lissa murmured, "I guess."

Hanna fiddled with her tiara.

He lifted a grungy eyebrow and questioned Andi. "Understood?"

"Yes!" She hopped from one foot to the other eager to get on with the adventure.

Nervous, Sophie pulled Hanna close. "Are you camping?"

"I'm working through a qualifying trial for a job with a security agency."

*Not a white-collar job.* "What must you qualify

in?"

His smile didn't reach his eyes "Survival skills."

Her heart took a nosedive. He didn't have a camp on the other side of the hill or a cooler filled with drinks and breakfast. "And the dirt on your face?"

"Swamp mud. Keeps the black flies at bay."

Still clinging to him, Andi's smile exposed the gummy hole in her mouth. "I told you he's our angel. He knows how to live in the woods." She tugged on his belt. "I'm seven."

His growl didn't dampen her enthusiasm.

Sophie introduced her daughters. "The one hanging on to you is Andi." She pointed to her eldest. "Lissa."

"I'm nine." Lissa tossed Andi a superior glare.

"The little one is Hanna. She's four."

Andi grinned at her angel. "Will we have to eat bugs?"

"Oh, yuck!" Lissa stuck a finger in her mouth and made retching noises.

A brief smile reached his eyes. "Only if you want to."

# Chapter 2

Four females gazed expectantly at Gray. What was he supposed to do with *four*? And three of them smurfs! This was God's way of punishing him for something he'd done in his less than illustrious past.

Moving at a rapid pace the last few days gave him a short window of time to help this bunch and not get too far behind on his trial. He'd gain nothing second-guessing his decision.

He'd committed to them. Like it or not, for the next few days he had a team to lead.

They were unlike any unit he'd ever been a part of. Poorly outfitted for one thing. The sandals and pink gown would have to go.

"What do you have in the van? Some things will be of use on the trail." He opened the rear door and paused. A colorful jumble of luggage and backpacks filled the cargo area. Snagging a bright pink pack as though it were a snake, Gray held it up. "Whose is this?"

The princess raised her hand.

He handed the pack to Sophie. "Empty it. Set

aside any food. I'll go through what you find to pick out what we can use." Handing the other two girls their backpacks with the same instructions he turned back to the van. He unzipped the largest piece of luggage, threw back the top and came to an abrupt halt.

Delicate underclothes spilled from the overstuffed suitcase and threatened to slither out of the van to his boots.

Gray's heart jack-hammered sharp blows against his ribs. His hand hovered above wisps of fabric so insubstantial he feared it would dissolve beneath his touch. *Breathe, Kerr. This is just another op.* He plunged his hand into the clingy softness. Just another mission. *Right.* By the handful, he tossed lingerie over the backseat. A startled gasp made him pause and look over his shoulder.

Hands on lush hips, Sophie glared at him. "What are you *doing*?"

"Going through the luggage." Gray swept away a wisp of sheer pink. Something brushed his pant leg.

Rings flashing and bracelets jangling, Sophie's hand shot between his ankles rescuing wayward bits of lace.

Doing his best to ignore her, he dug beneath the fluff and found a sturdy pair of jeans, a long sleeve tee-shirt and sneakers. "You'll wear these." Tossing her a pair of socks, he grabbed another to pack out.

He didn't let her angry huff stop him from opening the next piece of luggage filled with little girl clothing in pink, lavender, and yellow. The smiling flowers and big-eyed kittens were so sweet his back teeth ached. Pulling out the sturdiest articles of clothing, he handed them to her. "Have them change into these." He closed the lid.

"They'll need extra underclothes. A set for each day we're on the trail."

Gray shook his head. "We can't carry anything unnecessary."

"But, clean underclothes..."

"Are unnecessary."

Face crimson, she stomped away.

"And take off the jewelry. It'll only get in the way." Civilians. They didn't understand survival was a gritty, bare-knuckles business.

A half hour later, pleased he'd unearthed bug spray, a first aid kit, bottled water, cans of soda, snacks, and a few kitchen sundries, Gray went to inspect the women. The youngest tugged on her tiara and smiled at him. Her jeans peeked from beneath the sequined hem of her gown.

That worked. The costume added another layer of clothing. But no way could she hike in those glittery slippers with floppy bows. "Where are her shoes?"

Sophie held them up. "I'll be sure she's in them when we're ready to go."

He'd overheard pieces of the negotiation between mother and daughter about footwear. If he didn't nip the behavior now he'd be negotiating his way over every mountain between here and Bride Lake.

Taking the sneakers from Sophie, Gray crouched down eye level with Hanna. He held out the shoes. "Feet. Now."

She pulled a wet finger from her mouth and pointed at Gray. "No thank you." Sticking her finger back in her mouth, she ducked behind her mother's leg.

Heat crawled up Gray's neck. The smurf had

refused a direct order. Stonewalled by a four-year-old, he did what any self-respecting leader would do. Delegate.

He stood and thrust the shoes at Sophie. "When I head out she will have them on or she will be left." Walk away, Kerr. Leave them here and go find help. Send someone back to bring them out of this place.

Gray returned to the van and yanked the front door open. He grabbed the navy and red quilt tossed over the console and lifted it out. The woman's sweet cinnamon scent permeated the fabric and plucked at a lonely chord he'd buried years ago. With quick jerky motions he bundled the quilt in a ball. He'd endured more soft feelings in the previous twenty minutes than he'd experienced in the past twenty years. *Get a grip or get out, Kerr.*

Never before in his career had he contemplated abandoning a mission. Highly trained men who understood the rules and played by them had always surrounded him. How could he lead a bunch of females who didn't recognize a direct order unless, of course, *they* issued it?

A tug on his sleeve got his attention. The pixie stood beside him. She pointed to the backseat. "I put food in the cooler. There's water, too."

"Good job." Not that they'd tote a cooler, but he liked initiative in a man.

Except she was a woman.

Well. Not quite yet.

Gray rubbed his aching head. He'd given his word. Honor demanded he keep it. He would not walk away. Removing the cooler, he tossed the contents of the back seat and found a child's travel game.

Sophie approached, her hair pulled back from her face. She waved her hand over the small pile of items he'd collected. "Is this what we're taking with us?"

"Yes." He thumbed the battery cover off the back of the game. Jackpot! "These things will make the trek easier."

"You mean easier for us."

"You. Me. The smurfs."

"The 'smurfs'?" Her voice carried a note of warning.

Gray looked up from popping the battery out of the game. "They're short."

"They're *children*."

Now he had to explain himself. "In BUDS..." He'd already lost her. "During SEAL training, the men are grouped by height. Makes carrying the IBS..." Again, the blank look. "Carrying the 'itty bitty ship' overhead is easier." He pocketed the batteries. "The short guys are the smurf crew."

She took a deep breath. Her chest rose and fell.

The woman was a walking temptation. If God didn't already own a thunderbolt with Gray's name on it, one would surely exist by the end of this ordeal.

He tossed the game, now minus batteries, back into the car.

"But..."

He faced her. Less than an hour had passed and he'd already used up his daily allotment of patience. How would he manage several days of this?

"In that case, my girls are smurfettes."

At her unexpected answer his brain went blank.

"Thank you for helping us." Her features relaxed in a soft sweet smile.

As if holding a live wire, Gray's body jolted then kicked into overdrive. He watched her walk away with the growing realization he'd taken a direct hit and hadn't a clue what kind of artillery she'd used. Gray's fingers clenched around the batteries he held. The woman confounded him. Beneath her feminine charms beat the heart of an Amazon warrior ready to fight for her family.

He hoped she possessed the stamina to keep fighting. Some snack food and a quilt didn't take the place of three squares and a roof overhead.

Mid morning Gray finished going through the van and the toiletries Sophie gathered, choosing what they'd take and loading backpacks. Everyone had a pack to carry, even the little princess. Using two of Sophie's belts, he attached the tightly rolled blanket and quilt atop his pack.

Gathering the women together, Gray doled out the loads. "Lissa, no ear buds allowed while on the move. I want you able to hear. Understood?"

Lissa yanked on the wires popping the buds from her ears. With exaggerated gestures she stuffed the mp3 player into a pocket of her pack. The sour puss she wore promised trouble.

Certain he'd be keeper of the player by days end, Gray lifted his pack. "Ruck up, ladies."

They stared at him unmoving.

Sophie broke the silence. "Excuse me?"

If he had to explain every word he spoke this trek would never end. "Grab your gear and let's go."

That set them in motion.

"We're operating under the buddy system. Lissa and Andi, you stick together." He helped Sophie guide

Hanna into her pack and adjust the straps. "Sophie, you bring up the rear with Hanna. Hanna, do not leave your mother's side."

Playing with her tiara, Hanna didn't respond.

Her mother frowned. A sure sign she'd heard.

"We need to stay together. If I whistle, you come at once. If you can't see me, stop and call out, I'll find you." Gray slung a jury-rigged rucksack across his back and headed for the timberline. A quick glance over his shoulder confirmed the others followed.

Every mission involved risk. If he had assessed the situation accurately and stayed vigilant, they should arrive at Bride Lake without mishap.

Lissa tripped over a tree root and fell on all fours.

Or not.

# Chapter 3

Sophie followed the others along an obscure trail that wound up a rocky hill covered with scrub oak and mountain maples. The straps of her pack dug into her shoulders and her thigh muscles protested the hours of walking. If she sucked in one more bug while trying to get enough oxygen to stay upright, she'd throw up.

"Mommy." Hanna tugged on her hand. "I'm firsty."

"Turn around." Sophie undid the buckle of Hanna's pack and pulled out a water bottle. "Only a quick sip, honey."

Gray insisted everyone carry a part of the load. He'd doled everything out, careful not to give anyone more than they could manage.

Well, Sophie struggled. Lissa and Andi climbed like mountain goats, and if Hanna had longer legs, she'd be on her sisters' heels.

Occasionally Gray stopped to take a reading using the face of his analog watch and a short stick as a makeshift compass. Andi understood the process. Sophie needed it explained a few more times.

She recapped the bottle then slipped it back into Hanna's pack.

They followed a faint trail over what Gray considered a hill. With each step Sophie's muscles screamed 'mountain'. On the trail up ahead of her, she caught glimpses of Lissa and Andi's pink sweatshirts as they zigzagged between trees and rocks. The forest muffled their voices.

"Let's hurry, Hanna." Sophie willed her feet to move faster, prodded along by the fear of losing sight of her girls. She hoped she'd made the right decision in trusting Gray. Her chest tightened with anxiety. A few wrong turns off the highway and her dream of a fun family weekend had morphed into a nightmare, a dark prelude to the court appearance awaiting her back home. Missing the court date would only make matters worse. She *couldn't* lose her girls. Since Tommy's death they had become her reason for living and now his parents wanted to take them from her. The familiar spike of anger, less sharp now but still there, sliced through her thoughts. *Why did you have to die?*

Overhead, the canopy of green leaves waved in a light breeze. Sun dappled the knee-high ferns growing thick in the damp soil. Their steps stirred up the rich woodsy scent of leaf mold as the trail they followed wound between two monolithic boulders. Careful where she stepped, Sophie steadied herself with a hand on the rough lichen covered rock. She shivered. The warmth of the sun didn't penetrate the passage shaded by the huge stones. The cool dank air clogged in her throat.

Coming out the other side she paused and scanned the dense woods in search of Gray and her girls. No voices drifted back. No colorful bits of clothing flashed among the dark tree trunks. Her labored breath accelerated to choppy gasps. How far ahead could they be? *Think, Sophie.*

From the top of the boulder a chipmunk scolded with sharp chips. She clasped Hanna's small hand tight and closed her eyes in a silent prayer. Heaven help her, even with a guide she'd become lost.

A short, piercing whistle cut through the woodland sounds.

Gray!

Throat tight, she called out.

Dead leaves and woodland debris crunched beneath heavy footfalls before he materialized from among the trees, brow knit with impatience.

*Thank you, God.* Heart pounding, Sophie tugged on Hanna's hand and hurried towards him as fast as her aching legs allowed.

"You've got to keep up, Sophie."

She didn't answer. If she stopped to talk, all forward momentum would be lost.

Gray pivoted and moved a few paces ahead of her.

When they reached the bald face of the mountain where Lissa and Andi waited, Sophie let go of Hanna's hand and collapsed on a small rock opposite Lissa and Andi's granite perch.

The lofty height offered a breathtaking panoramic view of mountain peaks and valleys. A patchwork of alpine moss and low bush blueberries, the fruit still green and inedible, covered the bare open space. Rooted in the cracks and crevices, an occasional scraggy spruce tree braved the elements of a mountaintop existence.

Sophie slipped her thumbs beneath the straps of her pack to ease the throbbing pressure. An unexpected tug on the pack made her squeal in pain.

"Why didn't you tell me the pack hurt your shoulders?"

Too tired to respond, she stared at the toes of Gray's boots.

"Let go." His fingers replaced her thumbs.

He tested the fit of the straps and reworked them. "If that doesn't help, tell me and I'll figure out a way to pad the straps for you. The pack was made to fit someone smaller."

The insensitive brute! "Keep your thoughts about my size to yourself."

The words no sooner passed her lips then he was squatting on his heels, eye to eye with her. Or rather, they'd be eye to eye if she dared look at him.

He hooked a finger under her chin forcing her to meet his gaze. "Your rucksack is sized for a child." His eyes drifted as one side of his mouth quirked up. "I like that you're all grown up."

A blush prickled across Sophie's cheeks as his eyes warmed to molten pewter. Out of breath for a whole new reason, she pushed his hand away. How pathetic was she, letting an overbearing, unkempt tyrant set her heart to racing.

He squeezed on the rock next to her and held out a granola bar. "Chow."

Noting each of the girls had a bar, Sophie took the one he offered hoping he'd go away.

He didn't.

"You need to be vigilant about bringing up the rear guard. Don't want to lose one of the girls."

Sophie took a bite of her bar intent on ignoring the man and the turmoil he'd stirred up inside her.

Combing his fingers across his buzz cut hair he huffed. "If you fall behind, call out. Don't force me to come back for you."

The blame wasn't entirely hers. "I didn't know you'd disappear on the other side of those rocks."

He muttered a coarse word.

That did it! Sophie gave a shove with her shoulder.

Gray fell sideways off the rock. With lightening speed, his surprised expression changed to one of disapproval.

Before more foul words spilled from his lips, she shook her finger at him. "*Don't*. Don't speak another bad word."

His eyes narrowed to slits but Sophie didn't care. She preferred anger to the attraction that buzzed through her. "I will *not* listen to that filth coming out of your mouth and I don't want my girls to hear it."

From her perch on the rock Lissa leaned forward and looked down at him. "Mommy will wash your mouth out."

His eyebrows shot up. He clamped his jaw shut.

Andi chimed in. "And if you do it again, she'll pop you on the bee-hind."

The inappropriateness of Andi's comment sent another wave of heat across Sophie's already burning cheeks.

His anger appeared to dissolve as a speculative gleam shone in his eyes.

"Stop that."

Awareness sizzled in the air.

Gray rose to his haunches. "What?"

"You're thinking...stuff."

"What stuff?" Andi frowned, her gaze bouncing from her mother to Gray and back.

Glaring at Gray, Sophie swatted at a moose fly pestering her.

The corners of his eyes crinkled. "More stuff I'm sure your mother doesn't want you to hear. Now eat."

Andi sighed and peeled back the wrapper on her granola bar.

He bit into his scant lunch and chewed. "Never had a problem before with how I talk."

"You use too many bad words." Sophie's hand swiped through the air again. "Your coarse language is offensive."

The moose fly bit tender flesh.

Sophie squeaked and jumped up, hands beating the air.

"Stand still."

At his command she stopped, arms squeezed to her sides and eyes scrunched shut. A resounding clap reverberated close to her ear followed by a deep 'got it'. She opened her eyes to thank him, but he'd already turned away to speak with the girls. Sighing, Sophie rubbed the bloody bite on her arm.

***

"All of you. Shoes off."

Four identical expressions of disbelief faced him. Gray clamped his teeth together. *Newbies.*

Sophie recovered first. "Why?" She curled her feet close to the rock she sat on as though fearing he'd take her shoes in punishment for the gag order she'd imposed on him.

He'd start with the easy one. Crouched before Andi, he pointed at her shoes. "Off. Show me your feet." Seated on the rock, she toed out of her sneakers, stripped off her socks and thrust both feet at him. They fit in his palms as he checked each one for blisters. "You feel anything rub or sting, tell me immediately."

She nodded and he let go.

Lissa rolled her eyes and took her sweet time untying her laces.

Pleased to see Sophie undoing Hanna's shoes, Gray inspected Lissa's feet then moved on to check the princess. With foot inspection completed on the smurfs, Gray faced Sophie.

Her sneakered feet remained tight against the rock. "I'm fine."

*Showdown.* He'd expected one. Muzzling him had been only the first salvo in the battle of wills. He sat back on his heels. "I'll decide who's fine."

"I'm an adult and know when my feet are in need of attention."

Her prim declaration gave him an opening the USS Nimitz could pass through. To let the opportunity slip by would be criminal. "Believe me when I say I fully appreciate the fact that you're an adult."

Her eyes widened.

Was he being unfair teasing such an innocent? Gray rested his fingertips on her ankle. "Do you want to remove your shoes, or shall I?"

In a matter of seconds the shoes came off. Face as pink as Hanna's dress, Sophie avoided eye contact.

He looked down. The sight captivated him. Polished nails, buffed heels, toe rings and ankle bracelets. He'd never fully appreciated feet. In turn, he cradled each soft foot in his hand. Sophie had no worries about him forcing her to march barefoot.

Gray exhaled the breath he'd unconsciously held. He released her foot and stood. The feel of her sole remained imprinted on the palm of his hand. A phenomenon ripe with meaning if he allowed himself to think about it. "Show me your water bottles."

*Oh yeah.* Steam almost poured from her pretty ears. He expected to hear a whistle at any moment.

Sophie opened Hanna's pack and then her own. "Do you ever say 'please'?"

Ignoring her question, he counted the bottles of water that remained intact. That he didn't answer her question did not stop her from speaking her mind.

"We aren't soldiers."

No kidding, sweetheart.

"Saying 'please' and 'thank you' greases the wheel of cooperation."

Hanging on every word her mother said, Andi opened her pack and the one Lissa had dumped next to her. She glanced up at Gray wide-eyed. The concern in the pixie's eyes made him pause. She feared her mother would spout one cliché to many and scare him off.

He winked at her.

His chest tightened. As a rule, he did not wink. To do so meant a shared confidence or understanding. It meant he *cared*.

Before Andi turned away, a secret grin tipped up the corners of her mouth.

A curling sensation tightened Gray's gut. This was no time to get sick. "Ruck up. Time to go." He slipped into his borrowed pack and settled the straps he'd extended with luggage ties to fit his torso and shoulders. Only in a survival situation that didn't include the danger of being a target would he willingly wear a pack emblazoned with a cartoon character.

"At the bottom of this ledge we run into wetlands. The bog is too big to skirt. I tried yesterday when I came through this way. Stay single file behind me, and step where I step."

Winding between trees, Gray led his small band to the base of the rocky mountain. He used his knife to cut a sturdy sapling and stripped off the small branches. Stepping across a narrow strip of wet leaves and mud, he tested the ground with the pole. Cautious, he led them through muddy wetland thickets of alder and buttonwood. Tonight they'd have to deal with scratches and bug bites. He glanced back at Sophie. Sure enough, her jaw was locked and her lips stretched tight.

Mama wasn't having a good time.

\*\*\*

The going had been slow crossing the spongy ground that squished with each step. The late afternoon light gilded the tops of the thinning shrubby brush and made the winding ribbons of water glitter among the rocky knolls and tussocks of sedge. Nearby a bullfrog *ju-rummed*.

"You have *got* to be kidding!" Horror etched Sophie's face in stark relief.

Gray studied the log an enterprising hunter had laid across a watery bit of quag and shook his head. "It's the shortest way across this part."

"Andi, get back." Eyes wide, Sophie shook her head. "There has to be another way."

"Probably. But do you want to take time to wander around to find it? Someone was nice enough to build us a bridge. Let's use it. Give me your packs. I'll take them across."

Always up for a new experience, Andi immediately complied. The pixie would be a handful when she grew old enough to have some independence.

Gray collected the packs and crossed the log. He dumped them on dry ground near a patch of blooming sheep laurel alive with tiny orange-brown butterflies.

"Andi, you first."

She stepped on the log and took a tentative step. Arms stretched wide she dipped left then righted herself.

"Don't look down." If she fell in, guess who'd have to fish her out.

Andi tested the log with one foot. Stationed at the other end, Gray held out his hand. "Pretend you're at a playground."

A smile lit her face and with short rapid steps, she raced toward him.

Sophie's startled yelp drowned out his expletive.

Andi ignored his hand and flung herself at him. He closed his arms around her slim body, his heart painfully battering his ribs. He pivoted and deposited her on terra firma. Leaning over he growled, "You ripped ten years off my life."

Not in the least intimidated, Andi giggled and yelled across to her sister. "Lissa, it's wider than the balance beam at gymnastics."

Hands on her hips, Lissa scrutinized the bridge.

"Come on," Andi motioned with her hand. "You spin on the one at the gym."

*Spin?* Sweat popped out on Gray's brow. Sophie's expression turned apoplectic and in that moment he understood what she felt. "No spinning! For the love of Mike, just walk across the log and be done with it."

Lissa stepped up and with arms outstretched took a hop-skip and ran across the log. Prepared this time, Gray stood with arms outstretched.

The minx stopped short of the end. "Move."

Surprised and feeling foolish, for a split second he complied. His hesitation was enough for Lissa to take another hop-skip and cartwheel off the end of the log. She landed on her seat with a splat.

"What kind of a harebrained trick was that?" Gray's mouth ran off as his hands checked for broken bones. Not until he'd reassured himself Lissa was unharmed did he become conscious of her and Andi staring at him with their yaps hanging open.

Hot shame flooded through him. He clamped his mouth shut determined to keep a particularly colorful phrase to himself. He'd blown the no swearing rule. With any luck Sophie was too worried about her own trip across the log to call him on it.

He owed the girls an apology. "Sorry for what I said."

Andi shook her head. "We don't know what you said. You yelled at us in some weird language."

A reprieve courtesy of Uncle Sam, though the Pashto he'd spewed was in no way part of the Defense Language Institute materials. Under control, he helped Lissa to her feet. He didn't recognize his own voice, gruff with emotion. "You could've broken your neck."

She brushed at her wet fanny, tipped her head back and glared down her nine-year-old nose at him. "I dismount like that in gymnastics."

He leaned over, his older and bigger nose a scant

breath away from hers. "Which means you should know you don't do it without a beam that's high enough, mats on the floor and," she winced as the volume of his voice increased, "a spotter who knows what the..." *Try that again, Kerr.* "Who knows what you're going to do."

She had the good grace to blush before she flounced off to sit with Andi.

Gray had always expected to lose his life in the field to a band of terrorists or a rebel sniper. Never had the thought entered his mind he'd die of a heart attack brought on by a cartwheeling smurf.

*\*\*\**

Sophie tucked her trembling hands into the pockets of her hoodie sweatshirt. Lissa's dismount had left her shaking and light-headed but there was no time to indulge a well-deserved swoon. Uncle Sam's poster boy approached wearing an expression that said he was ready to feed her daughters to the slimy creatures living beneath the log he tread on.

Gray held out his arms for Hanna. She went to him as though he'd carried her over hurdles all of her short life. A princess worthy of her tiara, she gave him a sunny smile as he set her beside her sisters.

Sophie wiped her sweaty palms against her sore thighs. Balance. All she had to do was keep her balance. Place one foot in front of the other and stay upright.

"Okay, Sophie." He stood at the other end of the log, arm outstretched and waggling his fingers in a 'come here' motion.

Knees knocking, she stepped up on the log. The drum of her pulse and the rush of blood through her veins muffled Andi and Lissa's voices as they encouraged her.

"You can do it, Mommy."

"Go fast like I did."

Fast. Right. *Not*. Her feet stuck to the log's rough bark. *His* melt-in-your mouth voice cut through the racket in her head.

"Sophie, I have your daughters on this end of the log. Come across and you'll finish the trek with us. If you stay on that end, I'll have to take the girls on and come back for you."

His words, 'take the girls', caused a surge of hot terror to consume her panic and set her feet in motion. They were *her* girls. If he thought for one minute she'd let him waltz off into the forest with her daugh—

The log shifted.

*Help. Ohhelpohhelpohhelp.* Sophie froze three feet from the end.

"Take my hand."

She grabbed Gray's hand and lunged for the end of the log.

Straight into his arms.

Oh! *Ooooohh!* Powerful arms banded her waist and he unceremoniously hauled her off the log.

Dizzy with relief, she tried to ignore the awareness arcing through her as she leaned against his muscular frame.

Their gazes collided.

The longing in his eyes threatened to overwhelm her. He held her an instant longer than necessary then released her and stepped back. The girls crowded around Sophie.

She hugged Lissa, hiding her face in the warm

embrace. Wanting to forget what she'd seen in Gray's eyes, she wrapped her arms around Andi and hugged her. What did she have to offer a strong self-sufficient man like Gray? Nothing.

Nothing but love.

The still small voice echoed in her heart sending her to her knees. Why had the Holy Spirit picked *now* to speak to her? Sophie reached for Hanna. Oh, help. She was in deep trouble.

# Chapter 4

Sophie entered the derelict one-room cabin. The rustle of a small animal skittering out a hole in the back wall stopped her. The smell of rotted wood and damp dirt hung thick in the small space. Watery, late afternoon sunshine found its way through a hole in the roof and the dirty cracked glass in the window. A small table sloped to one side for the lack of two legs; the chair, in better shape, missed one.

Gray shed his pack and set it on the floor littered with leaves and other debris. "Home sweet home for tonight."

Sophie hung her pack from the rusty iron bed frame standing against the far wall. "How much farther to Bride Lake?"

"Day. Day and a half. Depends on how everyone holds up. Leafy branches will clean the floor." He hunkered down at the hearth, stuck his head in the rustic fireplace and looked up.

Andi dumped her pack beside Gray's. "I'll get them."

She pushed her way past Lissa standing in the

doorway, her lip curled with disgust. "Are there mice in here?"

Gray withdrew from the fireplace and stood. "Mice with wings. There are bats in the chimney."

"Eeew!" Lissa backed up and stood on what passed as a front porch. "Mooomm!"

Gray shot Sophie a 'deal with her' glare before he escaped out the door.

She sighed and helped Hanna with her pack. "Lissa, try to work with us here." Holding Hanna's hand, Sophie stepped out on the sagging porch. "Please take off your pack so you can help clean the cabin."

"I'm hungry."

"We're all hungry." *And tired. And sore.* "But let's count our blessings, shall we?"

"Like what?" Lissa poked her head into the cabin. "This place is dirty and it stinks. I want to go back to the van."

"We have a roof over our head for the night. Let's accept what God has provided and be thankful." Sophie held out a bottle of water.

Clicking her tongue, Lissa snatched it from her mother's hand and stomped off to sit on a log. Andi appeared from behind the cabin carrying an armload of leafy brush.

Sophie helped her pile it on the porch. "Where's Gray?"

Andi grasped several small branches in one hand and tested using them as a broom. "He went into the woods. Said he'd be back."

Sophie glanced toward the forest where shadows deepened as the sun sank lower. If he didn't come back what would become of them? Her already aching shoulders tensed painfully.

Clinging to God's promise that He'd watch over them and protect them, she followed Andi and Hanna into the cabin. Using an old board she found in a corner, Sophie scooped leaves away from the wall. At the bottom of the pile a rusty tin can rattled and scraped across the uneven floorboards.

Playing house, Andi and Hanna chattered with enthusiasm as they swept debris out the door and off the porch. Finding a long piece of wood, they propped the table up while discussing dinner, mud and leaves being primary ingredients.

Tired of her own company, Lissa joined them.

"Mommy, can we use a water bottle for flowers?" Lissa rummaged in her pack.

"Take one that's half empty."

The girls thumped down the creaky steps to gather wildflowers growing in abundance throughout the small clearing.

In a weak shaft of sunshine streaming through the roof, dust motes danced on the air currents. Pausing to survey what they'd accomplished, Sophie sat on the tippy chair and re-tied her loose shoelaces. Gray's surprise foot inspection had flustered her. A hard man, she hadn't expected gentleness in his touch. Even now, hours later, her heart raced and her feet tingled remembering his rough, warm hands wrapped around her bare feet.

His focused attention rattled her. So much so, when he'd finished inspecting her feet, she'd hurried to get her shoes on, haphazardly tying the laces. It was a miracle she didn't walk out of them crossing the log bridge. Remembering how Gray caught her in his arms at the end of the log roused another wave of shivering excitement.

The man dragged you off the log so you wouldn't fall in. That's all. Nothing happened. She tightened the bow in her shoelace.

*Except for the voice that whispered in your heart.*

She groaned and hid her face in her hands. He considered her and the girls nothing more than a nuisance. His honor wouldn't allow him to leave them stranded. Once at Bride Lake, he'd surely go his own way and leave Sophie to carry on with her plans. Perhaps she'd been mistaken about hearing God's whisper. The self-sufficient man didn't need her – for anything.

Tired of the thoughts circling inside her head, she stood and listened. She didn't hear any laughter or chatter outside the cabin. Unsure how long it'd been since she last heard the girls, she hustled to the door ready to call out.

Sophie swallowed back her words.

In a bright patch of yellow buttercups, her daughters sat with Gray. He held a buttercup beneath Hanna's chin. Sophie recognized a game she'd played many times as a child. If the shiny petals cast a yellow reflection on Hanna's skin the verdict was she liked butter.

Giggling, Andi and Lissa demanded their turn.

Gray's presence magnified Sophie's longing for Tommy. She missed the close relationship between a husband and wife, the shared dreams and secrets. Knowing how her man liked his coffee, the name of his favorite song, the sweet spot on his back he liked her to scratch. Without the intimacy of Tommy's love, her heart gaped dark and wide, an aching empty cavern.

Gray accepted the water bottle of blossoms from Andi. His voice drifted on the breeze, low and indistinct. All three girls wore huge smiles as he tucked a flower behind an ear of each of them.

There it was again, that unexpected gentleness that drew her like a powerful magnet. Sophie's insides softened and quivered. She pressed a hand against her stomach as yearning washed over her in warm waves.

The forest and meadow came into sharp focus, the colors enhanced as though viewed through a polarized lens. A breeze ruffled the leaves of the white birch trees. Dragonflies zoomed back and forth across the small clearing like tiny helicopters. A curious chickadee lit on the porch rail and hopped along the peeled pine log.

Like a drowning woman she drew in deep breaths and clung to the doorframe to keep her feet from walking down the steps for a flower of her own.

Disconcerted by her thoughts, Sophie stepped away from the door. She pulled the squeaky bed frame out from the wall and swept behind it, all the while berating herself for mooning over a man she barely knew.

The plank floor swept clean, she leaned her hip against the metal frame to push it back into place.

The bed didn't budge.

A quick inspection revealed one rusty leg stuck in a wide crack between the floorboards. Sophie wrapped her hands around the iron intent on lifting as she shoved. To either side of her white-knuckled hands, two larger hands joined in to help. Surprise zinged low in her belly.

The bed frame slid across the wooden floor and she lurched off balance. A strong arm snaked around her waist and held on.

"Ask for help."

Gray's warm breath fanned her ear and a delicious shiver prickled across her neck. Undone by her wayward emotions, she stepped back. "How is pushing around furniture any different from a forced march over a mountain and through a swamp?"

The muscle in his jaw jumped. "You did fine. So did the girls."

Sophie leaned against the wall. "I'm sorry." She absently waved a hand in the air. "I'm out of my element here. And we're losing so much time."

His eyes narrowed. "Before you set out on another trip, you better learn to read a map. And for the record, this stomp through the woods is costing me, too." He pivoted and left.

*** 

Through the hole created by missing roof shingles, Sophie counted the stars caught in a leafy branch that swayed in the night breezes. Beneath the quilt she shifted her hips searching for a more comfortable position on the blanket thrown over a fragrant bed of springy balsam boughs. Sleep would not come.

Beyond the walls of the cabin the dark forest vibrated with the buzz of insects and trill of tree frogs. The eerie screech of an owl raised goose bumps along her spine. From deep within, a childhood fear of the dark rekindled. She whispered a fervent prayer that the decaying cabin would keep out the danger prowling the forest at night.

The crackling flames in the stone fireplace

outlined Gray's silhouette in sharp relief. Earlier he ignited the fire with a 9-volt battery and the steel wool he'd found in her box of kitchen supplies. Sure of himself and his abilities, he'd taken control of Sophie's situation. Self-sufficient, he appeared not to need another person. But when he'd held her close at the end of the log, the longing in his eyes revealed heart-wrenching loneliness.

Sophie snuggled deeper into the quilt. Dinner had consisted of squirrel. Rodent wasn't her first choice for a wilderness meal, but certainly an improvement over the mud and leaves the girls had planned. She didn't ask Gray how he'd caught the animal.

Last night, stranded in the van, she'd bedded the girls down with the hope that morning would hold answers to their dilemma. During bedtime prayers Andi had asked for an angel. The next morning God sent them Gray. Tears of thanksgiving slipped from the corners of her eyes across her temples and into her hair. God had brought them this far. He'd see them through not only this time in the forest, but also the custody fight.

Beneath the quilt, the girls twined around her like a litter of puppies sharing body heat. She ran her hand across the pieced navy and maroon top. Her mother had made the quilt years ago as a high school graduation gift for Sophie. A mariner's compass medallion formed the center.

Her fingertips bumped along the many seams of the intricate pattern, her mother's words echoing in her mind. "Always seek God's direction, Sophie. Let His word be your guiding compass in life." *Lord, I need your guidance now. Help me to hear you.*

Restless, she shifted. Her eyes strayed to the fire and the man sitting beside it. Her gaze tangled in the glitter of his hard stare.

Breath caught in her chest, she couldn't look away. Her nerve endings buzzed and tingled with anticipation as if she'd clasped a live wire.

She flipped back the corner of the quilt before realizing her own intentions. Slipping out from beneath the covering, she hobbled on aching legs to the edge of the hearth and sank to the floor, sure she'd have to crawl back to bed. "Thank you for helping us." She reached her hands toward the flames, absorbing the heat.

Gray tossed a pinecone on the fire. The flames flared bright. "You're welcome." A soda can, blackened by the fire, held cooling boiled water.

Unable to gauge his mood, Sophie chose to jump in with the question niggling at her. "Will helping us disqualify you for the job?"

He shifted away from her and she could almost hear the walls falling into place. Finally he spoke. "I'll make up the time."

Time was crucial for Sophie as well. "The first of the week I have an appointment I can't miss. It's a court appearance."

The firelight washed across his face etching the hard planes in light and shadow. "A parking ticket?"

Determined not to let his prickly attitude bother her, she pulled her knees up and hugged them. His dismissive attitude stung. So did his determination to keep her at a distance. If she had any pride she would allow him to succeed.

"You can stop with the sarcasm." Evidently her

self-esteem chose to stay home this trip. The desire to tell him more burned in her chest. Sophie dipped her toasty fingers beneath the hood of her sweatshirt and wrapped them around the sides of her neck. She purred, enjoying the warmth. "It's a custody hearing." She glanced at him.

The turbulence in his eyes sparked a warm fire inside her.

"I don't want to lose my girls." Under his intent gaze, the rest of the world dropped away and a delicious heat bloomed low in her belly.

"Divorced?"

"No. Widowed. My husband died in a boating accident."

He glanced at the girls snuggled together asleep. "Who wants them?"

"Their grandparents."

"On what grounds?"

The accusations Tommy's parents had directed at her still rang in her memory. *Lazy. Neglectful. Unfit mother.* She couldn't say those words aloud. "I wrestled through depression." Sophie tightened her arms around her knees, the warm feelings evaporating. She had nothing to be ashamed of, but those dark days so full of anguish haunted her. "I barely functioned and the school suspended Lissa for bullying and fighting."

"Her response to her father's death." Gray frowned, his eyes on the lumpy quilt.

"And a blot on the Moore family name." Gerald and Suzanne never approved of Sophie as a wife for their son. After Tommy's death and Lissa's bad behavior they no longer saw the need to keep up any pretenses. "With the help of the school and doctors both

Lissa and I are better. But nothing I do is right in the eyes of Tommy's parents."

She pushed away the aching disappointment of the failed relationship. "I wanted a weekend of relaxation and fun with my girls before…before what could be the worst day of my life."

# Chapter 5

Gray poked at the burning wood. A crackling log rolled and a plume of embers flew up the chimney. The flickering flames bathed Sophie's features in a rosy glow. Earlier, he'd watched her gather Hanna into her arms and then lay next to the others. She touched each girl with a caress on the cheek or a kiss on the brow.

His skin tingled remembering her hand in his and the press of her body when he pulled her off the log. He couldn't imagine this woman neglecting her daughters. His own childhood had consisted of one long mission to survive his father's child rearing techniques. Sophie's ways were the exact opposite of his father's. She nurtured her girls with a gentle love. Was that the reason he was drawn to her like a heat-seeking missile locked on target? Her soft voice pulled his attention back to the present.

"I thank God you found us." Her lips quirked in a brief smile. "He works in mysterious ways, don't you think?"

It was a rhetorical question. No need to comment. But his pounding heart indicated he was about to go there anyway. "I don't know. I'm new to this whole God thing." His ears burned and he turned back to the fire.

"Ah. A new believer."

"Actually I'm more comfortable with the 'Christian soldier' handle."

She smiled. "Andi's right, you know. She prayed for help and God sent you."

"I'm no angel." Her soft chuckle flowed over him like warm honey.

In the firelight, her eyes shone. "Guess you'll have to settle for plain old hero."

Gray scrutinized her. "I've put you through h…" He coughed to cover his slip. Before he could reorganize his words, Sophie spoke.

"The only way I've survived the last year," she shot him a pointed look, "including today, is to believe that God is in control." In the warmth of the fire, Sophie pushed back the hood of her sweatshirt. "God sometimes uses trouble as the gift-wrapping for a lesson I need to learn." A self-deprecating smile slanted along her lips. "Other than the obvious, I'm not sure what He's trying to teach me this time."

Gray tossed another stick on the fire. Could the same be true for him? He believed his destiny lay with SeaMount, so why this detour from his goal? Guiding four women was a foray into alien territory. Men on the move didn't call out company-wide announcements for potty breaks or ask a million nonessential questions. The littlest smurf had picked up an invisible friend named Sushi somewhere along the trail. As if four living, breathing females weren't enough to contend with, he now had an invisible one to boot.

Did God have a lesson for him in all this? He wanted to successfully finish the wilderness trial and move on with his life. A life void of sweet voices, tiaras and pigtails. A life of self-preservation and caution.

Sophie blinked several times and yawned. She rolled to her hands and knees then got to her feet. "Good night, Gray."

"Good night, Sophie."

Clumsy with exhaustion, she climbed into the fragrant bed of pine boughs he'd cut and covered with the blanket. She snuggled close to the girls and fell asleep.

Like a monster wave, unstoppable in its fury, loneliness surged through Gray. The night stretched out before him, long and dark.

\*\*\*

Morning light filtered through cracked panes of glass. With a practiced eye Gray accounted for everyone. Sophie lay huddled in the center of the bedding. Poking from beneath the quilt he'd spotted the tip of Andi's braid wrapped in ribbon and Lissa's fingers decorated with chipped purple polish. Wisps of Hanna's white blonde hair completed the 'all-present and accounted for' tally.

He stepped outside and paused. The crisp morning air carried the scent of pine and wood smoke. The sun was still too low on the horizon for him to feel its warmth, but the day held promise. Slipping into the woods, he took care for his own needs then fetched more water to boil. By the time he got back Sophie had roused the girls.

Her welcoming smile faltered. "Where's Hanna?"

Only Lissa and Andi gazed up at him from the

nest on the floor.

A knot of foreboding twisted Gray's gut. The hyper-awareness that always accompanied trouble snapped into place.

Understanding flashed across Sophie's face. She ran to the door. "Hanna? Hanna!"

Heart slamming the wall of his chest, Gray tugged her back. "Stay here. I'll find her." He moved past Sophie down the steps and around the outside of the cabin. As team leader, losing Hanna was inexcusable. That she'd choose to leave the cabin's security hadn't crossed his mind. Dread crept through him.

Sneaker prints crisscrossed the clearing. A sparkle in the grass against the cabin's foundation caught his eye. He bent and picked up a sequin.

A soft moan spun him round.

Sophie leaned against the building, her face a deathly white. "I have to find her."

Fear for Hanna and anger over his own carelessness boiled up inside Gray. "I told you to stay in the cabin."

She stepped back. Hurt bruised her soft brown eyes. Gray reached for her and wrapped her in the warmth of his arms. She was a distraught mother, not a soldier disobeying an order. He wanted to reassure her, but until he found Hanna he couldn't give her any promises. "Come on, Sophie. Back inside. Stay with Lissa and Andi."

"I can help you find her." Frantic, she glanced around as though she expected Hanna to pop out from behind a bush.

He guided her toward the steps. "You do and I'll be searching for two people."

"I want to do something."

"Pray." He surprised himself, saying the word, but it had the desired effect.

Sophie hurried up the steps and stopped at the top. In the soft morning light, tears shimmered in her eyes. "Please, find my baby."

The curly thing bloomed in his gut. He managed a curt nod before he spun away and jogged to the edge of the clearing. The sequin he'd found could have dropped from Hanna's gown yesterday, but more would fall off. With a little luck and a lot of divine help he'd find them.

Gray circled the perimeter of the clearing. He'd almost completed the circuit when a glint of light caught his eye. Three steps deeper into the forest, he found two silver sequins on a pink thread dangling from a hobblebush. The thought of Hanna lost and frightened chilled him. Thankful he'd allowed her to wear the cheap costume over her jeans and shirt, he hoped the dense brush would tear off sequins and bits of thread with every step she took.

In silence Gray glided through the forest. If ever there was a time he could use help from above, this was it. *Are you listening, God? If you're handing out help today, I could use some.*

Even with her hair mussed from sleep and makeup smudged beyond repair, his attraction for Sophie remained strong. Would she hold Hanna's disappearance against him? As team leader, it was his responsibility to anticipate every problem. He'd failed on this one.

The forest thinned to a fringe of woody shrubs and bushes intent on taking over a meadow dotted with yarrow and orange hawkweed. He hadn't seen either a thread or sequin in the last ten yards. Did Hanna change direction and never reach the meadow?

Gray crouched and raked his fingers through the leaf litter. He'd have to go back to the last marker and begin an ever-widening circling pattern to find her sign. He studied the field. From this low angle his gaze raked through the knee-high grass and weeds.

Light flashed.

His breath caught in his throat as he watched and waited.

Another light breeze rippled the vegetation.

Another flash. Gray marked the spot and approached. On the tall grass, glittering in the morning sun, hung Hanna's tiara. Relieved he hadn't lost her trail he bent to retrieve it. A faint mewling cry raised the hair on the back of his neck.

Cautious, he advanced across the meadow. The sound, close by, gave the impression of floating up from the ground. Why didn't he see her? He dropped on all fours. Stones, dry brittle grass and nettles jabbed his knees and the palms of his hands. Undeterred, Gray followed the eerie cries.

"Mommy."

His insides jumped. "Hanna? Talk to me, Princess." Where was she?

Up ahead, a dark unnatural shape poked out of the vegetation. An old board, covered with a mat of dead grass and weeds jutted above the edge of a dark hole. Scrabbling to remove a thin layer of grass, he seized the splintered edge of rotted wood and yanked. The dank scent of decay filled his nostrils.

An old well.

Cautious, he leaned over the edge. A frightened, filthy princess peered up at him from the shallow depths.

"Hanna."

"I want Mommy."

His gaze scoured the hand dug well. Over time dirt and debris had sifted into the bottom making the hole shallow. "I'll take you to her as soon as I get you out."

If the wall caved in... His stomach clenched. With care, he moved back from the edge. A faint splash followed by a louder cry had him praying in desperation.

"Stand still, Princess. I won't leave you." Gray yanked off his shirt. Dry grass insulation showered down around him. Tying a knot above the cuff of each long sleeve, he inched forward on his stomach until his head and shoulders hung over the edge of the hole. Grasping above the knot in one sleeve, he lowered the shirt into the well. "Hanna, grab hold above the knot. Use both hands."

She reached for the dangling fabric and missed, falling on her knees. Muddy water splashed over her.

Her piercing cry made his heart give a painful leap. She struggled to her feet, slipped and clung to the dirt wall. "Try again. You can do it, Princess." Sweat beading on his brow, Gray coaxed her to use both hands.

Stretching one hand out, Hanna grasped the sleeve. Sobbing, she let go of the wall with her other hand and grabbed the cloth.

"Hold tight. I'm going to lift you out. Just hang on tight." Hand over hand Gray raised the shirt. A series of splashes set his pulse racing, but the strain of Hanna's weight on the shirt remained. He didn't breathe until he held one small forearm encased in his hand. Letting go of the shirt he gripped her other arm and rolled away from the opening bringing Hanna with him.

He sucked in a huge draught of air and jackknifed into a sitting position cradling Hanna in his arms. A pair of dirty hands snaked up around his neck. Relief spilled through his tight chest.

"I...I fell in." Hanna hiccupped and sniffed. "Sushi wanted flowers."

"It's okay, Princess. Everything's okay." Using the shirt he wiped the mud from her face and arms. He tried to set her away from him so he could check her for damage, but she refused to let go. She reeked of the rotten muck squishing in her shoes and coating her jeans and gown – and now him.

Lifting her in his arms, Gray headed back toward the cabin. His insides were raw, sliced and diced and stuffed back inside his body. Soon he'd have to confront the twisting pain in his gut.

"It'll be okay, Princess. Your mama's waiting for you."

# Chapter 6

Sophie sat on the floor and held Andi and Lissa in her arms. "Father God, please protect Hanna." Her voice broke and she gulped back a sob. "Please show Gray where she is. Bring them safely back to us."

"God," Andi sniffed, "I'm sorry I didn't let Hanna use my coloring book and crayons in the car."

Lissa wiped her nose on her sleeve. "I just want her back. Even if she does bug me sometimes."

A soft 'amen' whispered through the cabin.

Sophie pressed her lips tight holding back a sob. What kind of mother was she that her baby could wander off without her knowing? Last night, weary to the bone, she'd left Gray tending the fire and crawled into the bed of boughs falling asleep almost instantly. Upon awakening this morning and finding Hanna gone, she hadn't worried since Gray was also not there. She'd assumed they were together. But then he'd returned to the cabin – alone.

"I'm hungry." Andi rubbed her eyes, pink from crying.

"I'm not sure what Gray planned for breakfast."

Sophie's heart squeezed with remorse. Instead of asking questions and doing her best to be part of the solution, she'd spent the better part of yesterday feeling sorry for herself. Wrapped up in her own fears and discomfort, she'd contributed little of value to the situation.

"What's left of the snacks?" She stood and hurried to the bed frame stacked with backpacks. She hesitated a moment before picking up the pack Gray carried. Even though the pack and the items inside had come from her van, she felt like an intruder. Opening the pack, she went through the neatly organized contents. She found several granola bars and a bag of trail mix. In the other packs, she found equal portions of snack food and water bottles.

In a hidden pocket of an old schoolbag pulled out of storage for this weekend getaway, Sophie discovered two packets of peanuts bearing the logo of the airline they'd flown on a year ago. She had no idea if stale peanuts held any nutritional value, but they'd help fill the empty stomachs. Not wanting to eat food Gray may have allotted for future meals, she split a packet of peanuts and a bar between Andi and Lissa.

A shout followed by a clear sharp whistle cut through the crisp morning air. Heart leaping painfully within her chest, Sophie raced to the cabin door.

Gray stepped from beneath the trees carrying Hanna.

Sophie stumbled down the steps unable to breathe; afraid to blink for fear they'd disappear. Behind her, Lissa and Andi's feet thumped across the porch.

"Hanna. Oh, baby!"

"Mommy."

Mindless of the foul mud covering almost every

inch of her daughter, Sophie reached out to run her hands over Hanna. "Is she hurt?" Sparing Gray a glance, she wiped mud from Hanna's cheeks and whispered words of assurance between prayers of thanksgiving.

"Nothing serious." Gray didn't let go of Hanna. "Let's get her clean so we can doctor the cuts." He walked past the cabin to a sandy spot in the streambed and set Hanna on the bank in a springy patch of moss.

Ignoring the mud and odor, Sophie gathered Hanna into her arms. She couldn't hold back the tears any longer.

Gray spoke to Andi and Lissa then he knelt beside her. "They're getting soap and towels. You need to undress Hanna and clean her up."

"I will. I want to hold her another minute." She squeezed the mud from Hanna's hair. With a final hug, she let go. "Your gown has to come off, sweetie."

Hanna whined and clung to the skirt of the muddy garment.

"I'll wash it in the stream." Gray ran a finger across Hanna's tiny fist. "You want your dress clean and pretty again don't you?"

The gentle timbre of Gray's voice, at odds with his rough appearance and commanding nature, turned Sophie's knees to jelly. And he wasn't even talking to her.

Hanna's fist loosened and Gray nudged Sophie.

Brushing aside her astonishment she moved into action, stripping the tattered gown off Hanna and handing it to Gray. With Hanna's gown and his long-sleeved shirt slung over a shoulder, Gray walked down stream and out of sight.

Back from their trip to the cabin, Andi and Lissa helped peel off the rest of Hanna's clothes. Sophie handed them to Andi. "Take these to Gray. Lissa, please help me wash Hanna."

Velvety green moss carpeted the bank of the stream. Ferns swayed and a stray sunbeam made droplets of water glitter like diamonds. Like a tiny golden wood nymph, Hanna knelt on a mossy stone overlooking a shallow pool at the stream's edge.

Feet aching from the painfully cold water, Sophie coaxed Lissa, Hanna, and the invisible Sushi into the stream. They screeched and squealed with each splash of icy water against warm skin as they washed away the old well's foul brown mud.

"Is everything okay?" Andi stood on the bank, worry creasing her brow. "Gray wants to know what all the noise is about."

"Tell him he forgot to turn on the water heater." Giddy relief bubbled up inside Sophie. Like fizzy soda pop in a shaken bottle, a fit of giggles burst from her lips. She plopped down on a large rock to avoid falling headfirst into the water. Tears blurred her vision. *Hanna is here. Thank you, Lord.*

The bath complete, Sophie dried Hanna with one of the beach towels Gray had rolled inside the quilt. She hugged her close and whispered another prayer of thanksgiving. Bruised and scraped, Hanna suffered only two deep scratches on her arm.

Shaking out another towel, a sharp jab of irritation popped Sophie's bubble of joy. Due to Gray's dictate that first morning, Hanna didn't have any clean clothes to wear. Not even a pair of clean underwear to slip on beneath the towel. Sophie tried to tamp the festering irritability as she wrapped the pink beach towel around Hanna. But her discontent bloomed greater as she rubbed pale yellow hair dry. She wanted her girls to grow up as ladies. And ladies did not go commando.

Gray approached, the sun dappled his bare shoulders marked by war. Scars from an old injury marred the wide expanse of his chest. Above one hip, a round scar puckered his skin.

Sophie seesawed between the desire to run a soothing hand across the old injuries and the impulse to wring his dictatorial stiff neck. She didn't want to feel *anything* for this man. Exhausted beyond anything she'd ever experienced, her stupid heart had the energy to leap like a mountain goat at the sight of her helpful nemesis.

Anger at herself for losing Hanna and her fear of losing the girls forever jumbled with the unwelcome attraction to Gray. The emotional brew rolled into a hot ball of misery at Sophie's core.

Soggy clothes in one hand and a twinkling tiara in the other, Gray's watchful gaze scanned the scene before him. "All set?"

"No!" Sophie straightened up. The tumult inside her swelled to volcanic proportions, her insides too small to contain what boiled up hot as lava. "Because you didn't let me pack extra underclothes, Hanna has to go without!"

Eyes narrowed and locked on Sophie, Gray stood unmoving. "Andi and Lissa, take Hanna to the cabin. Give her a granola bar. We'll be right along."

"Stop issuing orders! They're *my* girls." Sophie couldn't stop the shudders plaguing every muscle in her body. "*I'll* take them to the cabin. *I'll* feed Hanna."

Gray dropped the wet bundle.

His hand snaked out lightening fast.

Sophie gasped as her face abruptly collided with the solid muscle of Gray's chest. His hand, warm against her nape, exerted only enough pressure to hold her still. His voice murmured soft, close to her ear.

"Don't do this, Sophie. Not in front of the girls."

Her hands splayed across skin chilled by the cold stream he'd washed in. In her ear drummed the steady beat of his heart. Beneath her cheek, his chest rose and fell. The masculine scent of Gray filled her lungs.

His fingers loosened and gently massaged her corded neck muscles. "Let go of whatever's eating at you."

She bit back a sob. "The only thing upsetting me is you. In so many ways I can't even begin to tell you. I wanted to bring extra underpants for them. But, noooo. *You* wouldn't allow me to." Gray's hand on her neck, so warm and comforting, melted the hard edges of her anger. She needed the anger to keep from dissolving into a tearful quivering heap. With reluctant hands, she shoved away from the warm solid wall of flesh.

He dropped his hands.

Bereft by the loss she moved away.

His hand touched her arm. "Look at me."

Sophie glared at the toes of his boots.

"Please." His swallow was audible.

She closed her eyes. One 'please' would *not* sway her into forgiving him. She lifted her head but obstinately kept her eyes shut. Something damp and soft caressed her cheek. Her eyelids flew up.

Cloth stroked the end of her nose.

Shifting her gaze, she clashed into a pair of eyes

the color of warm pewter.

"You have mud on your face from lovin' up Hanna." He offered her the scrap of olive drab fabric.

Sophie grabbed it and ran for the cabin.

\*\*\*

Gray watched her go.

The lack of a particular article of clothing wasn't the problem. Out of her element and emotionally fragile, he'd expected her to crack. Hanna's brush with disaster hastened the inevitable. He bent to pick up the wad of wet clothing and the tiara.

Sophie was dealing with more than an accidental trek through the wilderness. Between the death of her husband and the possibility of losing her daughters she was like a ship foundering in heavy seas.

On the porch, he draped the wet clothes over the railing in the sun. With no time for them to dry fully every bit of breeze would help. The murmur of voices drew him inside. He stood to one side of the door and let his eyes adapt to the dim interior.

Unaware of his presence, the Moore women sat in the center of the floor. Sophie tended Hanna's cuts with ointment and bandages from the first aid kit. The woman was everything he'd never had in his life and didn't know he wanted.

Gray shied away from relationships. Women wanted things he wasn't equipped to give them. A navy brat growing up in a home without a mother, he'd been expected to conduct himself like a seaman. His father knew only one way to relate to Gray. Dear old Dad issued orders and Gray carried them out. Survival. He'd developed the skill at an early age. To show tenderness exposed the soft underbelly of a person's defenses. His father had taught him well.

Hanna smiled up from her spot on the blanket.

He stepped away from the wall and joined them, holding up the tiara. A delighted giggle was his reward. He placed it on her damp hair.

"Thank you." Pink colored Sophie's smooth cheeks. Her quiet words wove through the girls' chatter to touch him deep inside.

Unable to speak past the lump in his throat, Gray nodded. The wanting to be a part of their warm happy circle troubled him. "Andi, come help me with the packs. Please." He turned away from Sophie and her soft smile. "I want to lighten Hanna's load."

By mid afternoon Gray wished he had the GPS that was in his pack at SeaMount. He stopped to check the bearings using his makeshift compass then compared the map from the van to the crude one provided when SeaMount dumped him in the forest. If they hustled, he could leave Sophie and the smurfs at the resort and get to the next checkpoint within the allotted time.

"Thank you for finding Hanna this morning." Munching on trail mix Sophie eased back against a rock.

Gray strapped his watch on and drank from his water bottle. He didn't deserve the thanks. He should never have lost Hanna in the first place.

Sophie rotated her shoulders and rubbed her thighs.

Keeping her in his peripheral vision, Gray's pulse jumped. He'd read enough of his Bible to know somewhere in it God had a command about keeping every thought under control. What was the good Lord thinking when He issued *that* order?

"I didn't see her leave the cabin. I should have since she's my baby *and* my buddy." Sophie sniffed. "I'm sorry."

Her self-condemnation hit him like a rocket-propelled grenade. "The mistake was mine. It won't happen again."

"Yours?" Sophie shook her head. "You paired me with her when we began this hike."

"I'm team leader. I'm responsible." He polished off his bottle of water.

Lips pressed together, she stepped away from him.

A fight broke out among the smurfs and he managed a sharp reprimand without a single cuss word. Lissa and Andi glowered at each other, finishing their granola bars in silence.

Sophie brushed a leaf from Hanna's hair. "How soon will we be at Bride Lake?"

"Not soon enough." Gray stepped back on the narrow game trail. "Let's go, ladies. Stick with your buddy."

\*\*\*

Water seeped from between layers of ledge creating a narrow runnel that wound down the face of the mountain. In the moist soil on either side ferns grew thick and wood sorrel bloomed. Rocks slippery with moss made the going treacherous. Rays of sunlight filtered through the forest's upper story and glittered in the running water. In one bright spot, wild strawberries poked up through the leaf litter.

Gray shucked his pack. "We'll rest here." The welcome statement prompted relieved groans from Sophie and the girls.

They'd hiked around a tightly woven thicket of pucker brush only to run up against a rock wall. Layers of exposed granite, dark with age and mottled with moss, towered high above.

Andi spied the berries and dropped her pack at her mother's feet. "Can we eat them?"

Gray nodded. "Stay close."

Dumping their packs, the girls knelt to pick and eat the treat. Sophie collapsed on a log and rubbed her temples with her fingers.

Gray eased the pack off her back. Her dry shirt set off warning bells in his head. "When did you last drink water?" She pushed the water on the girls, but he couldn't recall seeing her drink.

Befuddled by the question, Sophie frowned. "A short while ago, I think."

He unzipped her pack and pulled out three water bottles. One half full, two untouched. Uncapping a full bottle, he crouched on his heels and held it in front of her face. "Drink."

She dropped her hands and shot him a peevish scowl.

"Please." He took hold of one of her hands and slapped the bottle into it. "You're dehydrated. Drink up. And every time we stop for a break, you drink."

Sophie sipped and grimaced. "Boiled water tastes flat."

"It's wet. Your body needs it." He stood to check on the girl's whereabouts.

She muttered under her breath.

"What'd you say?"

Her angry gaze clashed with his intimidating glare. "I said I'm going to need a restroom."

He held back the laughter building in his chest. "And the problem is…?"

Her arm flung wide. "In case you haven't noticed, there are no restrooms out here. Not even a disgusting port-a-john."

He couldn't hide his grin from her.

"Go ahead and laugh."

The girls looked up from picking berries.

She lowered her voice. "It's not funny." Without thinking, she chugged several gulps from her bottle. "Between bugs that bite, poison ivy and some prickly weed thing out to get me, I'm tired of not having real facilities."

Though her offended sensibilities amused him, he'd have a real problem on his hands if she continued her current conduct. "If you want to keep up with your daughters, you'd better start drinking your water."

Grumpy and tired, she drank the rest then held the bottle up.

Taking it from her, Gray stowed it in her pack. "Good job. And if it helps, I'll scout any area you choose. I can't do anything about the bugs, but I'm pretty good at spotting poison ivy and prickly weed things."

She shoved hair out of her eyes. "Thank you."

Keeping his face straight, he nodded. "You're welcome." He left her sitting on the log and joined the girls. All three had lips and fingers stained with berry juice. "Hey ladies, how about picking a few for your mother?"

Lissa popped another berry in her mouth. "Why isn't she picking her own?"

Gray glanced at Sophie. "You can pick a few

61

berries for her to enjoy after all she's done for you."

A scowl settled on Lissa's face. "You're not my father. You can't tell me what to do." To prove her point, she pushed the ear buds of her mp3 player into her ears.

With a quick tug on the wires Gray popped them right back out. Taking advantage of her surprise, he snatched the player and slipped it into his pants pocket. "You're under orders not to listen to this while on the trail."

Face as red as the strawberry juice on her lips, Lissa bellowed. "Mooomm!" Tears followed the unearthly wail.

Sophie rose off the log and hobbled to Lissa's side. "Liss?" Exhaustion carved lines around her mouth. Her gaze bounced back and forth between Gray and her tearful daughter.

Standing his ground, Gray braced for a tongue-lashing. He didn't anticipate Andi jumping into the fray.

"She's acting like a baby."

Andi's pronouncement dried her sister's tears in an instant. "Am not."

"Are too."

Dueling tongues came out.

"Enough!"

Alarmed, both girls stared at their mother with wide eyes.

Gray crossed his arms and made an effort to keep the grin off his face. *Go, Sophie!* She sounded like him.

Sophie inhaled a deep breath. "Stop the fighting or I'll give Gray permission to... to..." She glanced at him.

He raised an eyebrow in question. *This oughta be good.*

"To do whatever they do to punish smurfs in boot camp." She frowned. "Or whatever they call it."

Not dropping his tough guy stance, he kept his grin in check and concentrated his gaze on Lissa and Andi. "One hundred push ups. Each. And that's only the beginning."

"He stole my mp3 player." Lissa wasn't ready to give up the fight.

"Good. The thing will make you deaf." Sophie twisted to face him. "Keep it."

Howling as though mortally wounded, Lissa stomped away.

Sophie swayed. Gray grasped her arm and helped steady her. "Andi, do you have any berries to share with your mother?"

Andi squatted to pick more, but Hanna was the first to present Sophie with juicy red berries the size of marbles.

"Thank you, baby."

Picking his own berries, Gray's attention kept going back to the tired woman half leaning, half sitting on a rock outcropping. She'd surprised him with her support in disciplining Lissa.

A part of him thrilled to the notion that for once he and Sophie were in accord. Another part of him – the loner – quaked with trepidation that this could become standard operating procedure. Unsettled, each berry morphed into a red caution flag, warning Gray of impending danger.

# Chapter 7

Determination kept Sophie upright. Thigh muscles burning, she tugged on Hanna's hand. "Come on, sweetie."

Pushing her cockeyed tiara back to the top of her head, Hanna plodded along in her mother's wake. Her gown, creased from the morning wash and wrung dry by Gray's heavy hand, clung to her jeans.

Slapping each other and bickering, Andi and Lissa followed close on Gray's heels at the edge of a small woodland meadow.

Gray stopped before a copse of birch and studied the area. "We'll stay here." A light breeze rustled through the leafy bower carrying with it the soft symphony of tree limbs knocking, insects buzzing, bird song and the timpani of burbling water.

"Where will we sleep?" Only four solid walls would keep Sophie's nightmares at bay.

He waved a hand at the stand of birch trees ringed with ox-eye daisies and orange hawkweed. "In among the trees. Should be trout in the stream."

She tamped back the dread of sleeping in the open.

"I know how to fish."

"I won't be long. I'll stay within hollering distance. Keep the girls in line." Hitching his pack higher, he pivoted and headed toward the water.

Sophie fought the urge to salute as he strode off.

Andi paused her disorderly pawing through her backpack. "Where's he going?"

"The brook. He's going fishing."

Lissa kicked at a tussock of grass. "I'll eat at Bride Lake."

Sophie sighed. "We won't get there tonight."

Wails of protest followed on the heels of that bit of news.

"Hush." Sophie allowed her quivering knees to give way. Her graceless descent ended with a bump as she settled among the flowers and tall grass. "I can't do a thing about it." Grasping her ankles, Sophie pulled her legs in tailor-fashion.

Hanna plopped in the middle of her mother's crossed legs. Overtired, she wiggled and whined to make room for the non-existent Sushi.

"Why aren't you fishing, Mommy?" Andi frowned.

"Gramps always took you fishing on Bride Lake." Lissa leaned back, her hands braced behind her.

"I don't have a rod and reel." Sophie straightened the tattered ribbons hanging from Andi's braids.

"What's Gray using?" Lissa blew her bangs out of her eyes.

"I'm not sure. Maybe something he found in the van."

Andi slumped in a dejected heap. "Wish we could go fishing, too."

Lissa poked her. "We'd need a pole and line, you dope."

Andi pointed at the woods. "We can use a stick for a pole and don't call me a dope."

"Girls." Sophie's reprimand silenced the squabble. She rubbed a hand across Lissa's narrow back. "What could we use for a line?"

"Andi's ribbons." Lissa made a face at her sister.

"Uh-uh." Andi clutched a braid in each hand, covering the ribbons with her fingers. "Daddy gave these to me."

Sophie patted one small fist. "What else is there?"

"My shoe laces." Andi thrust her feet out in front of her. The laces were round and brown with dirt. "But we need a hook."

Uninterested in the game, Hanna squirmed in her mother's lap.

Sophie grasped her above the elbows and shifted her slight weight to a more comfortable position. A flash of silver caught her eye.

"I have it!" With quick fingers, Sophie undid the large safety pin at the back of Hanna's princess gown and held it up. "A hook." Sophie pointed at Andi's shoelace.

Reading the intention in her mother's eyes, she reached for her shoe and pulled the lace from the eyelets.

Lissa curled her lip at her sister. "You need a pole."

Sophie shook her head. "I can fish without a pole." Arms around either side of Hanna, she tied the pin to the end of the shoelace and held them up for inspection. Primitive but possible. "All I need now is bait."

"We can search under rocks and logs." Andi glanced down the hill. "But Gray told us to stay here."

"No. He told me to keep you in line." Perhaps she could contribute to the next meal using her one and only wilderness skill. "Will the three of you promise to be quiet?"

"We're going with you?" Lissa rose up on her knees. "Really?"

"I won't leave you here alone."

Andi reached for Hanna. "We'll take care of her while you fish."

Muscles protesting, Sophie struggled to her feet. "Not a peep out of anyone. And no fighting."

Lissa tsked her tongue. "We know."

Sophie led the girls to the nearby stream. It ran wide and fast with feathery ferns and soft moss edging its rocky bank.

Andi rolled a half rotten log, leaned into the depression and picked a white grub from the moist earth.

Lissa cringed with disgust.

Taking the bait, Sophie settled the girls away from the bank and moved to the water's edge. Over time the current had undercut the bank of the stream. Exposed tree roots and a tangle of bushes formed a dark grotto. The perfect hidey-hole for trout. Soft springy moss beneath her knees, Sophie ignored the squeamish flutters in her stomach and hooked the grub on the pin. Lowering the baited pin into the water, it drifted into the dark cool cave beneath the roots.

Bam!

The hit came fast and hard. Sophie jerked the line

to set the hook then pulled up her catch. The sun glinted off the brookie's wet mottled skin as it flopped and wiggled trying to return to the water.

Andi and Lissa whooped with delight.

Sophie cut their celebration short. "Quiet. Remember?" She set the fish back from the water's edge. Using another grub, she dropped the pin back into the water. The waiting stretched out longer this time before the second trout took the bait.

Helping her mother, Andi placed the fish beside the first one before settling beside Lissa who held a sleeping Hanna.

By the time she caught the third trout, Lissa and Andi had fallen asleep as well.

Pulling her fourth trout from the brook, Sophie swung it ashore.

The fish landed on the moss – at the toes of size fourteen boots.

Uh-oh.

A masculine hand reached down, pulled the pin out and hooked a finger through one gill.

She wished he'd say something. A cuss word would be preferable to the heavy silence. He moved without a sound on the moss to where Andi, Lissa and Hanna lay sleeping near the other three fish. He stood over them in silence.

Sophie held her breath. Gray carried only three trout. A tiny frisson of satisfaction rippled through her. She'd helped catch supper. Finally, she met his gaze.

His eyes held an unmistakable challenge. "You catch them. You gut them."

Was that a universal law? Her grandfather had lived by the same rule. He'd taught her how to do the unpleasant task with efficiency.

Gray unsheathed his knife and offered it to her handle first. His lips tightened a fraction and he held the blade a moment longer than necessary before releasing the knife to her.

Sophie carried a fish to a flat rock at the water's edge. With the butt of the knife, she knocked the fish on the head. Holding it belly up, she deftly wielded the knife. With quick sure movements, she removed the entrails then rinsed the trout and her hands in the stream. She turned to place the cleaned fish on the rock and bumped against Gray squatting on his heels beside her. His strong fingers caught her elbow and set her back on balance.

Sophie's heart kicked. The challenge in his eyes had vanished, replaced by a twinkle and laugh lines. Warmth flooded through her.

"What would your manicurist say?"

The quiet humor was in complete opposition to what she'd come to expect of him. She examined her chipped nails and scratched hands. "He'd insist on a paraffin treatment."

"He?"

She glanced up into his frowning face and nodded. "Chen has done my nails for years."

His eyes narrowed to slits.

So long, soft side.

"I'll finish up here. Wake the girls and take them back to camp. Gather firewood along the way."

Sophie sighed. *Issuing orders again.* Happy to relinquish the grisly task to him, she went to wake the girls.

\*\*\*

Listening the gentle murmur of Sophie waking the girls, Gray set to work on the remaining trout. The woman had out-fished him! The image of her hands moving with assurance through the gory cleaning process stuck in his head. His chest tightened with the thought of another man holding her hands. Didn't matter that it was business. The fact didn't sit well. Especially after hauling her off that log to safety. She'd felt so incredibly right in his arms.

Gray flipped the flat rock into the water then disposed of the entrails farther down stream. He washed his knife and cleaned the area hoping predators wouldn't be drawn in by the scent. The wind carried the occasional high-pitched notes of laughter from camp. Sophie and the smurfs laughed a lot. They loved each other fiercely. Lissa and Andi could be locked in combat one moment and laughing together the next.

He leapt along the rocks on the bank of the stream. Out of habit he took care not to leave sign a tracker could follow. Not that it mattered this time. This mission didn't come with tangos. Good thing. Sophie and the girls had cut a swath across the meadow wide enough to accommodate a tank. Caution was ingrained in him much like Sophie's instinctive mothering of the girls. He marveled at her ability to love with a depth he'd never experienced.

What would a woman like Sophie find appealing in a wrung-out ex-military man? She had outright admitted he upset her in ways too numerable to count, the swearing being her first disappointment. The no cussing rule had pretty much muzzled him. Irritated by the direction his thoughts had taken, he sped up his pace.

The sun had slid behind the mountain when camp came into sight. Colorful backpacks leaned against a rock on one side of the grove, the women gathered in the center. Rocks the size of cannon balls ringed a small area bare of all tree litter. Andi had laid out the sticks for a fire the way he'd taught her last night.

He nudged Lissa aside and squatted opposite Andi to cast a critical eye over the pile of tinder and sticks. "Make it looser so air can feed the flame." He pulled out a few sticks. "That'll do. Good job."

Her face lit up and Gray had to look away. When he got back to civilization he'd see a doctor about the curling sensation in his gut.

An hour later, Gray checked the trout hanging on a stick above the crackling flames. "Fish are ready." The women gathered closer to the fire. Sophie knelt across from him; smoke drifting between them like a billowing veil.

He slipped the trout off the stick onto pieces of white birch bark.

"Eeew. The head is on it!" Lissa crossed her arms and wrinkled her nose. "It's staring at me."

Andi picked her fish up and swished it through the air in a swimming motion straight at Lissa.

"Andi. Don't play with your food." Sophie spared Gray a quick embarrassed glance before gingerly trying to remove the head of the fish with her fingers.

He unsheathed his knife and held it out.

With a smile of thanks, she removed the heads from the fish and returned his knife. "Girls, let's say grace."

Hanna and Andi reached out to take Gray's hands in theirs. His breath caught in his chest. They bowed their heads and Sophie said a prayer.

He didn't hear a word of it. Blood rushed in his ears, deafening him. With his eyes closed, nothing existed but the tiny fingers connecting him to their circle. Being a part of their tight-knit group was like free-diving in uncharted water. He had no knowledge of the depth or if he'd have air and stamina enough to get back to the surface before blacking out. The 'amen' chorus brought his attention back to the moment and he released the girls' hands as if he held two hot gun barrels.

"Girls, watch for bones." Sophie turned to help Hanna.

Holding up a piece of bark piled high with wet greens he'd washed in boiled water, Gray tried to ignore the tremor in his hands. "Found some watercress."

Sophie took a small helping and encouraged the girls to do the same.

Lissa held up a leaf and examined it closely. "I don't think I like this."

Red-faced Sophie's eyes darted to Gray then back to Lissa. "Gray went to the trouble of preparing it, Lissa."

Beside her, Andi picked out several leaves, stuffed them in her mouth and chewed. "Like radishes."

Lissa nibbled the pungent green. No sign of distaste or nausea followed. A good sign in Gray's estimation.

Their chatter swirled around him as they ate their supper. Meals in the field had been mostly silent affairs for Gray. You got hungry. You ate. This bunch made each meal a social event. One more sign he'd stumbled into unfamiliar territory.

Swallowing the last of his meal, he stood. "When you're done, toss the bark and bones into the fire. If you need anything from your pack, grab it. I'll be hanging them out of the reach of bears." Turning to police the area for bits of food, he noted Sophie's furtive glances beyond the campfire into the deepening shadows of the forest.

As darkness descended on the small camp he secured the backpacks high in a tree using the cargo net from Sophie's van. The soft din of nocturnal insects and frogs warming up for their nightly concert soothed him. Noisy critters were happy critters. If they went silent, then he'd worry.

Stomachs full, the weary girls bedded down with a minimum of fuss. As he'd done the night before, Gray covertly listened to the ritual of prayers followed by goodnight hugs and kisses. He'd spent the better part of his life with men who, out of duty and respect, would lay their life on the line for him just as he'd willingly die for them. He envied what Sophie had with her girls. It went further than loyalty to one another. Was this what love looked like?

He'd feared his father and respected the men he served with. When he wasn't worried about staying alive he'd spent time with women he found attractive. But those relationships had nothing to do with love. Observing Sophie and her girls drilled a hollow spot inside him that grew bigger with each hour spent in their presence.

With the girls tucked up for the night, Sophie returned to sit at the fire. He'd hoped she'd fall in with the girls. "Go get some rest."

She shook her head. "I'll stay up with you."

The woman had no idea what she did to him. "I can keep the fire going on my own."

"I don't doubt that." She studied her nails then chewed one.

"Here." Gray unsheathed his knife. "You want to trim them?"

She regarded the blade with apprehension.

He shifted closer to her. Warning bells clanged in his head, but he ignored them. "Give me your hand."

"Why?"

Her suspicious expression put a dent in his ego. "I'll trim your nails."

"With your *knife*?"

"I promise I won't slip. All your fingers will be intact when I'm done."

Hesitant, she extended her hand. His pulse fired like an MP5 on full automatic. He grasped her fingers and tension coiled between them. Her hand shook and he tightened his grip to steady her. With careful precision he used the finely honed blade to trim each nail still spotted with remnants of pink polish. Though he'd done this procedure on his own nails often enough, never had he performed this service for someone else. The intimacy tightened his chest and he had to remind himself to breathe. "Tell me about your late husband's parents."

"They hoped Tommy would do better than to marry someone like me."

"Better?" What more could they want?

Sophie nodded. "My family never had money or social status. Both are important to Gerald and Suzanne." She paused, cautious of the blade paring her ragged fingernail. "Mayflower connections would be acceptable, too."

Indignation on Sophie's behalf burned low in Gray's gut.

"I believe they want the girls because they see a bit of Tommy in each of them." Her ragged sigh ended in a tiny sob. "And now I'm going to miss the hearing if we aren't back by tomorrow afternoon."

He wished he could assure her she'd make it, but it was more than likely they wouldn't.

In the surrounding darkness a clamor as varied as the nocturnal inhabitants of the forest, rose in volume. Amid the buzzing, trilling and croaking, an owl hooted. A large animal splashed in the stream.

Sophie jerked. "What was that?"

"Hold still." Keeping his promise, Gray avoided slicing tender skin. "Most likely a moose."

"I hate the forest at night." She shuddered all the way to the tips of her fingers. "I'd forgotten how much until the night in the van."

He released her hand and slid his knife home in its sheath. "The wilderness at night can be frightening if you've never experienced it."

Sophie bent her knees up and wrapped her arms around her legs. "It's scary even if you have. When I was young, I spent my summers with my grandparents at the Whispering Pines Resort on Bride Lake."

"Where we're headed."

She nodded. "My cousins would often be there, too. We'd swim and canoe in the lake all day and after dark play hide and seek." She gazed at the fire deep in thought.

Gray tamped the urge to reprimand her. They

weren't in enemy territory where the split second it would take her eyes to adapt to the darkness beyond the fire could cost her life. He sat quiet, afraid she'd clam up if he moved.

"One night I hid farther away from the house than usual." She gulped. "I heard an unearthly scream and freaked." She shivered reliving the memory. "I ran scared then couldn't find my way home. Gramps found me at three in the morning, sitting on a rock crying. Said I'd probably heard a Canada lynx." Sophie blew out her breath. "I never again played outdoors after dark."

Gray added a log to the fire. He scrambled to find words of encouragement. "You're doing okay so far." *You stink at this, Kerr.*

She gave an indelicate snort. "It's not three in the morning yet."

"Did your grandfather teach you to fish?"

"Yes." She tossed a twig on the fire. "Every evening before bedtime, Gramps announced who'd go with him fishing the following morning." The warm glow of the flickering fire enveloped her. Her mouth curved in a gentle smile. She glanced at him sidelong. "Your turn."

"What?"

"Tell me about yourself."

He shook his head in automatic refusal. No way would he go there with this woman. She'd already broken through his defenses with nothing but the lightest of artillery. "Nothing to tell."

"I don't believe you." She yawned and glanced at her daughters in a tangled heap beneath the quilt. "Guess I'll try to get some sleep."

Good choice.

She tugged a stick the size of a baseball bat from Gray's pile of firewood, weighed it in her hand and smiled. "'Night." Dragging the stick with her, Sophie crawled back under the quilt and snuggled up to the girls with her back to Gray.

"Goodnight." He'd disappointed her, but he didn't want to expose her to the horrors of his world or to the darkness inside him. He was selfish enough to want her gratitude and Andi's hero-worship. Escorting them to Whispering Pines Resort was the first good and sacrificial thing he'd done in a very long time – if ever.

Hours later, Gray tossed more fuel on the fire. Sophie had been restless from the moment she crawled under the quilt clutching the stick. Moss could be soft but it wasn't memory foam.

Off to the west a loud grunt silenced the lesser beasts of the forest.

Sophie sat up, hair disheveled and eyes opened wide. Her gaze landed on Gray and stayed there.

"Go back to sleep." He set aside the log he used to poke the fire. "Probably just a bear."

## Chapter 8

"A bear?" Panic shot through Sophie.

Hearing her mother's voice, Hanna mewled.

Sophie rubbed her back soothing her to sleep before scrambling from beneath the quilt clutching her stick. She dropped to her knees and rubbed her sore hip. "Should I wake the girls and have them move closer to the fire?"

"No." Gray's eyes searched the meadow and dark forest beyond the shifting light of the campfire.

The stick's rough bark dug into her clenched hand. She fought to keep her terror in check. "Will the bear go away?"

"Most likely nosing around where we cleaned the fish." He glanced at her stick.

She ignored his questioning gaze. "Will it come here?"

"Might come by out of curiosity."

Oh, *that* was comforting. *Not!*

He frowned. "Didn't bears come through Whispering Pines when you were a kid?"

"Once in a while. I trusted the adults to keep me

safe."

"Then trust me."

To him it was that simple.

He selected wood from the pile beside him and added it to the fire. The flames crackled. A log fell with a hiss sending sparks and smoke up into the air. The firelight played across the sharp angles of his brow and cheeks. Even with the scruffy beard, his face portrayed resolve and strength of character.

Sophie pressed a hand against her chest trying to slow the pace of her heart. What was happening to her? This man was the complete opposite of Tommy. In the past two days her heart raced more times than she cared to admit. Tommy had never had this affect on her. They'd known each other all their lives. Perhaps the intrigue surrounding Gray fueled her attraction.

She set her stick aside and shoved her hands deep into the sleeves of her sweatshirt. Maybe if she knew more about him she'd dispel the infatuation. "The company you're hoping to work for, what do they do?"

His gaze never wavered from the dark woods.

Sophie shifted her position and rubbed her arms. She'd given up on getting an answer to her question when he finally spoke.

"They carry out diverse operations worldwide."

"What type of operations? Military?"

"No. Though most of the agents have military training." His gaze swung to her, focused and intense, captivating her. "They're a private investigative and securities firm. Federally sponsored though unacknowledged. If they go into a foreign country, it's without the official backing of Uncle Sam. Might be missionaries caught in the middle of a political uprising or people in trouble after a natural disaster. Wherever there's a need, SeaMount will send help."

"Sounds dangerous."

His lips tipped up on one side. "Yeah."

*Alrighty.* That told her a lot about the man. "You like going into danger?"

He turned toward her. His eyes glittered in the firelight. "In this job, I'd be facing danger for all the right reasons."

"Which are..."

"Rescuing the lost, protecting the innocent, helping people in need."

She'd have to figure out the wrong reasons for facing danger, but not tonight. "Kinda like what you're doing for us."

His face relaxed into a smile. "Yeah. Kinda like."

Sophie's insides melted like the center of a toasted marshmallow, all soft and gooey.

They sat in companionable silence. Sophie, sure she had loads more questions, couldn't remember what they were as the forest's nighttime music lulled her tired brain and body into peacefulness.

"Come on, Sophie."

She labored to open her eyes.

Bent over her, his hand on her elbow, Gray picked up her stick. "Time you got some shuteye." He helped her up and led her over to the quilt, lumpy with children. Flipping a corner back he let her climb under before tucking the fabric up around her shoulders and setting her stick close beside her. "Sleep well, Sophie."

\*\*\*

Sophie swiped at the itch on her forehead and drifted back toward sleep.

The tickle moved to her cheek.

She scratched it.

The tip of her nose itched.

A soft giggle penetrated the fog of sleep. Sophie opened her eyes.

An intent silver gaze held her captive. For one breathless moment, she remained frozen in place as her heart rolled in a slow labored somersault.

Andi dropped to her hands and knees next her mother, breaking the connection between Sophie and Gray. "Wake up, sleepy head."

Hooking an arm around Andi's neck, she pulled her down and rubbed a noogie on the top of her head.

"Mommy! It wasn't me."

Catching her breath, Sophie glanced at Gray.

He twirled a daisy between thumb and forefinger. "Time to break camp."

"You let me sleep." She sat up. "This will put us behind even more."

Noting the high cloud cover, Gray hitched his chin toward the fire. "Lissa has some berries and trail mix for you." He rose, taking her quilt with him.

*How rude.* Brisk morning air swept over Sophie and brought her fully awake. She rolled to her knees and pushed to a stand, muscles aching. "Will we get to Bride Lake today?"

"Hope so."

Last night's fireside chat hadn't improved his social skills one iota, though the daisy thing was a puzzle.

\*\*\*

Someone had loaded her pack with rocks. Hours later, Sophie was sure of that. It seemed pounds heavier today. She grunted and hauled herself up over an outcropping of ledge only to find the land dropped away dramatically on the other side. Below her, Gray and the three girls zigzagged down the side of the steep hill grasping trees to keep from pitching headlong to the bottom.

Breathing in the damp woodsy air, she leaned against a birch tree and caught her breath. *Lord, don't let me fall.*

In the distance, a deep rumble reverberated between the mountains. Above the green canopy of leaves, a solid layer of ragged gray clouds rolled in blocking the sun and the warmth of its rays.

Gray hadn't said anything about the weather, but before breaking camp he'd wrapped the packs and blankets in garbage bags confiscated from the van. All morning he'd hustled them along skipping the usual mid morning break.

Placing one foot carefully in front of the other, Sophie braced against trees and grabbed bushes as she made her way to where Gray and the girls waited for her. The way they stood lined up next to one another caused dread to well up inside her. *What now?*

A soft rushing noise hung in the air as she staggered to the bottom of the hill. Forcing one foot in front of the other, she went to stand beside Andi.

Her heart fell to her toes. They stood on a cliff overlooking a river several hundred feet below. The spectacular view caught at her already ragged breath. Awe battled with the aversion to another obstacle. Collapsing on a nearby rock her gaze swung to Gray.

His eyes were already focused on her, taking her measure.

"What now?" She hated to ask for fear of his answer.

He glanced skyward then back across the river. "We want to be on the other side."

"Wonderful." She rubbed her aching legs. "How do we get there?"

His only answer was to turn and walk along the ragged edge of the cliff.

Heart in her throat, Sophie stood and grabbed Hanna's hand. "Andi and Lissa, stay back from the edge." Whispering prayers, asking God to watch over their every step, she followed. Gradually, the uneven rocky slope dropped to meet the river. The narrow game trail they followed broke from the forest where the river had worn the face of solid bedrock as smooth as a beach stone.

They followed Gray across the rock to stand within inches of the water as it rushed from one stone terrace to the next in a series of small waterfalls.

"A water slide!" Andi edged closer to the water.

Sophie pulled her back. "Don't get any ideas." She didn't like the way Gray studied the water, as though he expected them to walk on it or something.

"We can cross at the top of the second fall."

Great. He'd boiled the choices down to 'or something'. "The girls will be swept away." Sophie shoved Hanna toward Lissa. "Get back on the dirt."

Lissa and Hanna happily did their mother's biding. A crestfallen Andi dragged her feet, peeking back every three or four steps.

She hadn't questioned Gray on any of his decisions. Well, not many of them. But this one was dangerous. "There has to be a different way."

He faced her, his silver gaze unblinking. "I crossed here. The water is only a few inches deep coming over the face of the rock."

"But you're an adult and can withstand the current." She waved a hand at the water. "If one of the girls slips, she'll be carried away."

The muscles in his jaw clenched. "Trust me on this, Sophie." He clamped both hands on her shoulders. "Do you think I'd take unnecessary risks with their lives?"

Like that made her feel better? "I don't want you to take *any* risk with their lives. Necessary or unnecessary."

He kneaded her shoulders, his face inches from hers. "I'll carry Hanna. I'll carry each of them across one at a time if that's what you want."

Pure bliss. Sophie wanted to forget about the fight for survival and just enjoy the strength of his hands massaging her sore aching muscles. Eyes closed she leaned towards him.

"Sophie?"

"Mmm?"

"Did you hear what I said?"

She opened her eyes. "Yes."

"So, I'll carry them across."

"No."

He let go and with a glance heavenward, blew out his breath. "If we're going to do this we have to do it now."

"I know you want to be rid of us."

"Don't assume you know what I want."

She waved away his interruption. "And as much as I can't wait to get back to civilization, I want to walk out as a family, all of us in one piece."

He turned back toward the mountain.

"What are you looking at?" Sophie spun around and for the first time saw the ominous black clouds enveloping the mountain peak.

"The river may become impassable if we wait." He called the girls to follow him.

"Maybe we should find shelter on this side of the river." Sophie increased the volume of her voice to be heard above the rush of the river and the gusty wind tugging at the plastic bags encasing their packs.

He halted on a narrow strip of dry rock and scooped up Hanna. A light shower of raindrops swept across the surface of the river and blew into their faces. *Lord? Why must the rain come now?* Praying for divine intervention, Sophie helped the girls remove their shoes.

Gray frowned at their actions but said nothing.

"Lissa, you'll come with me now. Give me your pack."

"Why me?" Lissa crossed her arms and glared at Andi. "Take her first."

Game for the adventure, Andi hopped up and down. "I'm ready."

But he would have none of Lissa's argument. "I'll carry Hanna and I want you with her on the other side while I come back for Andi."

With a click of her tongue and a dramatic sigh, Lissa dropped her arms and took his outstretched hand. He led her to the water and waded in. Lissa followed. Her high-pitched squeal pained Sophie's ears.

"It's cold!" Clinging to him with both her hands, Lissa bent in the middle like an old woman. She cried and screeched, high-stepping behind Gray through the bone-chilling water.

Loaded as he was with Lissa's pack as well as his own, and the two girls, Sophie stood in awe of the man's strength. Still wearing his boots, he forged ahead sure-footed and determined. "Lord, direct their steps. Take them across the river safely." She hadn't realized she'd prayed aloud until Andi said, "Amen."

Reaching the opposite shore, he slung Lissa's pack up on the high bank. He lifted Hanna and Lissa up then shucked his own pack.

Eyes riveted to the other side of the river, Sophie finally breathed with relief.

He spoke and gestured away from the bank. Lissa got up. Dragging a pack, she led Hanna away from the river's edge to the shelter of a tangled blow down.

Sure they were settled, Gray began to make his way back. Half way across a flash of lightning followed by the deep rumble of thunder heralded a heavier rain that soon pattered over the face of the rock in big, sloppy drops.

Sophie held Andi's hand with one hand and clutched at the hood of her sweatshirt with the other. The wind whipped the light pink fabric speckled with dark spots from the falling rain.

Gray surged forward, his expression tense.

Rainwater dripping off her chin, Andi waded in to meet him. Water swirled above her ankles. Feet braced wide apart, she handed her pack over to him.

"Be careful, Andi. You hold fast to Gray." Sophie dipped her toes into the frigid water. Sharp pains shot up her legs. Wiping rain from her face, she inched forward praying her feet became numb enough to withstand the agonizingly cold water.

With Andi's pack slung over one shoulder, Gray held out a hand. "Give me the shoes and your pack, Sophie."

Lightning flashed again and the boom of thunder vibrated in her chest. They stood exposed and vulnerable on the bald expanse of rock. The silver rain created a lacy screen separating her from Lissa and Hanna on the opposite bank.

Gray took up the pack with dangling shoes. "Andi, take my hand." He speared Sophie with an uncompromising glare. "Wait for me."

Raring to go, Andi followed Gray. Twice her bare feet slipped on the slick rock. Each time Gray was her anchor, hauling her back to her feet. Reaching the other side, she hooked her arms through the packs Gray handed her and joined her sisters beneath the fallen tree.

Bare feet numb, Sophie shuffled forward another few inches. In the short time it took Gray and Andi to cross, the current had become stronger. He waded toward her. Wet t-shirt plastered to his torso, his determined expression sent shudders of apprehension through her.

Lightening sizzled overhead. A sharp clap of thunder followed by a rolling crash jolted Sophie into action. Gasping, she stepped toward Gray, trying to cling to the smooth rock with numb toes.

His hand, wet and warm, enveloped hers. The muscles in his arm bunched. "Hang on tight."

The air crackled. The rain fell in torrents diminishing her vision. She tried to blink the water from her eyes.

Over the drum of rain and the rush of the river, a

shout rang out.

Someone screamed.

Lissa! With her free hand, Sophie pushed back the soggy hood of her sweatshirt and tried to protect her eyes from the pelting rain. "Lissa?" The icy water flowed fast and strong up to her knees, much deeper now than when the girls crossed.

"Sophie, move!" Gray pulled on her hand.

Unfeeling stumps had replaced her feet. Heart pounding, she let Gray pull her along. She slipped and struggled to regain her balance. A sizzle of lightning, clap of thunder, rushing water and screams created a discordant din.

Gray shouted and yanked on her arm. Pain shot through Sophie's shoulder at the same moment a large object rammed her legs.

She scrabbled for a foothold, but her legs below the knees were too numb to work properly. Clouds the color of smoke whirled in her line of vision. Frigid water cascaded across her hips and back. Gray's voice penetrated her shock but she didn't understand his words.

Pain exploded in her side.

She gasped and swallowed water. Pain seared her ribs. Her grip on Gray's hand slipped.

His fingers tightened. The dread of being swept away rocketed through her. The swift current scraped her across the slippery rock face. Her hips hung over the edge of the fall.

She slid some more. The current twisted her round and wrenched her hand from Gray's grasp. A mouthful of water silenced her scream. She hung suspended on the edge of the fall. Then the world dropped away.

Sophie hurled over the edge. The girls' faces flashed through her mind as she splashed down at the bottom of the waterfall. Water engulfed her, filling her nose. Terror fueled her thrashing fight beneath the water, unsure which way was up. Her lungs burned. Then her foot hit bedrock. Pushing hard, she broke through to the surface and sucked in huge draughts of air.

The racing current pulled her out of the pool. Her bottom bumped and slipped along polished rock. Andi's water slide comment cut through Sophie's panic as she tried to gain control of her direction. Frothy water splashed all around her. She craned her neck trying to keep her head above water. Then once again she was weightless and falling.

She drew in a breath and remembered to close her mouth before dropping into the next pool. The cold water sapped her strength and with uncoordinated strokes, she swam for the surface then treaded water.

She heard Gray call out.

Fighting the current she rolled toward his voice, struggling to stay above the foaming surface. The uncompromising river carried her across the next slab of slippery rock, scraping the backs of her heels and tearing her hands. Rolling over and over, she sank into a black cloud of pain. The world spun in a dizzying collage of twirling trees and wheeling rocks.

Then once again, she was falling.

# Chapter 9

Branches whipped Gray's face and scratched his arms as he scrambled over rocks along the river's edge. Agony speared his heart.

What had he done?

Powerless to stop her fall, Gray's heart plummeted as Sophie catapulted over another fall. Fueled by memories of friends lost in battle, his mind flooded with pictures of her broken and bleeding on the river rocks. Lungs laboring, he leapt from boulder to slippery boulder, reaching deep inside for the calm detachment that carried him through so many treacherous missions. But the objectivity wasn't there. Only terror – raw and painful.

If Sophie died, three little girls became orphans because of his actions.

He should've scratched his original plan when he saw the dark clouds gather around the mountain's peak. But he'd pushed on and when the rain blew in with a vengeance, Lissa and Hanna sat alone on the opposite bank. The storm released torrential higher up the mountain swelling the river and loosening debris and deadfall along the way. With unerring precision, a log had careened into Sophie.

Gray splashed through a shallow pool to reach the place he'd last seen her. In a web of leafy branches below, a patch of pink bobbed and swayed in the water.

"Sophie!" He scrambled over the boulders. One foot missed a step and he fell against the sharp edge of a rock. Burning pain shot through his upper arm.

He heaved to his feet. Blood from the gash in his shoulder mingled with rainwater and ran down his chest. He wouldn't be any good to her if he crippled himself. Using more caution, he worked his way over the last of the stones then slid feet first into the waist deep pool. Caught in the swirling eddy, he fought the current pulling at him. He surged ahead, heart hammering his chest like a battering ram. "Sophie!" *Please, God let her be okay.*

A foot splashed above the surface. Uncertain if the slight movement was the result of the river's current or Sophie fighting for her life, Gray advanced. Fearing she'd be pulled out of reach, he lunged the last small distance and closed his arms around her.

She kicked and thrashed knocking him off balance. A flailing hand clipped his jaw.

He held tight. He deserved worse. Regaining his footing on the rocky bottom he stood, lifting her head and shoulders out of the water.

She clung to him sputtering and coughing.

"I've got you, sweetheart. Relax. I won't let you go." He dodged an errant arm and waded ashore holding her close.

Finding a protected shallow at the river's edge, he paused. "How bad are you hurt?" He gently ran his hand along her limbs assessing damage and checking for broken bones. She flinched as he examined bloody scrapes and bruised flesh, but the cursory exam proved none of his worst fears had materialized. "Let's get you out of the water." He lifted her and set her on the riverbank.

Clumsy and disoriented, Sophie rolled to her knees and coughed hard.

Mindful of what was to come, Gray placed his hand to her forehead giving her leverage as her body strained to empty her stomach of river water.

Finished, she leaned weakly against him. He wrapped her in his arms and cradled her against his heaving chest. Her head rested beneath his chin and he allowed himself the luxury of pressing his lips against her wet hair. She was safe and whole. He didn't have the words to thank God, but the emotion welled up from deep inside.

"Mommy!"

Andi approached picking her way through the underbrush.

Sophie moaned through chattering teeth. Her apathy and the blue tinge to her lips spelled trouble. Hypothermia was the next real danger.

Andi dropped to the ground beside her mother, her face crumpled with tears. "Mommy." Her voice broke as she reached for her mother. Sophie rested a torn hand on Andi's arm. Her blood mingled with rain staining Andi's shirt pink.

Gray's vision narrowed and his chest tightened. He'd seen plenty of blood in his lifetime, much of it his own. But this was Sophie's blood. His gut clenched in an iron knot. She could have easily been a fatality at his hands.

Brush crackled. He whirled around.

Lissa and Hanna followed Andi's path along the shrubby bank. One misstep and they'd be sliding into the river. He hustled to pick up Hanna and lead Lissa back to Sophie.

Due to his own bullheadedness he now had four wet females to dry out and warm up.

On the side of the mountain, away from the reach of the river's treacherous flow, a monolithic boulder rose from the forest floor. Eons ago, in its glacial slide across ice and stone, a piece of the rock sheered off. When the boulder came to rest, the uneven side had created a low, sheltering overhang.

Gray pointed to the boulder. "Lissa, take Hanna up and stay with her. Andi, help me with your mother." He rested a hand under Sophie's elbow. "Can you stand, Sophie?" He hadn't found any broken bones, but the battering she received going over the falls may have caused damage he hadn't detected on the first hasty examination. She stood and swayed, whimpering with pain. He supported her as she took tentative baby steps on bare feet scraped raw in places. "Only as far as the rock, Sophie." Each slow awkward step was a triumph for her and a twisted a knife of pain in his heart.

Andi walked in front of her mother removing sticks and forest litter that might cause her to stumble and add to her pain.

Grateful Sophie could move under her own steam, Gray kept his arm around her waist and eased her along. She shivered as her body tried to maintain her core heat. Half way there they stopped and let her rest. He took the opportunity to adjust the twisted layers of her tee-shirt and sweatshirt. At the small of her back, a deep laceration on her pale scraped skin beaded with blood.

He settled her in the shelter of the rock. Her skin was cool and the bruise on her temple worried him. Following the simplest instructions eluded her.

Lissa stood close by, pale with fear and worry.

"Please stay with Hanna and your mom." For the first time she didn't respond with contempt but did as he asked hugging Sophie close sharing what heat her small body produced.

Gray showed Andi where to build the fire ring before leaving them to retrieve the packs. Finding the gear dry, he hauled everything back to the makeshift camp then stripped the plastic trash bags off the blanket and quilt.

"Lissa, get your mom, Hanna and yourself out of the wet clothes, wrap up in beach towels and bundle together in the quilt." He leaned to Hanna. "Can you sit with Mommy in the quilt to help her warm up?"

The princess nodded. "Sushi can, too."

"You be sure she does." With help from above perhaps the make-believe friend would add some warmth to the situation. "I'll be close. Yell if you need me."

Already unzipping her mother's pink hoodie, Lissa nodded her understanding.

Even though she didn't have the dexterity to undress herself, Sophie kept trying to help.

Gray caressed her cool cheek and stayed her bumbling hand. "Let the girls help you." Her eyes were void of their usual spark and his heart broke in his chest. "Andi, come with me to collect firewood."

Taking branches from the underside of dead falls where the wood was protected from most of the soaking rain, Gray and Andi soon had enough to start a large fire. Before going back to camp he went to the riverbank to check the water level. Though swollen, the rushing river flowed well below the lip of the bank. But storm clouds continued to roll in from the west bringing a light rain to the river valley.

Back at the camp Gray set about building a large fire. With Andi's help he added extra stones to the top of the fire ring, then balanced soda cans filled with water near the flame.

"I'm going after more wood." He studied the faces peeking up at him from the folds of the much-abused quilt. "The river is within its banks, but if it threatens to flood, we head for higher ground." The lack of response to the possible threat bothered him. He narrowed his gaze on Andi. "Understood?" Not fair, putting so much on the shoulders of a seven-year-old, but she appeared to be the only one listening to him.

She gave a serious little nod that ended with a body-racking shiver.

"Get out of those wet clothes and join the others. I'll be close by."

When he arrived back with the last load of wood Andi had snuggled in with Sophie and her sisters. The fire had warmed the sheltered area beneath the rock. Setting up a drying rack using forked sticks stuck in the ground and leaning against one another, Gray wrung out clothing then hung everything to dry. He rummaged through Sophie's pack for her extra pair of socks and retrieved the first aid kit from his borrowed pack, then knelt in front of Sophie. "Your feet need attention again."

Nose buried in the quilt, she didn't acknowledge his presence. His attempt to make her smile fell flat. What he would give to hear her tell him in no uncertain terms she'd tend her own feet, thank you very much.

He moved the edge of the quilt aside and peeled off her wet socks stained with spots of pink. Blood seeped from a deep cut on the top of her foot. Her heels were scraped raw and bruises smudged her pale skin. His heart ached seeing the damage and pain resulting from his decision. What remained of Sophie's foot jewelry he removed before swelling made the task impossible. He shucked his wet t-shirt and used it to handle the hot cans of boiled water. With his handkerchief and water, Gray bathed Sophie's battered feet, applied first aid cream and pulled on dry socks.

"Sophie, look at me." He beamed the flashlight into her eyes. She winced and turned away. "Let's try that again." The bruise on her temple worried him. Holding her chin between his forefinger and thumb, he once again shined the light into her eyes. The pupils contracted to pin points. He moved the light away and they expanded. Satisfied for the moment, he stood. He'd care for her other injuries when hypothermia was no longer a danger.

The extra stones he'd added to the fire ring had heated through. He kicked them over to where the women huddled beneath the quilt. Using the toe of his boot, he shoved the rocks under the quilt close to their feet. Having done all he could for the moment, he placed cans of boiled water nearby to cool. Grabbing the second blanket, he draped it across his back and slid between the face of the rock and Sophie's back.

"Lean against me." Encased in still damp pants, he bent his knees to either side of the quilt then wrapped his arms around her. She reclined against him, her head in the hollow of his shoulder. She trembled from the cold holding her in its grip. Her hair tickled his neck. If she knew the kind of man he had been before giving his heart to Christ, would she rest so close to him? Would she trust him so easily? Beneath the quilt the girls shifted and curled closer to their mother.

Gray poured warm water into an empty bottle and held it up in front of Sophie. "Sip on this." Her hands shook uncontrollably so he covered them with his and guided the bottle to her lips. This morning he'd rubbed a flower over her cheek and brow to awaken her. His first inclination had been to use his fingers. He'd wanted to touch the soft warmth of her skin. Instead, he'd used a flower to avoid temptation. Survival situations had a way of hacking away the trivial. With his back against a boulder and Sophie soft against him, this morning's concern ranked as absurd. He offered her more warm water.

She took several sips. "You're a f-furnace."

"Warming up?"

"Mmm." Sophie settled into his arms.

Gray closed his eyes and whispered a prayer of thanks. Only by God's mercy had they dodged an all-out disaster. His stomach roiled sick each time he recalled the feel of her hand slipping from his.

The *chicka-dee-dee-dee* of a curious chickadee broke the afternoon silence. Flame licked at the hissing wood. Keeping the fire stoked, Gray studied the women as one by one they fell asleep. Thankfully, Sophie's lips were no longer tinged with blue and her tremors had eased.

This fiasco he'd created would set them behind a day. He needed a plan. But first he wanted to savor the blessing of Sophie alive and in his arms.

# Chapter 10

A weight rested heavy across Sophie's middle. Her arms and legs were pinned down. Panic rippled through her as she struggled to break free, unable to see what held her wrapped in suffocating darkness.

"Sophie."

Gray. He'd help her. She tried calling out but the words wouldn't come. The world dissolved into a haze of hurt.

"Sophie. Wake up."

The weight shifted, still there but lighter.

"Mommy."

Lissa's voice pulled Sophie away from the dark shadows toward wakefulness, the last bits of her dream falling away. Powerful arms wrapped protectively around the quilt and her. The girls cuddled close, each one wearing a worried expression. She reached for them, but the quilt restricted her range of motion.

"You were dreaming."

Sophie glanced back at Gray and winced. The horror of being swept along by the river flashed through her mind and she shivered. Against her back, the rise and fall of Gray's chest steadied her. "I'm sorry."

Gray's bearded jaw rested against her temple.

"You have nothing to apologize for. The fault lies with me." His voice hummed in her ear.

The poor man was confused. "Because of me, we're losing time."

His chest expanded in a sigh. "How about this. Because of my stubborn insistence, you ended up in the drink and hurt."

For the sake of the girls, she attempted a smile. "Okay, you win."

"Thank you. I think."

She tried again to touch Hanna. "How long did I sleep?"

"Several hours." He lifted the quilt so she could move her arms freely beneath it. "How are you feeling?"

Reaching out, a shooting pain in her ribs made her wince and groan. "I hurt all over." She kissed Hanna's cheek. "Hi baby." Her actions slow and stiff, she hugged Lissa and Andi. Content to stay cocooned in the quilt with her girls, she studied their small haven. Every stitch of clothing worn by her and the girls hung from forked sticks and a crossbar near the roaring fire. The heat of a blush climbed Sophie's neck and cheeks as the hazy memory of Lissa helping her out of wet clothes and wrapping her in a beach towel surfaced.

Gray stirred behind her. "The rain has stopped. I'll replenish the water and wood. Your clothes may have a few damp spots but sit close to the fire and they'll finish drying on your backs. Girls, get dressed then help your mother into her clothes."

The three girls spilled from the quilt pulling at it.

Sophie grabbed a handful of fabric trying to keep herself covered. Pain sliced through her and she moaned.

Hands bunched in the quilt, Gray drew it up around her. "I'm so sorry, sweetheart."

Unsure if pain or the reaction to his soft-spoken words caused her trembling inside and out, she shut her eyes tight and concentrated on breathing.

"When I return, I'll doctor your back and all the other cuts and scrapes."

Her eyes popped open in alarm. *Oh dear!* She hurt all over. She'd let him think he could play doctor for now.

He rose and slipped the blanket from his back, exposing the grid of scars that nicked his shoulder and back. He spread the blanket over a nearby bush to create a privacy screen, then turned and caught her staring.

Her gaze ran over the scars she'd seen yesterday. She gulped back tears. She had no right sitting here sniveling over her own injuries. Whatever horrendous events he'd lived through surely marked his spirit as well as his body. And now, high on his shoulder, an angry gash was crusted with blood.

He retrieved his wadded up tee-shirt and paused. With the tips of his fingers he brushed her hair back from her brow. His eyes the color of smoke, roamed across her face as though trying to memorize it. The pad of his thumb brushed across her lips. Then he was gone.

Barely able to draw in a breath past her heart stuck in her throat, Sophie set the incident aside for examination later. The girls, busy climbing into their clothes, gave her time to check her injuries.

Sophie gripped a knob of the large sheltering rock

and pulled herself up to stand on throbbing feet. She swayed, waiting for the lightheadedness to pass before letting go of her anchor. With her back to the shelter's opening, she unwrapped the towel and took inventory. *Oh my.* Her new skin color consisted of black and blue. The darkest bruising marked her ribs and leg where she'd been struck. After being swept off her feet, she'd tumbled and rolled over rocks like a lapidary specimen. The abraded skin on her arms and legs stung. The white socks on her feet looked out of place against the dark earth beneath them and the rest of her naked self.

"Mommy?"

Moving with care, Sophie closed her wrap and turned to find Lissa fully clothed and holding the first aid kit. Stretching out her arm, she ignored the pain and embraced Lissa. "Thank you, sweetie."

Andi approached with a soda can of warm water. "To wash your cuts."

With the help of her daughters, Sophie cleaned and rubbed ointment on her injuries then dressed. Exhausted by the effort, she sat beside the fire wrapped in the quilt. Lissa climbed in with her and snuggled close.

"You okay, Liss?"

"Yes." Lissa sat quiet. "No." Her face crumpled and she buried it against Sophie's breast.

"Shh. It's okay, sweetie." Sophie rocked her in her arms, the hurt in her body minor compared to the ache she carried in her heart for Lissa and all she'd experienced since Tommy's death.

Drawn by their sister's crying, Andi and Hanna huddled close.

Lifting her face, Lissa knuckled her eyes. "I s-saw

you g-go o-over the fall and I thought you'd die like Daddy."

Sophie held her tight. The ache in her heart expanded and she cried, too. She'd missed the court hearing. At this very moment, Gerald could be accusing her of kidnapping her own girls. The terror of losing them pressed on her.

In time, the storm of tears petered out. Sophie dabbed her eyes with the quilt and looked up at the entrance of the shelter.

Motionless as a statue, Gray stood beyond the shelter, his arms loaded with wood. Seeing that she'd spotted him, he moved cautiously forward. Andi helped him pile the wood on one side of their sheltered camp. Avoiding eye contact with Sophie, he collected the empty soda cans and disappeared back into the forest.

She sighed. Not once in the past three days had the man shied away from her blubbering, so why this time?

Lissa's soft breathy snore vibrated from within the folds of the quilt.

Resting her cheek against her eldest daughter's hair, she closed her eyes to rest for a few minutes.

\*\*\*

A quiet *tink* woke Sophie.

Gray sat across the fire shuffling soda cans filled with water. Fish sizzled on a stick above the flame. Andi and Hanna sat on either side of him weaving leaves together to form small mats. Sophie's stomach growled and Gray looked up. A blush crept across her cheeks.

His smile didn't reach his eyes. "It'll be ready to eat soon."

Lissa awoke and uncurled from her mother's side.

Sophie brushed a kiss across her brow and let her go. "The fish smells delicious."

Andi held up her leaves. "We're making dishes."

"Andi says they took care of your injuries." Gray's intent gaze searched Sophie's face.

"Yes."

"The laceration on your back is deep. Any other serious wounds?"

Sophie frowned and shook her head. "Scrapes and bruises."

He checked the fish. "I want to look at your back."

Her heart jumped. "Lissa washed the cut and dressed it with ointment." Flustered, Sophie tightened her fists in the quilt.

"Thank you, Lissa, for helping your mom." His attention flicked back to Sophie. "I want to check it."

Her stomach fluttered nervously. Two could play this game. "Alright. You can check my back right after I attend the gash on your shoulder."

His eyes narrowed. "I'll take care of that."

Sophie bundled aside the quilt. Mindful of her many hurts, she stood.

Gray rose and moved to her side. "What are you doing?" He placed a hand beneath her elbow holding her steady.

"Being useful."

"What?" Perplexed, he glanced at the girls as though they would have the answer to his question.

"Please sit. Lissa, where's the first aid kit?"

"No." He crossed his arms and just as fast uncrossed them to catch her as she swayed.

Undeterred by his growl, Sophie took hesitant painful steps to stand behind the log he'd vacated.

When had he moved it into their small haven? "Sit here, please."

"You're ready to fall over."

"I'll lean against you while I work."

Exasperated, he sat so she wouldn't fall. "You don't have to do this."

"Yes I do. You've taken care of us for three days. It's my turn to care for you."

In one fluid movement, Gray stripped off his tee-shirt.

Sophie sucked in her breath. Pure feminine appreciation for the wide expanse of masculine muscle made her pulse dance but she refused to give in to the desire to trace each white scar with the tips of her fingers. Using a corner of a beach towel and boiled water she wiped away the crusted blood and washed the wound with gentle strokes.

He flinched and she stopped to examine the tender spot. Beneath a ragged flap of skin protruded the dark broken end of a wood sliver. "There's a splinter imbedded deep."

Rustling through the first aid kit, she found the tweezers then turned and braced one hand on his good shoulder. Noticing the play of muscle beneath the ridges and puckers that marred his skin, she leaned forward to better see the wound. His musky male scent enveloped her and for one brief moment she longed to press her nose to his skin and breathe deeply.

Tommy had never affected her so.

Her mind skittered away from the comparison as though it were a traitorous thought. She probed his flesh with the tip of the tweezers. He jerked and Sophie pulled back.

"I'm sorry."

"Just get it out." His voice rasped deep in his throat.

Heart thumping, Sophie pinched the wood with the tweezers and pulled extracting an inch long sliver. More blood oozed. Her hands shook as she cleansed the wound. This man had a way of upending her beliefs about herself and her marriage to Tommy. Spending every summer together, sharing childish secrets and eventually young love's first kisses, she'd married her best friend.

Mystery surrounded Gray. A seasoned warrior, he sat with the children and played the buttercup game. Hardened by war, he kept his emotions in check. The man was a mass of contradictions she couldn't figure out and being with him created feelings she'd never experienced with her late husband.

Sophie liberally smeared ointment on his wound then ran trembling fingers across the meshed threads of gauze and smooth tape. A longing to better understand this tough man poured through her. He'd touched a place in her heart unconnected to Tommy. She drew in a shaky breath. Was she falling in love? How could that be? This was too fast. Too soon. Too *everything*. Unsteady, she leaned against Gray.

*** 

Gray sat unmoving afraid Sophie would withdraw her hand.

Her fingers tightened. She brushed against the length of his back. His nerves jumped and quivered and he risked a quick glance back. Her eyes pooled dark against the pallor of her skin. She swayed. Rising and reaching around, he grasped her forearm. "Sophie?"

She stumbled and Gray wrapped his arm around her waist and lowered her to the log.

"I'm okay." She exhaled her words in a breathless rush that worried him.

"You've done too much too soon." Angry with himself, he snatched up the quilt and wrapped her in it. He hadn't put up much of a fight. Truth was, even as he'd shucked his tee-shirt hoping she'd turn away in revulsion, a part of him needed her touch, wanted to be the center of her attention.

Disgusted with his own weakness he crouched beside the fire and checked the fish. Doling out the meal, he helped Hanna remove the small needle-like bones. "We'll stay here overnight." Silence followed the announcement and Sophie's expression didn't change.

Wary, Lissa and Andi waited for their mother's response.

She nodded and resumed eating.

***

The meal finished, Gray threw the fish bones into the fire along with the leaf mats. He hoped the overnight rest would give Sophie time to recuperate enough to finish the trek under her own steam. Unfortunately, there was also the possibility that come morning she'd be so sore and stiff she'd go nowhere fast.

He took up the first aid kit. The time had come to tend her. Maybe she wouldn't fuss with a daughter present. "Lissa, come help me."

Alert to his intent, Sophie clutched the quilt tighter. "I told you, Lissa and Andi already helped me with my cuts."

Gray knelt behind her. "I'm fool enough to believe you when you say your other injuries aren't bad. But I saw the laceration on your back. I want to take a look at it." He lifted the edge of the quilt and doubled it up over her shoulders. Sophie buried her face deep in the folds.

Her tee-shirt stuck on the ointment Lissa applied earlier. Gray gently peeled the fabric off grazed skin blotchy with bruises. Anger over his stubborn stupidity rose to the fore. Sophie wouldn't be in this condition if he'd only waited to cross the river. Inspecting the deepest cut, he didn't find any debris or bits of gravel buried in her soft skin. "You did a good job cleaning the cut, Lissa."

The youngster straightened up a bit. A ghost of a smile whispered across her lips. "Thank you."

Determined to keep an iron grip on his wayward thoughts, Gray applied gauze with tape then pulled down the hem of Sophie's shirt and rearranged the quilt. He handed Lissa the first aid kit. "I'll bring in more wood."

"Can I come, too?" Andi stood ready to follow him.

"Stay with your mom and sisters. Keep the fire going."

The disappointment on the pixie's face almost made him relent, but Sophie called Andi to her side, so he ducked out from under the boulder and left them huddled together before the fire.

Gray slid down a steep embankment that brought him close to the river. The water ran at the same level as earlier. The rain had stopped. Water dripped from leaves and a sweet earthy scent hung heavy in the air.

Doubling back he quartered the area above their camp searching for broken limbs and blowdowns to fuel the fire for the night.

He'd broken one of his ironclad rules. He'd allowed himself to become emotionally invested in a mission. A rule easier to adhere to if everyone on the team followed the same code. But Sophie's nurturing nature had blasted his inflexible expectations to kingdom come. The walls that had always protected him from emotional involvement were rubble.

Looking back, he could now see how poorly he'd constructed his barriers. Satisfied to hem himself in and limit his contact with others, he hadn't anticipated someone breaching his defenses. And never had he expected he'd welcome the infraction or *want* to scramble across the wreckage of his heart to move beyond his rigid existence. Arms loaded with wood, Gray made his way back to camp troubled by his self-assessment.

*** 

A breeze puffed through the overhang, circulating wood smoke through the small shelter and out the other side. The rush of the river amplified the forest's nightly chorus. The creak of one tree branch rubbing against another accompanied the trill of tree frogs and the hum of insects. Wrapped in the blanket, Gray placed more wood on the fire. After Lissa applied more ointment to Sophie's various scrapes and cuts, they'd curled up on the boughs of balsam he'd spread for them. Exhausted, the little ones fell right off to sleep. He wished Sophie could do the same. Uncomfortable, she shifted position every few minutes.

He glanced her way. Her eyes were open, curious

and questioning. The woman hadn't a clue how to protect herself from men like him. Insisting he clean up his language didn't rid him of the haunting bleak shadows. He'd walked into the abyss and confronted every kind of ugly the world had to offer. Wading through the blood and muck of countless missions came with a price. The crud washed off but left a soul-deep stain. Sophie deserved better.

His heart thudding loud enough to deafen him, he raised his blanket-draped arm in invitation. *What're you doing, Kerr? Asking for trouble or trying to avoid it?* The next few minutes would prove which.

Her movements slow and clumsy, Sophie rose and came to sit beside him on the log. He cloaked her in the blanket and held her snug against his side. She sighed and relaxed resting her head on his chest.

"Better?"

She nodded and a stray wisp of hair feathered across his throat. "Everything hurts. I can't find a comfortable position to sleep."

"You're pretty banged up and it's my fault." Beneath his arm, her shoulder lifted in a shrug.

"I'll heal and probably not bear any scars." She gave a start. "Oh. I'm sorry." In the dancing firelight, her cheeks grew rosy.

He couldn't have asked for a better opening. "Sophie." He held her chin between his thumb and forefinger. Her trembling lips parted. "My scars don't bother me. They're just another part of me now."

She swallowed audibly. "What happened?"

He trailed his fingers the length of her throat before he turned back to face the fire. "I've been a warrior my entire adult life. I'm good at what I do."

As an idealistic kid, he'd fought to protect innocents like Sophie and her daughters. Like sheep, they trusted the men willing to play the part of the sheep dog. Fighting the wolves was his life. "Every battle cost me. Sometimes I paid with a hunk of flesh, other times a piece of my soul." He paused. It was time she saw him for real. "I began to believe my life was worth a great deal more than Uncle Sam was willing to pay me."

It was slight, but he felt her stiffen.

"What are you saying?"

"I fought for the money. Not some noble cause. A soldier of fortune. The shine wore off my honor years ago. I've stayed on the right side of the law working for security companies, but war is my life. Above all else, I chose to protect my own interests."

Her breath broke into choppy bursts. "So...you never fought against us... your own country... did you?"

He bit back a curse word and shook his head instead. "No. Never. And I never served in a foreign military. The possibility of being considered a criminal was all that kept me from crossing the line. That's about the extent of my integrity." He tracked a bit of ash drifting off on the smoke. "In the last few years the line has thinned and bent in places."

She no longer relaxed against him. Shoulders stiff, her posture telegraphed she no longer welcomed his casual embrace. Gray lowered his arm and let her move away.

Her gaze darted between his chin and her sleeping daughters. "I'll go get some sleep now."

Good luck with that, sweetheart.

Not meeting his gaze, she returned to the nest of pine boughs.

He'd squelched any misguided notions she had entertained about him. Mission accomplished. His gut burning as though shredded by a million tiny pieces of shrapnel, Gray sat the night watch alone.

# Chapter 11

At the base of the mountain, a variety of powerboats, canoes and kayaks dotted the sparkling water of Bride Lake. Small summer camps peeked from beneath the pines, their wooden docks extending into the blue of the lake.

Whispering Pines Resort rimmed the lake below them. Even at this distance the neglect was clear to Gray's practiced eye. Where clipped lawns had once sloped to the water's edge, hayfields dotted with sumac now grew. The boathouse leaned to one side on its pilings and a black gaping hole in the main dock testified of missing boards. Back from the lake's edge and in among the trees, cabins wound along a narrow dirt road. Their once white paint had weathered to a dull gray.

"You're sure this is the place?" Gray turned to help Sophie sit on an outcropping of rock. Her pallor worried him. Exhaustion and pain etched harsh lines around her mouth.

He'd done a bang up job last night convincing her he wasn't hero material. The moment there was enough daylight for walking, she'd roused the girls. She preferred the pain of travel to another unnecessary moment in his company.

Smart woman. That's what he wanted. Now he could get cracking and rebuild the protective walls she'd so sweetly demolished.

Sophie stared at the patched buildings below. "As a child, I climbed up here to look down on my friends swimming or playing baseball."

Andi came and stood beside Sophie. "Maybe it will be better up close."

"They always kept the grounds well-groomed." She pointed to the right. "That large building is the main lodge and dining hall. They serve breakfast and dinner. The cabins have small kitchenettes for lunches and snacks."

Her attention kept straying to a knoll where a forest fire had claimed four of the lakefront cabins as well as a large patch of forest. A tear streaked the dust on her cheek. She pointed to the charred remains. "My family cabin and Tommy's are gone." Disappointment and sadness tinged her words. "So much has changed."

Unease rippled up Gray's spine as he moved to sit beside her. "Why did you choose to come here? Why now?"

"I went through Tommy's things after he passed." She glanced at the girls. Lissa sat on a rock jabbing a small branch into the moss at her feet.

Running a hand down Sophie's forearm, he clasped her hand in his. That she allowed him the liberty revealed the depth of her bewilderment. "Go on."

"I found a pamphlet. I don't know how long he'd

had it." She tightened her grip. "The pamphlet reminded me how much I loved this place. I wanted to come and remember the good times."

"You called?"

She shook her head. "I mailed in the reservations using the form in the brochure. Tommy always talked about coming back. This is where we met. Our families rented cabins next door to each other every summer."

He squeezed her hand. "Which makes the betrayal of his parents that much more hurtful."

"Yes."

Smoke drifted from the chimney of the lodge. A rusty pickup truck sat outside the door.

"Was your check cashed?"

"Yes."

"Ow! Mommy, tell Lissa to stop poking me with the stick." Andi swatted her sister.

"Lissa, leave your sister alone. Drop the stick."

Ignoring her mother, Lissa whacked the leaves from a nearby bush.

Sophie sat up. "Lissa. Drop the stick."

Lissa clenched the stick with both hands and cast a mutinous glare at her mother.

Gray released Sophie's hand and stood. "Your mother gave you a direct order. Get rid of the stick."

Anger flitted across Lissa's face. "Oh all right." She threw the stick down. "It's just a stupid stick."

Gray stood and held his hand out to Sophie. "Come on. Let's go see what's up at The Whispering Pines Resort. If you're lucky they'll have a hot tub for you to soak in."

Her weak smile got tangled in the turbulent battle raging between Gray's heart and head. *Get them down the hill, Kerr. Then you can go back to your own mission.* Rather than cheering him up, the thought sent his mood in a downward spiral. He had the unsettling feeling he was moving in the wrong direction with every step he took down the mountain.

*\*\*\**

A hand-lettered sign nailed to the porch rail of the lodge proclaimed, 'The Bates and Tackle Sporting Camp'. The lodge emanated an air of neglect. Piles of leaves filled the corners of the front porch. Weeds crowded the sagging steps.

"This place is a dump." Lissa dropped her pack on the ground.

Andi held Hanna's hand. "Is this where we check in?"

Gray climbed the steps and tried the door latch. It released and he stepped inside. Sophie and the girls followed close behind.

"Hello?" his shout echoed around the gloomy room.

A soft tinkling floated through an open doorway at the back.

"Anybody here?"

"Cool," Andi ran across the room. "Mom, look at this." A sculpture made of aluminum beer cans occupied a tabletop.

Movement in the doorway claimed Gray's attention.

A stub of a man entered the room. His long matted beard made up for the lack of hair on top of his head. He tore at a strip of jerky with yellowed teeth. Beneath faded overalls, his long sleeve undershirt bore stains and holes in the elbows. A long-eared brown goat followed him into the room. "You're late. Expected you days ago." He stopped short, his rheumy gaze on Sophie and the girls.

To Andi and Lissa's delight, the goat trotted their way. Hanna screeched and leapt into her mother's arms.

"Moose! Quit scarin' the wim'min." The man nodded at Sophie and bared his teeth in what Gray assumed was meant to be a smile.

"We were held up." He stepped into the man's line of vision relieved Sophie's reservation had been received. "When did this place become a sport camp, Mister...?"

"Bates. But everybody calls me Sharky." He didn't extend his greasy hand for which Gray was thankful.

"That fancy resort went into foreclosure 'bout eight years ago." Sharky stepped behind a reception counter cluttered with papers, a hunting knife, a bottle of Cornhuskers Lotion and a stack of dirty dishes. He waved the piece of jerked meat to encompass the room, his eyes going back to Sophie as she fussed between the girls and the curious goat. "Place was closed for three years before I took over." Shuffling through the debris on the counter, Sharky pulled a yellowed guest book out. "Sign here, Mr. Moore."

Gray plucked a pen from a tin can holder. The man had a death wish looking at Sophie like that. Signing the register, he noted another guest, George Frost, had signed in three days ago.

Sharky turned the book, squinted and read the signature. "Gray Moore." He fingered his greasy beard. "S. Moore made the reservation."

Gray drilled him with a look. "That would be the

lady."

Taking another chew of meat, Sharky wiped his mouth with his shirtsleeve. "One adult and three kids. That's what the reservation said."

"Spending time with them is an unexpected bonus." *How unexpected you'll never know.*

"Will cost you extra."

"Start a tab."

"Never had a fella bring his wife and kids with him. This ain't no highfalutin' place with room service."

Gray tapped the counter. "As long as we have clean sheets and two meals a day, we're good." For Sophie's sake, he hoped the sheets were clean. As for the food, if he got his way they wouldn't stay long enough to eat two meals. "Some place nearby where I can buy fuel?" He didn't have any money on him, but when packing the women, he'd made sure to include Sophie's wallet.

"In town. Ten miles east of here." Their host frowned. "I didn't hear you drive up."

"Van ran out of gas a ways back."

"City folks." Sharky shook his head.

Gray ignored the comment and the condescending smirk meant to make him feel like a fool. He'd wrangled with bigger, more dangerous men than Bates.

Sharky rubbed his bristled jaw and bit off another chew of jerky. His gaze drifted to where Sophie stood beside a stuffed black bear. "My boy can take you into town. It'll cost you, though. I'll put that on the tab, too." He retrieved a key from the pegboard and tossed it on the counter. "Fourth cabin on the right. The Perch."

Palming the key, Gray paused, "We'd appreciate a

bite to eat."

"Ain't making nothin' fancy. I didn't know you'd be here for supper." Sharky fished a toothpick from his pocket and dug at his teeth.

Gray took Hanna from Sophie, herded Andi and Lissa away from the goat, and hustled them toward the door. "Give us thirty minutes." Outside, he headed for the cabin. "Come on, ladies. Let's see what amenities The Perch has to offer." He led the way between pine trees and up the crooked washed out path.

If one ignored the skulls of indeterminate animals nailed to the peak, the cabin wasn't so awful from the outside. The door hinges creaked and the acrid odor of damp ashes greeted them as they stepped inside.

The walls were paneled with aged dark pine. A lumpy couch and two overstuffed chairs, their fabric worn and stained, sat before the fireplace. An odd collection of mismatched chairs surrounded a battered table, which held a worn deck of cards. Tucked in a corner, a small kitchenette completed the room.

To the right a small bedroom held a set of bunk beds butted against one wall and a twin bed against the opposite wall. Between them there was barely enough floor space to turn around. A full size bed and dinged chest of drawers filled a second bedroom.

He'd hoped for better. "Home sweet home for tonight."

Silence followed his statement.

The whistled *tew-tew-tew* of a pine grosbeak broke the quiet and a small hand wormed its way into his.

Andi stood beside him. "It's better than the cabin with the hole in the roof."

"That it is."

Bone-weary from the ordeal of the past few days, discouragement flowed off Sophie and the girls in waves. He turned to Sophie. "What do you think?"

Tired, she stood outside the bedrooms looking lost and defeated. "They were such pretty cabins." She shook her head. "I should have planned a movie night at home instead of a weekend away."

Morale was in the tank. Time to rally the troops. Gray slid his arm around her and squeezed. "But you would have missed so much."

"Like what?"

"Like me." Going with his gut, he swooped in and gave her unhappy lips a kiss. *Oh yeah. He* felt much better.

Not waiting for a reaction, he dropped his arm and released Andi's hand. "Come check out the beds." He flung back a threadbare orange spread and revealed camouflage sheets. "Not exactly the Marriott."

Hearing no comment, he twisted round. From the doorway, four pairs of eyes round with surprise stared at him. One pair appeared a bit dazed.

He turned back to the bed. Call him a fool, but wanting her close appealed more to him than chasing her off. He hoped she'd have sense enough to set him in his place, because he was doing a poor job of keeping away from her. "Check these out, Sophie."

She snapped out of her shock and pushed him aside. Lifting a corner of the bedding to her nose, she sniffed. She ran her hand across the sheet. "I believe it's clean." A thread of surprise laced her words. Next she picked up the pillow, smacked it and lifted it to her nose. "Not as fresh, but passable."

While she assigned beds to the girls, Gray poked his head into the small bath. Chipped tiles, cracked mirror and stained porcelain with all the necessary plumbing. It would do. He stepped aside for Sophie's inspection of the facilities.

"Better than I'd expected. Sharky should expand his cleanliness to include personal hygiene."

"Let's talk." Taking her dimpled elbow in hand, he steered her away from where the girls studied a deer antler floor lamp. "There's something you need to know."

A guarded look shadowed her eyes. "What?"

"Sharky believes we're married."

"What would give him such an idea?"

"Maybe because I signed the register 'Gray Moore'."

"You *what?*"

Three curious pairs of eyes watched them.

"Why would you do that?"

Hoping to keep the situation from spiraling out of control, he reached for Sophie's hand. He addressed the girls. "Stay here. Your mother and I are going outside to talk."

\*\*\*

Sophie ignored the tingle of awareness racing up her arm as Gray dragged her through the cabin door and down the steps to the dirt. Her swollen feet throbbed with each step.

"Are you crazy?"

"I did it for your protection. He assumed my last name was Moore because of your reservation."

"But that's not the truth." She brushed a greasy strand of hair from her eyes.

"Sharky made an assumption and I went with it." His eyes lit with inspiration. "Maybe this is divine protection."

"Don't do that!"

Gray rubbed a hand over the back of his neck. " What?"

"There is right and there is wrong. But you...you take black and white and...and make it gray!"

His lips quirked up on one side. "My life in so many ways."

How did he do it? One half-smile and all her indignation evaporated to nothing. What if she'd shown up here with the girls Friday night as planned? Sophie shivered and stepped closer to the warmth he radiated.

"If I'd had a better option, I would have taken it." He reached out and ran his hand along her arm. "After we eat, I'm leaving with his son."

Panic rocketed through her. "You're leaving?"

His eyes darkened as he burrowed his hands beneath her hair and cupped them on the sensitive spot between neck and shoulders.

Sophie stiffened her knees to prevent them from buckling. He was world-weary and, with the small glimpse of his life he'd allowed her, more than a little scary. But it wasn't fear that set her pulse racing. The attraction was undeniable. She didn't know how to stop her heart's headlong gallop into what was surely harm's way.

"I'm going with his son for fuel then I'll bring the van here."

She exhaled the breath she didn't realize she'd held.

"You've trusted me this far, Sophie. Trust me a

little longer, okay?" His thumbs gently caressed her jaw.

Tongue stuck against the roof of her mouth preventing speech, she nodded.

A thump from the cabin drew his attention. He dropped his hands and the haze of attraction clouding Sophie's mind cleared. She turned to see what had captured his interest.

Three small faces pressed against the grimy windowpane.

Mother mode snapping into place, she stormed the cabin clapping her hands. "Go wash up, ladies. We'll eat then come back for showers."

\*\*\*

Sophie had a new appreciation for convenience foods and eating utensils.

The cheese sandwich, barely grilled on one side and charcoal on the other, was accompanied by lukewarm vegetable soup from a can.

She bit down. From between the two thick slices of bread the tang of sharp cheddar cheese melted over her tongue. Sharky's cooking skills weren't the best, but the less-than-perfect meal beat roasted rodent.

Occupied with their food, the girls didn't fill the room with their usual chatter. And if she ignored the occasional bit of sandwich they sneaked the goat, their table manners were stellar.

On edge, Gray's hard gaze roved ceaselessly around the room and out the windows. He studied their host's every move. The front door opened and his gaze swung in that direction.

A young man outfitted in camouflage hunting clothes thumped across the wide plank floor toward the kitchen.

Sharky charged out from the back. "Where you been?"

The young man pulled at his jacket. "Lookin' for sign."

Sophie strained to hear the few words he mumbled. Across the table, Gray took another bite of his sandwich and studied the newcomer.

Beside him, Andi wiped her mouth with a cheap paper napkin. "There aren't any signs in the woods." She turned to Gray. "We'd have seen them. Right, *Daddy*?"

Sophie spewed soup.

Gray choked on his sandwich.

Hanna patted his shoulder while Andi banged on his back with her fist.

Nose burning, Sophie wiped soup from the front of her shirt, desperately trying to pull together a coherent thought.

Gray cleared his throat. Through leaking eyes, he nailed Andi with a hard look. "*What*?"

Andi sent Lissa a covert glance.

A smug grin on her lips, Lissa fed Moose a crust of bread.

"You little devils. You heard us talking." His voice barely audible, Gray encompassed all three girls in a steely-eyed scowl. "Spying on your mother is not nice."

"Everything alright, folks?" Eyes bright with curiosity, Sharky's gaze moved from one to the other before stopping on Gray.

"We're good."

Sophie wished the floor would open up and

swallow her whole. Cheeks burning, she blessed Andi and Lissa with her best 'you're-both-in-such-big-trouble' glare before mopping up the soup she'd sprayed across the table.

Gray polished off his sandwich. "Andi, the 'sign' they're talking about is the evidence an animal leaves when it moves through an area. Shows the places they favor."

Sharky approached the table. "This here's my son, Daryl."

Gray rose and held his hand out. "I appreciate your help."

Daryl took the hand Gray offered. "I'm leaving soon."

"I'll be ready." Gray remained standing.

The young man retreated to the kitchen.

Moose bumped Sophie's elbow, demanding a bite of her lunch. "Stop that." Dreading Gray's departure, she returned to her meal with less enthusiasm.

Bristly lips nuzzled her neck.

"Agh!" Sophie cringed and flipped up her hand, shooing the pest that shuffled behind her.

"Go away, you old goat!"

"Who you calling an old goat?" The throaty murmur in her ear raised goose bumps on the back of her neck. Turning her head slightly, her gaze tangled with smoky eyes smudged with warmth.

Gray stood behind her chair leaning over, his face even with hers. Laughter crinkles fanned out from the corners of his eyes.

"If the shoe fits…"

He pulled a hank of Sophie's hair from the goat's nibbling lips and shoved the animal away.

She palmed Gray's bearded cheek. "Maybe we can go with you?" Staying with the girls in the rundown cabin left her uneasy.

"No can do." His breath whispered across her face. "The cab of the truck isn't big enough for all of us." He straightened, surveyed the empty plates and bowls and reached for Hanna. "Come on, Princess." Careful that her gown's tattered skirt didn't snag on the chair arm, he lifted her. "I'll walk everyone back to the cabin before I go."

# Chapter 12

Reluctant to leave Sophie and the girls, Gray watched in the pickup's side mirror as the camp receded from view. Before leaving he'd lit a fire in the fireplace and made each of them promise they wouldn't leave the cabin. He regretted not having time to explore the resort and check out the one other person registered as a guest.

The truck bumped off the rutted gravel road and onto pavement. Tires hummed on the road that snaked like a black ribbon between the tall pines.

The way Sharky looked at Sophie was disturbing. Short of bringing all of them with him there was nothing he could do to change the situation. The van needed gas so he could take them home.

Gray jerked upright.

When had he decided that *he'd* be the one driving them home? Swiping a hand across his face, he sank back into the ripped vinyl seat. What about *his* mission? To abort the trial could mean throwing away his one shot at being part of the elite agency. His gut churned hot. He couldn't walk the ragged moral edge again.

He'd be lost for sure.

*Daddy.* Andi's voice echoed in his mind. None of them understood how that one simple word made breathing difficult. He'd been called many things in his lifetime, but he'd never allowed himself to believe he'd ever be a father. The example he'd had growing up almost guaranteed he'd fail at the job.

A sharp turn brought them to the outskirts of town past a combination feed store and restaurant to a gas station stuck in the early twentieth century. A winged red horse perched on the roof. Tacked on the building, faded signs hawked everything from motor oil to soft drinks.

Daryl wheeled the truck into the station's lot and pulled up next to the garage bay. With a glance at Gray, he got out. Taking the hint, Gray followed him through a door smudged brown by greasy hands.

The door was a portal into another time.

The sour smell of oil and rubber caught in Gray's throat. Hoses and belts hung from beams overhead. Dusty shelves held boxes of filters, cans of oil, assorted tools and car parts. Old and yellowed packaging sat next to the new, mixing the past with the present. Over the door, a clock advertising tires marked each passing second with a loud click.

Daryl spoke with a man built like a tank before joining two other young men in the corner by a stove.

The man stepped forward and extended a beefy hand, the creases permanently embedded with black grease. "I'll fix you up."

Gray shook his hand. "Thanks. Appreciate it." He followed Tank out back to a stack of dinged metal gas cans.

"One of these'll do you." Tank clattered through the pile till he found one that fit criteria privy only to him. "Here you go."

Leaving the silent Daryl with his equally silent buddies, Gray headed out to the vintage pump. Taped on the glass, a faded curling piece of paper stated all sales rang up in half gallons. After filling the can, he returned inside to pay.

Tank stood behind the counter thumbing through work orders. Daryl wasn't anywhere in sight.

Fishing out the money Sophie pressed into his hand earlier, Gray peeled off several bills. "The phone work?" He motioned to the dark shadowy booth in the corner.

"Not too good, but up here better than most of those fancy cell phones."

Gray dropped the money on the counter. "I'll give it a try."

Counting change Tank slammed the antique cash register shut. "Go easy on the cord. Might have to jiggle it."

Squeezing into the booth, Gray shut the door and sat on the narrow bench seat. Back pressed against the wall, his knees touched the opposite side of the enclosure. People must have been smaller back in the day. He twirled the rotary dial with a fingertip, praying he'd remembered the red line number correctly and the call would go through. Gray wiggled the cord near the receiver and heard the ring on the other end.

"SeaMount."

He recognized the deep gravelly voice of the founder and director, Sam Traven.

"Kerr here."

"We...where...time...ack." The intermittent connection made conversation impossible.

"A situation needs checking out. My trial is on hold at the moment." Hoping Sam heard enough to take action, Gray fired off the little information he had about Sophie and the issue with her in-laws. The director would probably surmise he'd lost his mind, but after four days in the woods with her, Gray had an unwavering certainty that Sophie was more than competent as a mother.

Static crackled in his ear and a high-pitched tone signaled a dropped call.

White knuckled, he gripped the receiver fighting the urge to slam the thing into its cradle. He'd have to hope Traven had heard him. Exiting the booth, he waved his thanks and headed for the door.

The can of gas sat on the stoop where he'd left it.

Daryl's truck was gone.

Behind him the screen door squealed on its hinges. "See the kid left." Tank took a wad of chew from a tobacco pouch then offered it to Gray.

His gut grinding, Gray shook his head. With effort he kept the rage from his voice. "Know where he's off to?" Delay was unacceptable. The more time he spent separated from Sophie and the girls, the more horrific the scenarios he dreamed up. It didn't help that in each one Sharky played a major role.

Tonguing the tobacco into his cheek, Tank shrugged. "Could be most anyplace."

Gray's insides chilled. The good old boy was having fun at his expense. "Did he say anything about coming back?"

"Nope. Boy doesn't come and go on a schedule."

To let his frustration show would only get him more of the laid-back know-nothing answers. He set the gas can down. For all the grease and diffident attitude, the man standing next to him was shrewd. Gray lowered himself to the edge of the step, forearms braced against his knees. "Is there a coffee joint nearby?"

'Yep."

He counted to fifty before asking the next obvious question. "Where?"

"East about three blocks."

"Thanks." Gray stayed seated. Only when a customer drove up, did Tank leave the stoop.

\*\*\*

No kid. No traffic of any kind.

Gray drained cold sludge from the bottom of a foam coffee cup, the bitterness matched the anger eating at his insides. He'd wasted time waiting for Daryl's return thinking the kid would come to collect payment if nothing else.

Tossing the cup in a trash bucket, he squinted into the soft evening light. A distant rumble grew louder and soon a log loader rounded the bend. Uncomfortable with the 'praise the Lord' stuff, Gray recognized this as a hallelujah moment without any doubt and offered up a quick thank you. He hefted the gas can ready to flag down the truck, but it slowed and pulled to the side of the road without any signal from him.

The driver climbed out sparing Gray a glance before loping across the road and into the station.

Gray waited. The door of the red cab displayed the company name, M & B LOGGING. He prayed the driver was either M or B. A hired hand might adhere to company rules and not take a rider on board.

Exiting the building with a cola in hand the driver's attention jerked away from his drink and zeroed in on Gray. His eyes slid to the gas can then back his face.

Gray hooked his thumb toward the truck. "Need a ride."

"Where to?"

Giving general directions, he hoped the logger knew the area better than he did.

The man's eyes narrowed. "What are you doing out there? Nothing in them parts." A hint of a sneer communicated the unspoken 'dumb tourist'.

"Nothing at all." Reining in impatience, Gray concentrated on dancing the dance. He shook his head. "Wasn't me that got lost. Found a woman with three kids stuck out there. No sense of direction."

"No sense, more like it."

He let the comment go. "They're holed up in a sporting camp."

"How'd you get here?"

"Rode in with the Bates kid."

The logger's gaze sharpened. "Daryl Bates?"

Gray nodded.

Hand reaching up for the door handle, the man paused and studied Gray as though taking his measure. "Hop in."

He stepped to the other side of the truck, wedged the can between two wood chocks and climbed into the cab. Wheels started rolling before he'd shut the door. Gut in a knot, he shoved aside a pair of leather gloves, a sweatshirt and a roll of duct tape. Resting his feet on a coiled chain, he turned to the driver. "Want to share what you know about Bates?"

The man glanced over at Gray then back at the road. "Name's John Mercer."

The 'M' half of M & B. "Gray Kerr."

John gave a curt nod of acknowledgement. "The kid..." he shook his head. "Not one of the best this county has to offer."

"Expected him to take me to the van after I bought fuel."

John shifted gears and settled into his seat. "Not surprised. Kid's nothing but trouble."

"What about the old man?"

"Woods queer. A man spends too many years alone in the woods and he turns peculiar. Not sure the kid is even his. Rumors and such. The camp's a dump. Who'd want to go there?" John glanced at him. "Didn't mean anything by that."

Gray waved a hand. "It's okay. Sophie remembered the place from years ago. It was different then."

John nodded. "Years back the camp was top-notch. A nice family place. Now it's for sportsmen." He paused. "They come up to fish. Mostly they drink and Sharky is happy to supply the booze."

"Must cause problems for the locals." Gray studied the road, memorizing the way for his return trip.

"Every season the volunteer firefighters pull a few of them out of the lake. Bates doesn't bring in the most upstanding people. Bunch of rowdies." John shook his head. "No place for a woman and kids."

"I appreciate you taking time to give me a ride."

Almost an hour later the van came into sight.

"Will be full dark soon." John squinted at Sophie's van sitting dead center in the road facing him.

Gray opened his door. "I'll back into that wide patch so you can go around me.

"You okay getting out of here?" His questioning gaze snared Gray's. "Don't want to end up back here tomorrow searching for you."

"I'm good. Coming in with you from this direction helped." He climbed from the cab and grabbed the gas can. "Thanks again." With a quick salute, he headed toward the van. Grateful for the truck's headlights he went about the task of filling the gas tank. Once in the van, he backed up to the wide weedy shoulder of the road. With a blast from the air horn, John drove past and Gray sat alone in the deepening darkness.

Maneuvering the van along the winding dirt road, he kept the need to race back to Sophie in check. He had a full gas tank, but if he got reckless, a broken axle was a possibility.

*** 

The deepening gloom of early evening settled around the cabin as Sophie tucked a faded blanket around Hanna and leaned over to give her a kiss. The strong scent of medicinal shampoo hung in the air. Had they been home, the shampoo wouldn't have gotten near a single hair on a Moore head. But the current predicament was far from anything she'd ever experienced and the plastic bottle left by a previous visitor was a gift from God and used liberally. Clean hair, even smelly clean hair, was a wonderful thing.

The cabin had an abundance of blankets to bundle in while they washed clothes in the shampoo and hung them to dry on chairs pulled close by the fire. Through the flimsy walls, Lissa's high-pitched warble accompanied the rush of the shower. The last to take advantage of the hot water, she was fully enjoying the experience.

Wrapped in a scratchy blanket that rubbed against her scrapes and bruises, Sophie leaned back against the lumpy chair cushion. Tomorrow they'd be home. *Thank you, Lord.*

"Mommy, when will Gray get back?" Bent at the waist, hair flipped forward, Andi finger dried it before the fire.

"I don't know, sweetie." Disturbed by what Gray shared last night she had tried all day to suppress the attraction. She'd expected him to keep his walls in place. Then they'd arrived at Bride Lake and they'd no sooner stepped into the cabin and he kissed her. After that, he seemed determined to close any distance he'd created the night before. Her own emotions were like those of a lovesick teenager, confusing but thrilling.

The girls hadn't been the least bit repentant about their eavesdropping and the following episode at the lodge. Especially since they'd seen Gray kiss her. Sophie touched her fingers to her lips. The man bulldozed through her defenses so easily he left her breathless. For the hundredth time, she went to cabin window to peek out, willing him to appear. Her heart leapt with surprise as a man emerged from the stand of pines. But her hope was dashed as he drew closer walking on the trail that past the cabin toward the lodge.

He wasn't Gray. Shorter and thinner, he didn't stride along the path with confidence. He slowed down as he drew abreast of the cabin. His gaze caught Sophie's.

Startled, she drew back from the window and

whipped the curtain back into place. Pressing a hand to her thumping heart, she moved to the side of the window and nudged the curtain fabric away from the window frame to create a sliver she could peer through. His intense interest in her cabin sent goose bumps rippling up her arms. She waited for him to move on, disappearing in the ever-deepening darkness, before hurrying to check the locks on the door and windows. How she missed Gray's protective presence.

The fire snapped and a log fell with a crackling swoosh. Andi added another stick and nudged it with an iron poker into the flames.

Four days ago Sophie would have yelled at Andi for getting too close to the fire. But under Gray's guiding hand, her daughter had learned to build and tend a fire with confidence. His patience with the girls amazed Sophie. Another trait of his that undermined her attempt to put distance between them.

A loud bang followed by a thump, came from the bathroom.

"Mooomm!"

Sophie lunged from the chair.

Lissa skidded around the corner clutching a threadbare towel around her slim body and trailing water. "It broke!" Shampoo suds billowed around her face.

Wrapped tight in the blanket, Sophie geisha-walked across the room. "What broke?"

Lissa thrust out her hand. The aged chrome shower handle rested in her palm.

Nudging Lissa aside Sophie entered the tiny bath. She whispered a frantic prayer and snapped back the curtain. Water cascaded into the stained shower stall.

Taking the handle from Lissa's outstretched hand, she tried to fit it on the rusty rod to no avail. She pinched the rod between her fingers to give it a twist but that didn't work either. "There must be a shutoff."

Elbows akimbo, Lissa stood in the doorway shivering.

Tugging at her blanket, Sophie knelt and opened the cupboard beneath the sink. A pipe with a knob ran through the cruddy interior. Squeamish a spider or snake might lurk in the dark corners; she reached in and grasped the knob.

It didn't budge.

Wrapping one hand around the other, she tried again.

Nothing.

Water continued spraying from the showerhead at a fast clip. Pulling the curtain closed, Sophie hurried from the bathroom. Butterflies ricocheted off the walls of her stomach at the thought of leaving the cabin. "I have to go to the lodge." She snatched wet jeans and a top off the wooden chair back and made a beeline for the bedroom.

"But, Mom," Andi's voice seeped through the crack in the door. "Gray told us not to leave the cabin."

"We can't drain the well dry, Andi." Sophie shivered as she stepped into her wet jeans and tugged at the material to pull them up her legs.

"Besides, you're afraid of the forest after dark."

Just once she wished her middle daughter wasn't so practical. "I have no choice."

"I'll come with you."

Sophie paused in her clumsy gyrations, shirttail rolled up across her shoulder blades. "But that leaves

Lissa and Hanna here alone."

"Buddy system, Mom. Remember?"

"Yes, I remember." Gray said it so many times, who could forget? Struggling to unwrap herself from the wet cloth without opening any healing scrapes, Sophie grunted. "Okay, Andi. Get your clothes on. It's you and me."

Andi's muffled whoop faded. Through the seam of the door, Lissa whined. "What about my hair?"

The small bath had become a sauna as hot water continued to stream into the shower stall while Sophie dressed. Sweeping a hand beneath the water she found it remained comfortably warm. "Come in here and rinse out the shampoo. Be quick about it. Hanna, sit on the potty lid while Lissa finishes up."

Stepping out of the cabin, Sophie threw a blanket around her shoulders to ward off a chill. She made Andi do the same. Locking the door, she tucked the key into her pocket. Two feet beyond the light shining from the windows, the night enveloped the cabin and woods.

A thin beam of light cut through the darkness.

Andi, bless her, remembered to grab the flashlight from Gray's pack.

"Follow me, Mommy."

Knowing she'd be a fool to argue, Sophie trailed Andi down the steps and into the night whispering a prayer of thanksgiving for a daughter with an unerring sense of direction.

Andi shined the light on the ground. "When will Gray be back?"

Careful to step between exposed tree roots, Sophie hugged her blanket close. "I don't know." She refused to give into the urge to worry. He, of all people, could

Out of the Wilderness

take care of himself.

The dark bulk of the lodge loomed ahead. Andi climbed the creaky steps and unlatched the heavy plank door and pushed it open.

From the bushes on Sophie's right came a bright flash. She screamed, throwing her hand up in front of her face as the light flashed once more. The rustle of twigs and leaves scrapping against fabric was followed by an ominous chuckle.

"Who's there?" Momentarily blinded, Sophie's heart hammered. She reached for the step railing. "Sharky, is that you?"

"Naw. But I'm getting some good pictures of the wildlife in these parts."

"Who are you?" Her foot found the bottom step at the same time the beam from Andi's flashlight captured the lean face of the man who'd passed their cabin earlier.

"Give me that flashlight, you little brat." He rushed for the steps, shoving Sophie aside. Smaller and quicker, Andi dodged his hand and scrambled through the lodge door.

Sophie dropped her blanket and pounded up the steps after him, sore feet and muscles protesting.

The interior light flicked on.

The man ducked back into the shadows of the porch with a curse then pivoted to leave. Acting on instinct, Sophie stuck her foot out. He tripped, stumbled forward and pitched head first down the steps. Lunging through the door, she slammed it shut. Andi stood beside her, hand on the wall light switch.

Breathing hard Sophie held a finger to her lips silencing her daughter. Outside the man groaned.

139

Cursing, he left.

She sighed with relief.

"Who was he, Mommy?" Wide eyed, Andi stared up at her.

"I don't know. But he's gone now." Shaking, she hugged her arms close around her middle.

"What do we do now?" Andi clicked off her flashlight.

In the overhead lamp's dim light the aluminum can sculpture cast an eerie shadow. The stuffed animals appeared ready to come alive at any moment. Mustering her courage, Sophie approached the counter and banged her hand on the desk bell. The *ding-ding* bounced off the peeled log walls. She eyed the door afraid the man might come back. *Gray, where are you?*

Another slap on the bell brought Sharky through a door at the end of the hall yanking on a shirt. The tails flapped as he hustled along the hall, Moose following at his heels.

"What is it? What now?" His eyes lit on Sophie. The glitter of speculation in them made her step back and pull Andi close. "Our shower is broken."

He licked his lips. "How'd you break it?"

Repulsion snaked through Sophie. "The handle broke and I can't turn the shut off valve."

"I *knew* having wim'min here was bad business." Sharky shook his finger at Sophie. "You'll pay for this."

Sophie blinked back the tears burning behind her eyes. She wouldn't let him see her cry. "This is not our fault." Something tugged on her sleeve. Moose stood at her side nibbling her clothes. The main door squeaked open and Sophie spun around afraid it was the stranger.

Daryl Bates stepped across the threshold.

"Where you been for so long?" Sharky snapped his suspenders in place. Moose gave a nervous *naaaa-aaaa* and leapt on top of a low table.

Daryl slumped into a chair. "Out."

Sophie wrapped her arm around Andi. "Is Gray on his way back in the van?"

Staring at the worn carpet, Daryl shrugged. "Dunno."

Her heart sank. "Didn't you take him to the van after getting the fuel?"

"Nope." Picking at his fingernail, Daryl glanced at his father then back at Sophie before studying the carpet again. "Got back to the garage and he weren't there."

Sophie's mouth felt dry as the ash of a long dead campfire.

"Well now. Ain't that interesting." Sharky stepped out from behind the counter and stepped close to Sophie. "Your man must've took off by his self."

*Lord, help me.* Keeping a tenuous hold on her fear, Sophie swept aside her worry for Gray. One crisis at a time. "Please fix the shower." She gave Sharky a pointed look, hoping he didn't hear her knees knocking.

Andi squeezed Sophie's hand. "Daddy will get here soon."

Minutes later, armed with a large wrench and an equally large flashlight, Sharky led the way back to the cabin.

Retrieving the blanket from where she'd dropped it earlier, Sophie followed with Andi close on her heels. The beams of light from their flashlights danced along the path before them. Close by on the left, the brush snapped and crackled. Swallowing a squeal of fright, Sophie sped up. "What was that?"

"Some critter." Sharky pointed his light toward the noise. Within the yellow circle, twigs and branches wove together in a tight leafy web hiding from view whatever had made the sound.

The cabin window glowed like a beacon.

Sharky's silhouette crossed through the light, his booted feet clomped across the wooden porch. The doorknob rattled under his hand. "You gonna let me in?"

"Lissa?" Sophie limped up the steps. "Let us in."

The door opened. Wrapped in a blanket and her hair up in a towel, Lissa held Hanna's hand.

Sharky glanced over his shoulder at Sophie then forced his way past the girls into the cabin. "I'll charge you for parts and labor." In the tiny bathroom, he continued to grumble.

Uncommonly quiet, the girls gathered around Sophie. Lissa brushed a drop of water from her ear lobe. "Where's Gray?"

The tingle of apprehension crawled up Sophie's spine. Before she formed an answer to Lissa's question, Andi jumped in, her voice edged with anger. "We don't know."

Lissa stuck her tongue out. Andi let go of Sophie and swiped at her sister.

"Stop it!" Sophie grabbed Andi as Lissa danced out of reach. "Stop it, both of you!" She caught a glimpse of fear in Andi's eyes. The same fear growing in her own heart. "Gray is getting the van." Sophie glared at the girls. "Fighting doesn't help our situation."

"Yep. Gotta situation all right." Sharky stepped

out of the bath wiping greasy hands on the towel Sophie used earlier to dry her hair. "Shut off the main water valve." His beard shook with each word. "Not a smidge of water comin' into this cabin now."

"But..." Sophie shook her head. "We need water to use the bathroom."

Sharky's thin lips bent into a smirk. He ran a calculating look the length of Sophie. "I got empty rooms at the lodge."

# Chapter 13

Missing the road into The Bates and Tackle Sporting Camp, Gray swore under his breath. Full dark had settled over the mountains. He'd been away from the women far too long. The van's headlights illuminated the tunnel created by the dark forest on either side of the road as he searched for a place to turn around.

Thankfully, the punk kid ditched him in a public spot. Sharky wouldn't win businessman of the year with the locals, but that didn't automatically mean danger for Sophie and the girls. But a score of terrible scenarios continued to march through his mind and every one of them ended in disaster.

How had he come to care so much for Sophie and the smurfs in four short – okay, make that very long – days? They were exactly what he'd always thought he didn't need. A family. They stuck together finding their strength by loving and caring for one another. Pushing Sophie away was the right thing to do, but the desire to be a part of their circle plagued him.

"Getting soft, old man." At a wide spot in the road

he made a U-turn. Traveling slower, he watched for the sign and the road leading to the camp.

Daryl's beater sat in front of the darkened lodge.

Gray ignored the urge to haul the kid out of bed and vent the anger coiled in his chest. The need to check on Sophie and the smurfs kept him in the van negotiating the narrow potholed lane.

Warning bells clanged in his head as he pulled into the gravel parking space in front of the cabin. In the black of the night, he could just make out the small building against the dark towering pines. Indoors, Sophie and the girls slept in real beds, the fire warming the room.

The fire.

No light flickered behind the curtains.

He leapt up the steps. *Probably died down and went out.* Though he'd taught Andi how to build and bank a fire she was still green. He gave the door a quick rap and reached for the knob. It turned beneath his hand. His heart kicked.

"Sophie?" He flipped the light switch beside the door. The living room was tidy. The bedrooms were empty. Keeping a lid on his growing alarm, he worked his way through the cabin finding evidence of their occupation. Damp towels, open cupboards and finally a small white sock.

The bit of cotton rested soft in the palm of his hand while in his chest a hot band of anger unfurled. Had Daryl left him stranded on purpose? Fists clenched tight, he tried to control the fury boiling inside as he charged out the door and down the steps. He ignored the mini van and took off on foot. If Sophie or the smurfs had come to any harm, Sharky was a dead man.

The main door of the lodge banged against the wall and then bounced closed with an equally satisfying crash. *Oh yeah. He'd* let *them hear him coming.*

"Bates!" The one word, delivered as a roar, rang in the rafters. Gray flipped on the light and stomped across the bare wood floor to the counter. He slammed his hand on the desk bell – several times.

Scrambling movements came from the back. Fighting the black fury that tunneled his vision, Gray stepped to the side of the counter.

In a shaft of moonlight, Sharky lurched into view at the far end of the hall. "Hold your water. I'm coming! What happened? Did you break..." His voice thinned to nothing.

"I'll break something alright. Your neck if I find out you harassed Sophie or the girls." Gray reached out and thrust Sharky against the wall. The old man's sour breath sickened him.

Sharky grabbed Gray's forearm. "I don't know what you're talking about! I haven't done nothin'."

His voice a low growl, Gray rammed his fist against Sharky's chest. "They're not in the cabin."

Eyes bugged, Sharky gasped for breath. "I moved them."

"Where? Why?"

"The Trout. Closer to the lake."

"Why?" He didn't relax his hold.

Sharky's eyes shifted.

In one swift maneuver, Gray hauled Sharky up on his toes, swung him around and threw him into Daryl's path. The two careened into the beer can sculpture and fell to the floor amidst the clatter of aluminum.

Gray circled past them to stand near the door.

Scrambling to their feet with knees bent and hands fisted, Sharky and Daryl postured like the hotheaded barroom brawlers they were.

"You want to live? Don't even think about it." *Breathe. Focus.* Gray stood his ground. "One more time. Why did you move them to a different cabin?"

Sharky shifted his weight. "They broke the shower. I turned off the water going into the cabin." He shook his fist at Gray. "I told your wife she'd pay for the damages."

*Wife.* He struggled to ignore the ping in his gut. "They better be where you say they are and unharmed." He spared Daryl a glance. "Good of you to show up."

Clothing skewed, Daryl flexed his fingers and knotted them back into fists. "When I got back to the garage you'd gone."

If he stayed he'd do something he'd regret. Kicking aside a beer can, Gray opened the door, his back to them. He wished they'd jump him and give him an excuse to use up his anger in a down and out fistfight. Disappointed, he got out the door without incident.

His gut screamed at him to hit the path at a run, but the uneven ground and darkness held him to a cautious pace. Only when he stood before the remote cabin, smaller than the first, and saw the uneven flicker of firelight through the thin curtains, did he relax. He climbed the steps to the porch and rapped on the door. "Sophie!"

A thump was followed by a whisper of movement. "Gray!"

Her voice set his blood singing and his heart racing. The door rattled and opened. He stepped inside.

One instant she stood before him, pale and shaken. The next moment he was in her arms, unsure how he got there. He couldn't have said who reached out first. It didn't matter.

Gray wrapped Sophie in his arms and pressed her cheek to his chest. He buried his face in her golden hair, breathed deep – and came up gasping for air.

She cried and talked and he didn't understand a word she said. His eyes watered unmercifully. He blamed the waterworks on the industrial strength medicinal smell emanating from her. He held her and tried to hush her, but she either didn't hear him or chose to ignore him. The three girls huddled on the bed watching their mother with wide frightened eyes. He offered them a smile and held out an arm. Tripping over the blankets that swaddled them, they hurried over to snuggle close.

"Sophie." He framed her face in his hands. Tears glimmered on her cheeks. He smoothed them away with his thumbs. He caught and held her gaze. "I'm here now."

Her lips quivered. A temptation too sweet to resist, he feathered a tender kiss across them. She sighed and he pulled her closer. Fear for her safety melted away in her warm embrace and with the urgent kiss they shared.

Shaky with relief, Gray loosened his hold, broke off the kiss and leaned his brow against hers. So much for keeping his distance.

Her soft shoulders glowed pearly white against the drab brown blanket she held close. An endearing mix of surprise and bashfulness played across her face. And then they both laughed softly, breathless and shaken by the depth of their emotion. Gray wrapped her in a bear hug and rocked her back and forth.

"When you didn't come back with Daryl, I got scared."

Her fear, clear in her whispered words, pained Gray. Having someone worry about him was a new experience. "I'm sorry things didn't go as I'd planned." Releasing her and untangling the girls, he ushered them to the couch and encouraged them to sit while he added logs to the fire. They sat like birds on a wire, not an inch of space between them, and stared at him as if they expected him to vanish in a puff of wood smoke.

"Now will one of you please tell me why you're in this cabin?" Much smaller than the first one, there were no separate bedrooms.

"Lissa broke the shower." The disdain in Andi's voice set off a battle of dueling tongues.

"That's enough, ladies." He sliced them a quelling look before going to Sophie and crouching in front of her. Hanna, thumb in her mouth and tiara slipping to one side, clung to her mother.

"Sophie, what happened?"

"It's true. Lissa broke the shower handle. I couldn't stop the water so I had to go to the lodge to get Sharkey." She shivered.

Imagining Sophie outside the relative safety of the cabin chilled him.

"Andi went with me."

He glanced at Andi and nodded his approval. She tossed her hair over a shoulder and stuck her nose up at her sister.

Sophie held Hanna closer. "He shut off all the water. With no bathroom facilities we didn't have a choice."

"And he didn't," Gray stopped to clear his throat, but his voice continued to rasp. "Sharkey didn't bother any of you?"

A pink blush stained Sophie's cheeks. Her eyes dipped and she shook her head. "At first he wanted us in rooms at the main lodge."

A cold chill rippled along Gray's spine and formed an icy hard ball in his gut. "But you're here."

Arms crossed, Lissa scowled. "That place is creepy."

"Lissa cried." Andi's comment earned her a slap from her sister. Undeterred, she spoke louder. "Like a baby."

Lissa shoved Andi. "A banshee. Mommy said I cried like a banshee." Her head whipped around. "Isn't that what you said, Mommy?"

"What's a banshee?" Andi executed a well-placed elbow punch.

"Girls." Sophie's gaze rested on Gray's nose, chin, ears, any place but his eyes. "Hanna cried, too. The noise was too much for the man. He led us to the cabin farthest from the lodge."

Not overlooking the fact the old reprobate may have had other reasons for sticking them way out here, Gray's gaze flicked to Lissa. "Good job." Her pleased smile had him adding, "But don't try that tactic on me."

Andi piped up. "I didn't like the man with the camera."

"What man?" Gray glanced from Sophie to Andi and back to Sophie again.

She waved her hand as if trying to brush the incident off. "Some man said he was taking pictures of the wildlife."

"But he was taking pictures of Mommy so I shined my flashlight in his face to see how *he* liked it! " Giving a satisfied nod, the warrior pixie crossed her arms with a *'humph'*.

"It wasn't Sharky or Daryl?"

They shook their heads.

An unknown man shooting pictures of Sophie after dark. Someone was up to no good. Only one other person was staying at the camp.

George Frost.

Before morning Gray would know more about Mr. Frost. "One last question." He paused considering each flushed face peeking out from a blanket. "What's that smell and why are you dressed in blankets?"

Sophie's cheeks turned a bright pink. "That's two questions."

"Humor me."

"Someone left medicinal shampoo in the other bath. We used it to shampoo and wash in. I rinsed our clothes, too." She motioned toward the jeans and tee-shirts draped over wooden chairs and hanging from doors. "We wanted to feel clean."

"By the smell of it you're lucky you have any hair and skin left." A bruise the size of an egg discolored the curve of her shoulder. He reached out to touch it, but pulled back and instead ran his hand across his beard. He needed to get a handle on this thing happening between them. He hadn't planned on kissing Sophie. The lack of control appalled him though he had no regrets. Given half a chance he'd kiss her again. "The van is at the other cabin. I'll get it so we can start early in the morning."

As one, they bounced off the couch and reached

for him.

"Hey, it's okay." He brushed his fingers across Sophie's cheek, then reached down and ruffled a mop of spun gold hair, tweaked a nose and patted a shoulder. "I'll be back."

Sophie stiffened. "We're going with you." She turned to the girls. To the last smurf, they nodded. "The buddy system, remember?"

He tried to hide the smile twitching on his lips. What other gems had he spouted? They'd come back and haunt him for sure. "Okay, ladies. Put on some clothes and let's go round up the van."

While they prepared to leave, Gray did a little recon on the cabin's interior. He checked window locks and the fire, becoming familiar with the new digs. He'd known of ops, only minutes from successful completion, hitting the skids. That wouldn't happen here. Getting them home was paramount.

"We're ready." Sophie stood near the door with the girls gathered close. They looked at him with the same expectant faces they'd had four days earlier while standing next to their disabled van.

"Let's roll." Gray opened the cabin door. Out of habit he swept the perimeter with his eyes before leading his small group down the steps.

A snick followed by a beam of light whirled him round.

Andi held the flashlight shining on her mother's feet.

His gut churned. The light exposed them as easy targets for anyone watching, but Sophie and the smurfs moved faster with it. Uneasy, he hustled them along the rutted pathway and narrow lane.

The women set upon the van as though greeting a long-lost member of the family. The girls climbed in exuberantly embracing the clothing and toys he'd pitched into the backseat four days ago. Bits of lace flew up as they dug through the pile squealing and giggling.

Girls made an awful lot out of nothing when the mood hit them. "Find a place to light so I can drive."

Sophie settled them in the back seat on top of the clothing before she climbed in to ride shotgun. Gray keyed the ignition.

Reaching out, she rested her hand on his forearm. For one breathless moment her gaze held his. A million unspoken words flew between them before she whispered, "Thank you." Her fingers squeezed and she let go. The imprint of her fingers on his arm stayed with him on the drive back to the cabin.

\*\*\*

"Everything inside." Sophie leaned into the backseat and wrapped her arms around a bundle of clothes. "I want to repack tonight."

"Sophie, it's late. You should rest. The girls, too."

Rest? If she stretched out flat she'd float a foot off the bed. The man could kiss! When she tried to remember why it was a bad idea to get involved with him, her lips tingled and her thoughts flew to the comfort of his strong embrace. "Please, Gray? I want to do this. Tonight." She stretched her neck to see over the load she carried. "Tomorrow I'd like to leave as early as possible. Civilization is calling me."

His low rumbling laugh rippled along her spine. He was bossy and drove her nuts, but she would miss him when he left tomorrow. Worse than ever now that he'd kissed her like he meant it.

"Would it be cheating on your trial if I drop you off at your next checkpoint?"

"What?"

She turned. His intense eyes peered at her from above an armload of pink terrycloth, lace and ladybugs. "I said—."

"I know what you said." He passed her on the path and climbed the steps into the cabin.

*Now what?* Placing each foot squarely on the next wooden step, Sophie made it half way to the top when muscular forearms brushed against her wrists.

Gray took the pile from her and deposited it on the couch next to his. He turned back to her, his face set in an uncompromising mask. "I'm driving you home."

She shook her head. "No. I have the map..." He quirked an eyebrow and heat flooded her cheeks.

"I've gotten you this far, I'm taking you home."

Sophie turned back to the pile of clothes. The girls stood next to the couch listening. She shook out a set of pajamas and folded them. "What about the job with SeaMount?"

"I've contacted them and told them I'd temporarily suspended my trial."

"You can do that?" She clutched a small pair of pants his words sinking in. "When did you call them? How?" She had to contact her lawyer, Mr. Vole. He'd be *furious* that she missed her court appointment. Tommy's parents might already be guardians of the girls. The frightening thought caused her heart to plummet.

"The place I bought fuel had an old-fashioned phone booth still in operation."

A tear slipped down her cheek. "Gray, I have a call to make. Can we go there in the morning?" She glanced at the girls not wanting to say much in front of them.

He tugged the pants from her hands and tossed them back on the pile before pulling her into his arms and holding her close. Breath warm against her ear, he murmured. "We'll be long gone before they open. I told Sam why I suspended my trial and asked him to work on your situation."

Sophie tried to stop the tremors rolling through her. She'd be silly to let embarrassment get in the way of her fight for her daughters. "What did he say?"

His hand rubbed across her back. "The connection wasn't great, but I told him what information I had before the call disconnected. How much he got or what he'll do about it, I'm not sure."

She exhaled, fear and frustration warring for the top place inside her.

"Hang in there, sweetheart. You're not in this alone anymore."

At her first sniff, his hand burrowed through her hair. He drew her head against his chest, his shirt absorbing her tears. Surrounded by his warmth, she wrapped her arms around him and leaned into his solid strength. Against her better judgment, she let the door to her heart creak open a little wider.

He nudged her chin up with his thumb. "Now finish packing so you can go rest."

She took a deep breath and stepped back. "Okay."

Gray ran his hand across the top of his head. "You packed a lot for a weekend away." With a resigned sigh he went out the door.

Sophie handed each of the girls a set of pajamas. "Go change, girls. Be quick about it." Tomorrow would be a long day.

Gray dumped the last load of totes and duffels on the floor then sank into a worn overstuffed chair. He leaned his head back and closed his eyes.

In the process of sorting and folding, Sophie paused to study the man who'd found them and then guided them through the wilderness. Even relaxed with legs stretched out in front of him, he exuded an aura of power. Light from the fire etched lines of fatigue in his masculine face. The temptation to reach out and smooth away the tension caused her heart to pick up its tempo.

Dressed in pajamas, the girls squealed with delight as they pawed through their duffels.

"Shh." Sophie glanced at Gray. "Quieter please, girls."

"Hair stuff!" Lissa held up a plastic bag. She opened it and began clipping multiple bows and barrettes in her hair.

Opening a tangerine duffle, Andi pulled out a small video game. She sat back with a sigh and soon faint beeps filled the tiny cabin.

Hanna occupied the rug at Gray's feet. She'd put on all the bracelets she'd brought from home, which happened to number a great deal more than Sophie expected. The plastic bangles covered Hanna's arm from elbow to wrist.

Sophie smoothed the wrinkles from a shirt. This could be an ordinary evening at home... with the exception of the six foot four inch man slumped in the chair power napping.

# Chapter 14

From beneath his eyelashes, Gray studied Sophie. Her gentle smile and warm, sleepy eyes warmed his blood. Did the woman even realize what her eyes were saying when she looked at him like that? He poured every ounce of control he possessed into keeping his butt in the lumpy chair.

He almost sighed with relief when the small plastic case she held claimed her attention. Digging through it, she lined up colorful bottles, tiny tubes and puffs of cotton on the low coffee table. Clutching something in her hand, she sat back amidst the piles of clothing and set to work on her fingernails.

*Ahh. A fingernail file.* The concentration and detailing she put into each nail gave the word 'manicure' new meaning. Gray now understood why she'd cringed when he'd pared her nails with his knife.

She slipped off her shoes, swept aside her collection and balanced a foot on the edge of the table to inspect each toenail. The tip of her tongue licked across her full bottom lip. Gray held back the groan building in his chest.

Hanna bounced across the room a bit of cloth in her hand. "Tie up my hair please, Mommy?"

Sophie set aside the file. "Turn around." Long fingers raked through white gold strands, twisted the stretchy cloth and Hanna's hair was up.

How would his childhood have been different had his mother never been killed in an automobile accident? Gray couldn't remember her and the one time he'd asked his father what she looked like, he'd gotten a backhand across the mouth. He never asked again.

"Can you braid my hair?" Andi leaned across the arm of his chair, her face close to his.

Sophie glanced in his direction surprised before turning her attention back to Hanna.

Gray sat up. The pixie staring up at him hadn't bought his ruse, which was down right disturbing.

Andi scooted around the chair and plopped to the floor at his feet offering him a view of the back of her head. She slung a hairbrush over her shoulder. "One braid, please."

*Right.* He'd never braided hair, but how hard could it be? He fumbled the small pink hairbrush, hesitated then tried to imitate what Sophie had done with Hanna.

"Ow!" Andi slapped a hand to the crown of her head. "You pulled."

Gray cleared his throat. "Sorry." He balanced the brush on his thigh and picked and pulled at the silky strands. Whiffs of industrial strength shampoo teased his nose. "Hold still." The girl could wiggle. Taking the brush in hand, he ran it through Andi's hair, this time without a hitch. He divided the sleek skein into thirds and braided one long rope.

She held up a stretchy circle of cloth.

He secured the end of the braid then let go to inspect his handiwork. An odd little bump bulged out half way down but otherwise it looked good. "All set."

Andi sprang up. "Thanks." She joined Hanna on the rumpled bed.

Her casual acceptance of his accomplishment pricked his ego. He glanced Sophie's way. Her dark eyes shone with a warm light. Her tender smile had his gut doing the curly thing.

"Andi's braid came out nice."

He resisted the urge to take a deep breath and puff out his chest. Instead, he grinned like a fool. "Thanks."

Sophie zipped closed a purple duffle and placed it on the floor next to the other bags and totes. "These are ready to go into the van." Her large suitcase lay open on the bed waiting to be filled with clothes including the intimate apparel he'd manhandled that first morning.

Rising, he went to the pile of luggage. He remembered too well the soft insubstantial weight of all that lace and silk. Loaded down with duffels and packs, he paused at the open door. "For a short weekend, why did you pack so many..." He lifted his chin in the direction of the froth of feminine skivvies. Her blush set his heart pounding in his ears.

"I wasn't sure what I wanted to wear."

He shook his head. *A woman thing.*

***

Near midnight Gray checked the fire one last time. The van was packed. The girls were in bed asleep. Sophie stood next to the couch hands tightly clasped together, her face lined with fatigue.

"Time you hit the rack."

159

Her brow wrinkled. "Where will you sleep?"

"The van."

"You'll be cold."

"I have the quilt and the van's heater." Gray reached out, took her hands and separated them. "Relax. I'll be okay." Staying in the van allowed him the freedom to patrol the area around the cabin without waking anyone. Something she didn't need to know. "Good night, Sophie." He squeezed her hands and let go. Time to leave before he made a move that required an explanation.

As the door closed behind him, he heard a quiet, "Good night, Gray."

An hour later, satisfied Sophie had settled in for what was left of the night, Gray exited the van to prowl the resort in search of one George Frost. Close to the lake he found an occupied cabin and a truck with Connecticut plates. He approached the cabin with caution.

Wavering light from the fire silhouetted a man, SAT phone to his ear, pacing the floor. A boom of laughter covered any whisper of sound Gray made as he crept closer.

"That's right. You'll be pleased with what I got." Average build and balding, the man wouldn't stand out in a crowd. He turned toward the window and Gray pulled back.

"I'm almost finished here. Just one more stop then I'm leaving." Floorboards creaked and his voice faded as he paced the other direction.

Time crucial, Gray retreated from the window and focused on the truck parked at the side of the cabin. He tried the passenger door.

Unlocked.

He opened the door and the overhead light flicked on. With no windows on this end of the cabin, he used the light to his advantage. He riffled the glove compartment for the registration and insurance card. Both bore George Frost's name and address. Committing the registration number and address to memory he stuffed them back where they belonged.

A search beneath the seat turned up an oily rag, a crumpled candy wrapper and a pair of work gloves. In the bed of the truck he found a coiled chain and an empty cooler. Nothing to give him a clue why Frost was at the sports camp off-season.

Thumping and shuffling noises came from the cabin's interior, Gray's signal it was time to slip away.

He circled back to Sophie's van. Climbing in, he pulled the quilt up around his shoulders. A faint whiff of cinnamon and pine teased his senses. The trek had taken a toll on the quilt. Batting puffed out where hunks of fabric had gone missing. Some seams had split and the edges were dark with dirt. Hoping the thing wasn't destined for rags, Gray hunkered down and waited.

Not long after headlights punched a hole in the black night. Beams of light bounced wildly as the truck lumbered over the rutted road. Reaching the narrow pull off at Sophie's cabin, the truck slowed then revved and took off, shocks protesting the abuse.

The knot in Gray's gut loosened. He leaned his head back and closed his eyes. George Frost had spotted the van. The man wouldn't come back.

\*\*\*

As night melted into predawn, Gray pulled the unused map from the glove compartment. With a yellow crayon he'd dug from Hanna's pack, he traced the route he planned to take out of Maine. He'd pick up a Southern New England map when they made a pit stop and finish tracing the route all the way to Sophie's hometown a few miles inland from SeaMount.

His discovery of Sophie and the disabled van had been pure luck. A quiet nudge to his heart brought him up short. "Okay, God. Not luck. You. But she should learn to read a map. If I'm not around..."

If? What do you mean 'if', Kerr? You're not going to be around. You have a trial to finish and, hopefully, a job waiting for you. Gray ran a hand the length of his face then rubbed his eyes. He felt like road kill. Flat.

The first rays of sun had gilded the treetops with a golden light when the door of the cabin swung open. Fully dressed, Sophie stepped out of the cabin. She held a sleepy Hanna in her arms.

Gray bailed out of the van and took the child. "Morning." Hanna's tiara, now missing two plastic gems, clipped him under the chin. Tension hummed around Sophie. A passel of problems waited for her at home. He buckled Hanna into her car seat then helped Lissa and Andi, groggy with sleep, climb into the backseat on either side. The van's engine turned over without a hitch.

Passing the dark lodge, Sophie sighed. "I owe that horrid little man more money."

"You owe him nothing."

His threatening growl made Sophie's eyes widen.

"I'll take care of any extra charges." Gray's gut curdled at the thought of further contact between Sophie and Sharky.

They hit the main road and he relaxed his grip on

the steering wheel. Next to him, Sophie dug through her bag and pulled out a cell phone. She plugged in the car charger, switched the phone on then snapped it shut and flashed him a weary smile.

"Pull out the map."

She pushed the button and let the glove compartment door drop open. "I can't read it."

"Just open it and tell me what you see."

Paper rustled as she unfolded the map then turned it right side up. If she spread her arms any wider he'd have to hang his head out the side window to see the road.

She tsked. "It's ruined! There's a yellow crayon line on it."

He couldn't help but smile. "That's our route home and I want you to follow it as I drive."

"Me?" Her voice squeaked. With a great deal of crinkling, she lowered her arms. "You're sure you want *me* to read the map to *you*?" Her incredulous expression was priceless.

"I know where we're going. You're going to follow the map so *you* know, too."

Puzzled, she fingered the coated paper.

"It's the easiest way to figure out how to read a map. Refold it so the northern most part of the yellow line is showing."

After a bit of fumbling and figuring, Sophie folded the map to lap size.

"Now put your finger at the top of the line."

Sophie poked at the map as though it would singe her fingertip. "Okay. Now what."

"There's a small white circle. The name of the town is next to it."

"Beryl. That's where the resort is. I mean, where we are!"

"Congratulations, Sophie. You read a map."

She grinned and he fought the urge to pull over and plant a smooch on those chapped pink lips. "Follow the yellow line and find the road that intersects this one that we're on. Got it?"

"Yes."

"Keep your finger on that spot until we arrive there."

"That's all?"

"When we get there move your finger to the next intersection or the next town along the yellow line. That's the way home."

In the backseat one of the girls moved in her sleep. Sophie reached back to adjust the quilt tucked around them. "My beautiful quilt."

Gray glanced in the rearview mirror. "Pretty cruddy at this point."

Beside him, she nodded. "My mother made it for me." The sadness in her voice activated the curly stomach thing. "I'm hoping someone can restore it."

Knowing zero about such stuff, Gray's assessment placed the quilt beyond repair. For Sophie's sake, he hoped he was wrong.

Fidgeting with her phone, her attention shifted between the map and the passing landscape. He sensed her restlessness had nothing to do with the ruined quilt.

"Want to talk about it?"

Her long fingers sifted through golden curls. "I have to call my lawyer."

Though he'd called SeaMount from the garage, the question remained how much Sam had heard and understood. Did he do anything with the information? The man had bigger irons in the fire. "What's your lawyer's take on your case?"

The face she made looked so much like Lissa that Gray bit his tongue to keep from laughing out loud.

"God bless him, he's a nice man. I'm not sure, but he may believe the girls would be better off with Tommy's parents."

"What?"

"Keep your eyes on the road."

Gray's grip on the steering wheel tightened with frustration. The 'nice man' needed a reminder that Sophie was paying him to win this case for her. Unless.... "How'd you find this lawyer?"

"Actually, Mr. Vole was Tommy's lawyer. He came with the marriage, if you know what I mean."

Oh, he knew all right.

"Unlike Gerald Moore, I don't have unlimited resources to plow into the fight."

Could Sophie's lawyer be taking money under the table to throw the case? If the man owed loyalty to the Moore family, he might try to undermine Sophie's chance of keeping her girls. Suspicion flaring, Gray stomped the gas pedal a little harder. He'd find the truth with or without help from SeaMount.

\*\*\*

"There's our gas station!" Lissa bounced in the back seat.

Sophie folded the map and tucked it away. Another ten minutes and they'd be home. The closer they got, the more excited the peanut gallery, which was the complete opposite of the quiet brooding coming from the man in the driver's seat.

After breakfast at a small diner, she'd overseen the restroom visit with her girls, washing sticky maple syrup from pink cheeks and chins. Borrowing her cell phone, Gray excused himself to go outside and make a call.

When she herded the little ones out to the van, he'd joined the group, silent and on edge. He took extra care settling the girls and helping Sophie find the correct place on the map. They'd played out the same scenario at lunch in a fast food restaurant.

With each passing mile, as the time together drew closer to an end, an unexpected sadness descended on Sophie. Five days ago she didn't know this man, but the isolation in the wilderness had created a bond forged by intense daily contact and dependence. She would miss him. Would he miss her and the girls? They'd held him back, kept him from finishing his survival trial.

He negotiated the turn on Sunnyside Drive. Cresting the hill, Sophie's gray ranch came into view.

An enthusiastic cheer erupted in the back seat.

Gray leaned forward eyes trained on the black SUV parked across the street from the house.

"Who's that?"

"My ride." He turned into the drive and parked the van.

Warm happiness flowed through Sophie. She was home. The fearful times in the wilderness when she'd wondered if she'd ever see her home again were behind her. Breathing a prayer of thanksgiving, she unbuckled her seat belt and stepped out of the van.

In an excited frenzy, Lissa and Andi burst into the warm sunshine. Andi turned a cartwheel on the lawn.

"Girls, grab a backpack to take into the house."

Sophie unbuckled Hanna. Turning to open the back of the van, she halted.

Three men in casual dress crossed the street to meet Gray. Unsmiling and formidable in their carriage, she suppressed a shiver. Scars disfigured the face of the man in the lead. A slight hitch in his gait testified to other injuries. Torn between the meeting in her driveway and the need to get indoors to the warm embrace of her home, Sophie chose the house.

Loaded with backpacks and toys, the girls crowded her on the top step. Too tired to reprimand them, she fumbled her key before getting the door unlocked. The familiar scent of teaberry greeted her. Andi bolted through the door first followed by Lissa.

A shriek of surprised panic rang out followed by a loud thump.

# Chapter 15

Sophie stepped across the threshold, her heart in her throat.

Andi lay sprawled across a tumble of pillows on the floor. Stuffing puffed from sliced couch cushions. The television and lamps lay on the floor, cracked and broken. Moving forward she stumbled. Her mother's ivy plant was torn from its pot, roots exposed and the dirt spilling across floorboards.

Disbelief gave way to nausea. Shaking, she turned to the hallway. Glass from the pictures pulled off the wall crunched beneath her feet. In her office, file cabinet drawers hung open. Paper littered every surface. Across the hall in Lissa's room clothing hung out of dresser drawers. The bedclothes were stripped from the mattress.

She turned to her bedroom. Drawers torn from the bureau and nightstand lay upside down on the floor. Her closet door gaped open, a dark hole. The clothes flung in every direction, draped the bed and carpeted the floor.

A strong hand grasped her arm.

Gray stood beside her. Behind him, the other men

moved in and out of the rooms, weapons drawn.

A cold knot settled in Sophie's stomach. Icy tendrils crept along her arms and down her legs. What if they'd been home when this happened? Her heart thudded heavy in her chest. Home meant comfort and peace. A safe haven from a harsh cruel world.

"Sophie."

That world had invaded and destroyed her home.

"Sophie!" His hand clamped hard and shook. "Look at me."

She gazed into eyes the color of winter ice and shivered. His hand moved to the nap of her neck. The icy terror holding her in its grip cracked. He enfolded her in his arms. She leaned into his strength absorbing his warmth.

"Listen to me."

Face buried in the hollow of his shoulder, Sophie drew a shaky breath.

"Some of the best in the business are in this house. They...*we* will find out who did this.

*Lord, help me.* Her arms and legs trembled.

"I need you to take the girls outside. Wait for me there."

Sophie reached for Hanna, then Andi and Lissa. Their fear-filled eyes wrenched her heart. Broken china and food littered the kitchen floor making it impossible for her to take them out the back way. On shaky legs she herded them past the men she didn't know and out the front door. Fear warred with anger as she led them around the corner of the house and down the gentle slope into the back yard.

"Mommy. Who did that?" Lissa's voice wobbled with tears.

169

Andi tweaked Hanna's ear. Hanna struck back. "Bad guys did it. Gray will catch them." She picked up a stick and beat it against the trunk of the apple tree. "They'll go to jail."

A large wood swing set occupied a corner of the yard, one of the last gifts Tommy bought for the girls. He and his friends had joked and laughed like small boys putting it together.

Andi climbed the frame to hang upside down by her knees. Lifting Hanna, Sophie sat on the glider next to Lissa. She struggled to think clearly. Her thoughts careened wildly from blind panic to anger before settling on vulnerability and a sense of loss.

The certainty that Gray would not leave her to face this new trial alone provided a measure of comfort. She also wanted peace. The kind only God could give her in the midst of this storm. "Bow your heads and pray with me, sweeties."

With one foot, Sophie rocked the glider. The back and forth motion and the quiet squeak of wood rubbing against wood soothed her. Putting an arm around Lissa, she drew her close. Voice trembling with tears she struggled to think clearly. "Father, thank you for sending Gray to us. We don't understand why this happened. Don't know who did this horrible thing. But you know so we leave it in your merciful hands. Please watch over us and protect us... and Gray and the other men, too." She couldn't think of anything more to add so settled for "Amen."

Sniffing back tears, she rested her cheek on the crown of Hanna's soft hair. She'd ridden away from the cabin this morning relieved to put the wilderness ordeal behind her and anxious to speak with Mr. Vole. In her safe world, she never imagined she'd be faced with this feeling of violation and loss. *God, where are you in all this?*

A memory verse from 2 Corinthians came to mind. "My grace is sufficient for you, for my power is made perfect in weakness." That's me, Lord. After the past four days, I have no strength to battle through this new crisis. And I still have the worry of losing the girls. Fresh tears trickled down Sophie's cheeks and into Hanna's hair.

Gray strode around the corner of the house and approached the swing set. Concern flashed in his eyes before dissolving beneath a hard professional mask. "Sam wants to speak with you." He glanced at the girls then back at her. "Alone." The muscle in his cheek twitched.

He didn't like the 'alone' part any more than she did. "He's the director of SeaMount?"

"Yes. He calls the shots."

"Do you still have a hope of working for him?"

"I did what was necessary and right under the circumstances." He reached for Andi. She grabbed him around the neck and slid off the crossbar to the ground. "They're here to help, Sophie. Sam has the resources to find who did this."

The intensity in his expression melted the hard knot in Sophie's stomach. She rubbed her cheek over Hanna's hair. Violence had never touched her ordinary life. Crimes happened to other people - not to Sophie Moore.

He wrapped his hands around her wrists and urged her to release Hanna. "Come on. Help us find who did this."

Shaking, she released Hanna. She didn't want to face the questions. Didn't want to know who could be so hateful they'd invade her home, tear it apart and frighten her children.

Gray lifted Hanna into his arms and started back toward the house. Sophie followed with Andi and Lissa on her heels.

As they made their way toward the deck, a policeman stepped from the walkout basement door with a roll of yellow crime scene tape in his hand. The scarred man stood on the side deck off the kitchen. Another man, dressed in a suit jacket and tie, joined him.

As if he knew her courage was faltering, Gray turned and held out his free hand. Grateful for the support, she took it and climbed the steps beside him.

"Sophie, meet Sam Traven."

Sam grasped Sophie's hand in his. Ridges of scarred flesh pressed against her palm.

"Hello, Sophie. I'm sorry we've had to meet under such trying circumstances." His deep voice had a rough gravelly edge to it.

Gray shifted Hanna to his other arm. "I'll take the girls around front to wait."

A look Sophie couldn't decipher passed between the men before Gray led the girls away.

"Thank you for your help." She glanced through the sliding glass doors into the kitchen. The first rush of panic gone, she saw details she'd missed earlier.

Open cupboard doors revealed bare shelves. On the counter, oatmeal and crackers mixed with shards of floral patterned china and crystal glassware. Broken eggs smeared the floor, ketchup and mustard dripped from the walls.

Blackness edged Sophie's vision. "To do this...so much anger..." Sam helped her to a deck chair. Head in her hands, she drew in deep breaths to calm her stomach and keep from throwing up. *God, who did this?*

"I'm sorry." He gave her a wary smile. "I need to ask you some personal questions."

She nodded and braced her hands against her knees.

Sitting in a chair opposite her, he pulled out a small pad and pen. "We'll begin with the easy questions, full names and birth dates for you and the girls."

Concentrating on the basics helped Sophie focus. After ten minutes of answering questions about everything from the name of the neighbor with an emergency key to the details of Tommy's accident, nausea no longer threatened to cut the interview short.

Sam leaned forward in his chair. "Tell me about your financial situation."

"My finances?" She shook her head, puzzled where this line of questioning would lead. "Tommy said our investments took a nose dive in the economic crisis, but he'd managed to recoup a bit of the lost money."

He scribbled in his notebook. "Did he owe money to any one? Friends or family?"

Sophie played with the zipper on her sweatshirt. "I'd have known if that were the case, Mr. Traven."

"Call me Sam. Tell me about the custody battle for your daughters."

She waved her hand in the general direction of the

house. "What does this have to do with my girls?"

"Just covering all possibilities."

She took a deep breath. "Tommy's parents wouldn't... They love the girls. Suzanne, Tommy's mother, always complimented me on my home. She'd never come in and do... *this*!"

"When did you last see Tommy's parents?"

"About a month ago at Hanna's nursery school graduation."

"Both grandparents attended?"

"No." Sophie rubbed her hands along her thighs. "Just Suzanne. She said Gerald couldn't get away from the office."

"Is it unusual for him to miss an important event?"

"Yes." At the time she had thought it odd. "Gerald has always made time for the girls. He'd never intentionally disappoint Hanna. His fight is with me."

"So tell me about that."

Memories, both happy and sad, played through her mind. "As children, Tommy and I were inseparable. We spent the summers together in Maine." She paused remembering the carefree days filled with love and family fun. A longing for that simpler time swept through her. "Our parents were close then."

"That changed?"

Sam's question brought Sophie back to the present. "Gerald's business grew successful. He bought a new car, a bigger boat. Money was no object."

"And your family?"

"My folks never tried to keep up with the neighbors. We weren't wealthy, but we never lacked for anything, either. By the teenage years, I'd become 'that girl' next door."

"Were you forbidden to spend time together?"

"No. I think Gerald knew enforcing anything like that would be next to impossible. Instead, he invited wealthy friends with sons and daughters about Tommy's age to come and stay at the resort."

"How did Tommy feel about that?"

"Whatever adventure they cooked up, Tommy included me."

"And the wedding? How did that go with his parents?"

She shifted in her chair. "We eloped."

Surprise flared in his eyes.

Sophie smiled at the memory. "We wanted a great adventure."

He rubbed his mustache with his forefinger. "So you eloped?"

"Saying our vows was only the *beginning*. Tommy said our marriage was the adventure that would last a lifetime." Sadness enveloped her. They were so full of plans for the future, never expecting the tragedy that would cut short their time together.

"I think I would have liked your husband."

Sophie blinked back tears. "Are we done?"

"Almost." Sam glanced at his notepad. "Did your husband have a will when he passed away?"

Her throat tightened. "Yes."

He leaned forward in his chair. "Do you remember any unusual bequests in his will? Anything that could create dissension within the family?"

"No." She rubbed at her eyes. "The will was straightforward. Life insurance, investments and a trust funds for the girls."

"Do you know the terms of the trust funds?"

"Only that I'm the trustee and they receive the money when they turn twenty-five."

"That will do for now. Thank you." Sam closed his notepad.

He stood and helped her up. "Call me if you remember anything unusual or have questions. When the forensics team finishes we'll go through the house with you."

Sam escorted her down the steps and around to the front of the house. "A team will be working through the night. I have security posted outside. I don't believe anyone will be foolish enough to revisit the crime scene, but I don't want to take a chance."

Gray gently pushed Hanna in the old-fashioned tire swing hanging from the oak tree at the front of the house. Andi and Lissa sat on the ground leaning against the trunk. Spotting their mother, they sprang to their feet. The girls studied Sam's disfigured face but didn't ask any questions much to Sophie's relief.

Stopping the swinging tire, Gray helped Hanna dismount.

One side of Sam's mustache kicked up at the sight of Gray holding Hanna's hand. "You've all had a hard week." He turned to Sophie. "Please stay at SeaMount while we work through what has happened."

"Thank you." Sophie wrapped her arms around her middle. Sam may have framed his words nicely, but his command of the situation didn't leave room for a 'no'.

He addressed Gray. "One of the men will take them to SeaMount. Come find me once they're on their way."

A man hurried toward them with a clipboard in his hand. Sam excused himself.

Only a few hours ago she'd dreamed of tucking the girls in their own beds tonight. Now strangers had the full run of her home.

\*\*\*

Gray waited for Sam to leave before he palmed Sophie's elbow and ushered her toward the curb. "Time to go." She would never win at a game of poker. Every thought, every emotion played across her pale face. He motioned for the girls to follow.

"But..." She rubbed her brow.

"There is nothing more you can do here. Go, have a bite to eat and settle the smurfs for the night." Coming across as a hard-nose helped him keep his emotions in check. Angry with himself for letting them enter the house alone, Andi's scream continued to echo in his mind. He shuddered, imagining what could have happened if they'd entered the house with the perpetrator still on the premises.

A black passenger van idled at the curb. The driver, dressed in jeans and a cowboy hat, leaned against the fender. "Ladies." He touched a finger to his hat. "Whit McCord at your service."

Put out by the way the other man studied Sophie Gray rested his hand on the small of her back and opened the door. "Hop in."

"What about clothes?" Sophie dragged her feet.

"Your mini van is filled with clothing and toiletries. I'll ask to have it brought to you at SeaMount."

Her lips formed a perfect O.

"You'll have what you need." The SeaMount staff

177

had the resources to care for them, he was certain. He buckled Hanna into the car seat provided and Andi and Lissa climbed in on either side of her. Their subdued behavior concerned him. Andi, shouldering a burden too big for her age, watched her mother protectively.

Gray tweaked a frizzed braid. "You and Lissa follow orders till I get there, you hear?"

Andi nodded and reached both arms up for a hug. He closed the side door marveling at the ease with which he accepted the show of affection.

Riding shotgun, Sophie placed her palm against the closed window. He pressed his hand to the shatterproof glass covering hers. The van pulled away and his hand fell.

"Come help secure the crime scene." Sam limped up the walk and stood to the side of the open front door. "You willfully disregarded orders and took on your own mission."

Gray held the other man's gaze, unwilling to apologize or show remorse. "A rescue much like those SeaMount executes all over the world."

Sam glanced at the activity inside. "Your wilderness navigation skills are excellent and you brought four inexperienced civilians out with you. We're following up on this situation at your request, but I still have questions about your suitability for a job with the agency. We'll discuss it at another time."

Gray had figured his actions wouldn't go over well. Wondering at his lack of regret for putting his goal of a job in jeopardy, he scrutinized the scene beyond the yellow tape. Through the open door into Sophie's living room he tried to see beyond the damage to find the home she had created. A home unlike any place he'd ever lived.

The walls glowed a warm yellow. Treasured school portraits, glass cracked, lay scattered on the glossy hardwood floor. Next to the couch a small end table lay on its side; a bowl filled with sea glass and shells had shattered, the contents spilling across the floor.

In his childhood home the end table had overflowed with a full ashtray and empty beer cans. There had been no such thing as a school portrait on display or plants in need of water. Utilitarian would the kindest way to describe his father's house.

The arrival of a high-ranking police officer with golden 'scrambled eggs' on the visor of his cap pulled him back to the present. Sam turned to greet the Chief with a friendly handshake.

Taking the opportunity handed him, Gray ducked beneath the tape. A reckless move and one he'd be called on no doubt, but he needed to see for himself the broken pieces of Sophie's home.

Halfway down the hall he caught a whiff of cinnamon. An open bedroom door revealed floral sheets, pink blankets and articles of clothing cascading from a queen size bed, the mattress skewed on its frame. In the closet one lone blouse dangled from a hanger. Satin, silk and lace hung from open dresser drawers in a rainbow of colors.

Sophie's bedroom.

In the midst of the mess, a woman wearing gloves snapped photographs and jotted notes.

Careful where he stepped, Gray continued the length of the hall stopping at each door, visualizing what took place to create such wholesale destruction.

Someone knew precisely how to strike at Sophie's heart.

The need to avenge the losses she suffered, both the physical and the emotional, mushroomed inside him like an atomic blast. He would help find the person who did this and see justice meted out in full measure.

"Kerr, you don't belong in here." Jack Conroy waited at the end of the hall, the stuffing from a ripped couch cushion billowing at his feet. "You're here to keep sightseers out, not be one." The lean muscular man the other agents called 'Preach' held Gray's narrow-eyed glare with his own unwavering blue gaze. "She got to you, didn't she?"

Riding the dark determination to punish whoever destroyed Sophie's home, Gray didn't deny the accusation.

"Don't let your feelings for her get in the way of doing the job."

"Won't happen." The words grated past Gray's jaw locked tight with tension.

Unfazed, Preach gestured toward the bedrooms. "Sam's pulled together a good team."

"Are you two finished?" Stony-faced, Sam stood framed in the front doorway. "Because if you are, I'd appreciate it if you'd get outside and dispense with the spectators."

The black and white police car parked in the driveway had brought out the concerned citizens and nosy neighbors. Kids on bikes edged closer to the house with each sweep across Sophie's lawn.

Sam held up the yellow tape.

Gray ducked under followed by Preach. "We'll take care of it."

# Chapter 16

The rolling thunder of waves breaking against the shore carried across the sand dunes. On a bluff overlooking the ocean, the immense building SeaMount called home came into view, lit up like a cruise ship against the night sky. The modern re-creation of a historic hotel that had once occupied the bluff glowed in a golden wash of incandescent light.

Riding in the passenger's seat of the black SUV, Gray's gaze hunted along each balcony. Someplace within this building, Sophie and her girls were settling in for the night. Soon after they'd left the house with McCord, Sam had followed, leaving the team at Sunnyside to continue with the tech work. Preach turned the vehicle into the service entrance parking lot.

On the unlit loading dock the burning red tip of a cigarette arced upwards, paused, then drifted down again.

Muttering under his breath, Preach stepped from the vehicle and slammed his door shut. Shoulders back, his long stride ate up the asphalt beneath his boots.

Gray followed at a distance. The one evening he'd spent in this place he'd met only Sam and Preach. The pecking order within the group remained an unknown.

"Hurst!" Preach charged up the steps. The dark recessed corner of the loading dock swallowed him up. "You're not where you belong." He stepped back into the light holding a scrawny kid by the back of his shirt collar.

Futile as his attempt was, the kid fought. "Leave me alone." He swung a fist.

Preach clamped a hand around the skinny wrist. "Your orders are to be in your rack at twenty-two hundred."

Draped in scruffy clothing too large for his skinny frame, the kid dropped the butt of his cigarette and ground it under the heel of his dirty high top sneaker. "I don't even know what time twenty-two hundred is." His bravado dissolved into an annoying whine.

Showing no mercy Preach hauled him through the service door and down the hall. "You better learn quick. We're your last chance." He gave the kid a shove. "Keep up this idiocy and you'll be doing more than quarterdecking."

"Oh man." The whine escalated. "My muscles are already killing me."

"You want to go back to juvie? Have to explain to your mama why you're there?" Preach glanced over his shoulder at Gray. "Davie here is Sam's special project."

The service entry hall opened into a small foyer dominated by an open stairway leading topside to the sitting room. At the base of the stairs, floor to ceiling glass windows offered a view of the gym.

Preach shoved his captive past the quiet gym and into a tile and concrete room where a rhythmic *splosh splosh* echoed off the hard surfaces.

"You better hope The Man's in a forgiving mood, Hurst." Keeping the kid on tiptoe, Preach approached the end of the saltwater pool.

Curious to see how this drama played out, Gray took up a position just inside the door.

Sam powered through three more laps before he surged up the steps and out of the pool. Water streamed off him to reveal shiny ridges on his chest and shoulders and puckered flesh on his thighs.

The sight hit Gray like a punch to the gut. His own battle wounds were mere nicks compared to the heavy scarring on Sam's torso and legs.

Sam stood erect and faced the boy.

"Found him on the loading dock smoking." Preach adjusted his grip on the kid who stared in horror at Sam.

"Your bed out there?" The overhead lighting etched deep shadows in the harsh lines of Sam's face.

The kid mumbled.

Preach yanked on his collar as if correcting a recalcitrant dog. "Look at the man when you speak."

Davie gulped. "N-no." His gaze touched nervously on Sam's chest, arm, leg and face.

Unabashed, Sam stood his ground. "Take a good look. I should be dead."

Davie winced.

"The only reason I'm not is because your father got to me before he was killed." Sam plucked a towel from a lounge chair. "Out of respect for your father, I'm giving you a chance. Blow it and you're out of options." He whipped a towel around his neck. "Go to your room. We'll finish this discussion in the morning." Sam nodded for Preach to release his captive.

With false bravado, Davie shrugged his shirt back

into place and sauntered to the door where he abandoned his attempt at cool and ran for the stairs.

The thud of Davie's footsteps still echoing in the foyer, Sam nailed Preach with a hard look. "Where'd he get the smokes?"

Preach shook his head offering no explanation.

Sam's eyes narrowed and the air in the room chilled with tension. Without another word, he walked past Gray and crossed the lobby to the spa.

"That went well." Preach rubbed a hand across the back of his neck. "Let's go eat. Nights like this, Aggie serves in shifts. She'll have a late meal ready."

His stomach gnawing at his backbone, Gray followed Preach up the wide stairs.

Men sat in quiet conversation before a fire crackling in the beach stone fireplace of the lobby-turned-sitting room. So many alpha males living under the same roof had to make for an interesting time.

With a brief nod at the group, Gray entered a dining room with the ambience of a five-star restaurant. Round tables covered with linen and set with crystal and silver surrounded a large central floral arrangement involving orchids and polished black stones. The air was heavy with the aroma of meal preparations. Gray sat and fingered the cloth napkin. Yesterday he'd eaten fish from tree bark.

Preach settled in his chair. "Aggie believes the finery soothes the savage beasts."

"Beats any mess hall I've eaten in."

Other men filtered in and Preach performed introductions.

Whit McCord pulled out a chair across from Gray and shoved back his Stetson. "Amazing story how you found the Moore women in the forest."

Caution prickled along Gray's shoulders.

"That little one with the braids, what's her name?"

"Andi."

"She's a firecracker." Whit leaned an elbow on the table. "Has you right up there between Santa Claus and the Second Coming." He flashed a good-natured grin. "You let me know if you need any help with that bunch."

*Over my dead body.*

The arrival of food grabbed McCord's attention saving Gray from having to answer.

A roast beef dinner served up family style came out of the open exhibition kitchen. Not for one minute did Gray assume the tiny wizened woman overseeing meal production gave culinary classes. The open kitchen allowed her to keep an eye on the men in the dining hall. Not the other way around.

She approached with a steaming basket of biscuits in each hand. "Take your cowboy hat off in my dining room, mister."

"Stetson." Whit snatched the hat off his shaggy blonde head. "I'm a horseman. Don't particularly like cows." He swiped a hot biscuit, slathered it with a thick hunk of butter and took a huge bite. With a happy sigh he leaned back in his chair and chewed.

"Never saw a man like his biscuits and butter so much as you do, Whit McCord."

"Yes, ma'am. I dearly love biscuits."

Preach cleared his throat. "Think you could thank the good Lord for what He's provided *before* you eat it?

Whit's satisfied smile remained in place. "Tasting them first makes me twice as thankful."

Following the blessing, platters of meat and bowls heaped with mashed potatoes and vegetables were passed, emptied and replaced with refills until every man had a full plate before him. Conversation consisted of fragmented sentences and appreciative grunts as the hungry men devoured the meal.

His stomach full and adrenaline ebbing, exhaustion crept into Gray's bones. He lingered over his coffee reluctant to go to his assigned room. The last time he'd fallen asleep there he'd awakened in Maine. He stood. "Where are Sophie and the girls?"

The muted conversation ground to a halt.

Across the table, impeccably dressed for dinner and blessed with a face created for Hollywood, Caleb Fallon spoke. "Bedded down in luxury under Aggie's direction, I'd assume."

"I'd like to check on them before turning in."

"Good luck with that." Caleb refolded his napkin and tucked it neatly under the edge of his plate.

Preach pointed at Aggie, who was approaching with a platter of chocolate chip cookies. "She's your ticket." He wiped his mouth, wadded up his napkin and dropped it on his empty dinner plate.

Aggie clucked and grasped Gray's arm with boney fingers. "No need to worry. I fed them good. My how them girlies do eat. Showed them to their room hours ago." Her bright eyes snapped in her wrinkled face.

He wanted to say goodnight to Sophie and see that the girls settled in okay.

Aggie, so compact she could walk beneath his extended arm without disturbing a hair in her tiny tight bun, wasn't the least intimidated by his size or his glare. She lifted a hand and pointed one gnarled finger at him,

186

silently forestalling any argument.

"Uh oh." Whit muttered. "Don't wrangle with the finger, *amigo*."

Resigned, Gray stepped away from the table. Maybe it was for the best that he cleanup and got some sleep. Saying goodnight, he left the dining room.

He walked through the sitting room past the fireplace, the baby grand piano and open stairway leading below deck to the gym and spa. He caught a whisper of movement. Instinct spun him around face-to-face with a dark mountain of a man. Cautious, Gray widened his stance.

The man's craggy face relaxed into a wide smile. He held out his beefy hand. "Name's Ethan Thomas."

Remaining guarded, Gray shook his hand. "Gray Kerr. You weren't at supper."

"Ate earlier. Been sitting on the deck listening to the ocean and stargazing. Wishing I could see heaven." A soft drawl added a musical lilt to his words.

*See heaven?* Unsure how to respond Gray said nothing.

Ethan crossed his hands behind his back. "Wanted to say you've nothing to fear tonight."

"Why would I be afraid?"

The giant man rocked back on his heels. "Your last time here ended abruptly."

"You can sure as h..." Gray covered his slip with a cough. "Yes. It did."

"I helped carry you out."

"That so." The man's size gave his words a ring of credibility.

Ethan shook his head. "Didn't like that business."

"Why'd you do it?"

"Sam's ways don't always make sense, but good always follows. What would have become of Sophie and her girls if you hadn't shown up?"

"Sam didn't know they were out there."

"No, he didn't." Ethan smiled as though that explained everything.

Gray scratched his head, mystified by the conversation. He needed sleep in the worst way. A heavy hand clapped him on the shoulder, raising his hackles and irritability factor a notch. Only a man sure of his own strength and ability to fight would take such a liberty.

"Sleep well tonight, Gray Kerr."

"Yeah. Thanks." He turned, aiming for the hall, forgoing the elevator in favor of using the stairs. Passing what, in another era, would have been the hotel's registration desk, he heard his name called out. Now that he'd decided to hit the rack everyone wanted to talk to him. He backtracked a few steps and leaned his elbows on the tall counter. "That'd be me."

A thin young man sat at a desk loaded with paperwork and several computer monitors. The rough wooden nameplate prominently displayed on his desk had the name 'Charlie' spelled out in dry pasta. "Meeting in the Club Room at oh nine hundred."

Gray waved a hand in acknowledgment. "Got it."

His room was as he'd left it that first fateful night, his gear stacked in the corner and a minimal supply of toiletries in the bathroom. Locking the door, he opened his pack. It had traveled the world with him, each mile evident in the worn heavy-duty canvas.

Pulling out a length of monofilament line and duct tape, he stepped up to the window and looked out beyond the common sundeck and the dunes to the wide expanse of the ocean. The black water reflected the shimmer of moonlight on its ever-changing valleys and swells.

He shut the blinds then used his knife to cut a small strip of ribbon trim from the curtain. Setting the components on the writing desk, he detached the smoke alarm from the ceiling and set about rigging an alarm on the interior hall door.

The task complete, he stepped out on the deck. A light wind pulled at his clothes as he studied the ocean side of the eight-storied SeaMount building. Sided with yellow clapboards and trimmed with white gingerbread, the building and grounds blended well with the large historic 'summer cottages' of the rich and famous. He hadn't yet uncovered where Sam Traven acquired the money to raze the original Victorian era hotel and then recreate it with all the modern conveniences.

Atop a portion of the second floor, a sun deck complete with lounge chairs, water fountains and cold drinks bar carved the third floor and the stories above into a U-shape. His room, situated on the end of the residential wing, offered an unobstructed view of the ocean. The opposing wing housed the dining room, offices and Sam's private residence.

Following the curve of the exterior deck around the end of the building to the street side, Gray looked out over the rooftops of the small seaside village and the narrow streets that wound down to a river harbor where festive lights twinkled on moored yachts.

Built on a bluff with the Atlantic Ocean on one side and the mouth of the Pawcatuck River on the other, SeaMount was strategically located for a strong defense. Not that the necessity would arise. Just seemed like a good thing to know.

Gray retraced his steps back to his room. Securing the door to the deck with a small rubber wedge, he shoved the writing desk in front of it for good measure. He kicked off his boots and headed for the shower.

\*\*\*

The raucous call of seagulls and the gentle roll of surf filled Sophie's room as early morning light filtered in through sheer curtains. Visible through the open door of the adjacent room, the girls slept in a king size bed.

Tones of brown and sand prevailed throughout the suite. The décor centered on the beach and the ocean stretching to the horizon. The pictures that hung on the wall depicted seascapes and each bathroom towel was embellished with an embroidered seashell.

A tear tracked down Sophie's cheek. SeaMount was lovely but it wasn't home. Longing for Tommy and her home arrowed through her. She wanted the life she'd lived before Tommy's death when each day had been predictable and filled with happiness.

*God, why did you take him?* Like the hundreds of times she'd prayed in the past, God remained silent.

The light blanket covering the girls shifted. A quiet huff of breath followed.

They'd stayed up late last night enjoying hot baths, food aplenty and exploring the large common deck dotted with umbrellas and lounge chairs. Within fourteen hours Sophie and her girls had gone from staying at a grungy ill-kept sports camp in the wilderness to sleeping in an opulent mansion on the beach.

Anxious about what lay ahead, she slipped from

beneath the puffy duvet and went to stand before the small mountain of luggage Charlie and Ethan had stacked in the corner. Neither the quilt nor the blanket was in the mix. Perhaps the men had left them in the van.

Pulling on fresh underclothes, Sophie dressed in the soft apricot shift and matching sandals Aggie had provided last night. The dress fit as though made for her. Finding a pad and pen in the corner writing desk, she printed a simple note and propped it against the pillow on her made-up bed. After their explorations last night, the girls would have no trouble finding her.

She entered the sitting room where white orchids with delicate pink labellum adorned occasional tables, the massive beach stone fireplace a perfect foil for their delicate beauty. The tantalizing aroma of frying bacon drew her to the dining room.

"Morning, Sophie." Aggie nodded toward the coffee urn. "Fresh made. Help yourself."

Sophie breathed in the aromatic steam drifting up from her mug and wandered to the open windows overlooking Block Island Sound. A soft breeze carried a salty tang and the rhythmic roll of waves against the shore. Gulls glided and dipped on invisible wind currents. In the far distance, the clear blue sky joined the deep blue of the Atlantic Ocean. The wide-open vista of sand and sea soothed her.

"Breakfast's ready."

Turning from the window she went and sat in a tall chair at the counter positioned for viewing the activity in the gleaming stainless steel kitchen.

A tall man she'd seen at her home the night before set plates and flatware on the counter. "Everyone has eaten. You slept in."

Sophie glanced at the clock over the door. "Should I have risen earlier?"

Aggie set a jar of homemade strawberry jam in front of her. "Nope." The tiny woman shot a pointed glance at her helper. "Don't mind Preach. He knows the Old Testament backwards and forwards but can't make small talk worth beans."

"You're a minister?" He didn't have the demeanor of any man of the cloth she'd ever known. Tall and whipcord lean, he exuded the same strength and command that rolled off Gray. She couldn't picture him confined to a schedule of bible study, preaching and visitation of the sick and the elderly.

He shrugged. "I lead the prayer meeting when I'm here."

Aggie snorted. "He can preach so powerful you expect to look out the window and see the ocean part." She cracked eggs into a stainless steel bowl and whipped them to a frothy pale yellow. "The men named him Preach." She turned back to the stove. "It fits."

Giggles interrupted the conversation. The girls skipped into the room followed by Gray.

Sophie drank in the sight of him clean-shaven and dressed in jeans and a button down shirt. She wanted to reach out and touch him, but here in this place, his world, she suddenly felt shy. His eyes were pewter warm and he looked about to say something, but the girls ran to join her at the counter, cutting the moment short.

Drawn to a large pot of herbs, Lissa sat on the end. Andi climbed into the chair on one side of Sophie while Gray helped Hanna up on the other. Squeezing Hanna close, Sophie breathed another prayer of thanksgiving. Due to God's intervention they were safe and well. Whatever happened today, God would help her through it. He'd already provided Gray and SeaMount.

Aggie and Preach set platters of scrambled eggs, bacon, muffins and home fries on the counter. Sophie led the girls in saying their table grace then helped Hanna fill her plate while Gray helped Andi and Lissa.

"Can we go swimming?" Andi licked bacon grease from her fingertips.

Before Sophie could formulate an answer, Gray spoke.

"Smurf rule number one around here – if you're near water, an adult better be present. Got that?"

Both Andi and Lissa sighed in resignation.

"Got it?" Gray waited for the two girls to answer him. "Your mom has a meeting this morning."

Sophie shot him a questioning look. "I do?"

He nodded. "In the Club Room."

The memory of her home in a shambles created a rush of dread so strong her heart hammered in her ears. The jam and toast turned to cardboard on her tongue. All last night she'd reminded herself the broken pictures, ruined ivy and destroyed furniture were just *things*. Things could be replaced, but still her heart ached with the losses.

The girls cheered in happy chorus pulling Sophie from her thoughts. She glanced at Gray, bewildered.

His smile collapsed. "You weren't listening?"

She shook her head. Aggie patted her hand.

"You have a busy day ahead. The girlies will help me bake cookies. Then we'll go into the village for a ride on the carousel."

"Thank you." Sophie bit her lips to keep them from trembling. She hadn't thought about childcare. Here again, God had provided.

Gray stood. "Come on, Sophie." He ruffled Hanna's hair. "Be good for Aggie, you hear?"

The clatter of dishes mingled with the happy chatter of her girls as she left the dining room. Gray led her by the hand to a room suffused with the air of an exclusive men's club. Dark paneling on the walls and ceiling were accented with shiny brass fixtures to reflect the recessed light. Two men she didn't know talked in low tones before the unlit fireplace. Their conversation halted when they saw her. Only Gray's firm grip kept her from fleeing the room.

Seated at a small conference table, Sam had several files and papers spread before him. At his signal, the others moved to join him.

Gray held out a chair for her. She cast a longing glance at the sofa positioned for overflow seating, but took the seat he offered. He sat close behind her in an armchair. Pressing a hand to her stomach, she tried to calm the cloud of butterflies swirling there.

Taking a deep breath, she studied the room. Bookcases filled with leather-bound editions flanked the fireplace. On the wall above the conference table hung a flat screen for video conferencing. A wall of windows intersected by a door in the center opened to a private deck and the ocean beyond. Not a typical conference room but appropriate for the male-dominated culture within SeaMount.

"Right this way, sir. Mr. Traven is expecting you." Charlie, the young man Sophie met last night, entered the room followed by Leonard Vole.

# Chapter 17

Surprise and relief cascading through her, Sophie twisted in her chair to face Gray. "Did you know he'd be here?" Her words, whispered louder than she meant for them to be, caused the others to spare her a brief glance before turning their attention back to Sophie's lawyer and Sam.

Gray's noncommittal smile made her butterflies take flight again.

"Thank you, Charlie." Sam motioned for Mr. Vole to take the seat opposite Sophie.

Charlie left the room closing the door as he went.

"Hello, dear." Her lawyer adjusted his wire-framed glasses.

Sophie wanted to hop up and hug the man. "Good morning." She wanted to tell him all that had happened, but Sam didn't allow her the time.

"Mr. Vole, you received a report on the incident at Mrs. Moore's home. A team of investigators worked through the night with local law enforcement. The police are holding all evidence."

Sophie jerked around to Gray. *They found*

*evidence?* This time she mouthed her words.

He shrugged and twirled his finger as if stirring a cup of coffee. She took the hint and turned back.

Pushing his glasses up on his nose, Mr. Vole cleared his throat. "Thank you, though my preference is that the police department exclusively handle this case."

Sam lowered the papers he held. "May I remind you we're a private investigative and security firm with a forensic lab used by law enforcement agencies throughout the country. I chose to offer our services for this investigation," he nodded toward Gray, "because we're already involved with Mrs. Moore."

"But that's the very reason I hoped you would not have a part in processing evidence..."

Sam's eyes narrowed. "Are you implying we'd falsify our findings to suit our own purposes?"

The room hummed with tension.

Mr. Vole didn't answer Sam's question. Instead, he turned to Sophie. "I'm surprised you involved SeaMount. Mr. Moore will be unhappy with the publicity."

Sophie's heart jumped with panic. She didn't want that kind of attention.

"It's a small town, dear. A burglary is big news."

"Burglary?" Sam's gaze raked over Vole. "Do you know something we do not, Vole?"

The little man shifted in his chair. "No, of course not. But it stands to reason someone had a purpose for breaking and entering."

Sam's gaze flicked to the big burly man at the opposite end of the table. "Detective Brown, you'll interview Attorney Vole?"

"Now see here." A damp sheen glowed on

Leonard Vole's brow. "I'm only stating the obvious."

The detective smiled benignly. "And you also stated you wanted local law enforcement involved. I'd like your insight on what's happened."

As though the unpleasant exchange hadn't taken place, Sam turned back to his notes. "We're digging into the fiscal matters of Gerald Moore's holdings."

Mr. Vole made a choking noise. "You're looking into my client's finances?"

"Your client is Sophie Moore."

"Of course she is. Of course." He shifted in his chair. "Please understand, I've known the Moore family a good many years."

Sam nodded toward the man sitting on his right. "Meet Michael Drew. He'll be working with you on the custody case."

The angelic smile on Drew's face was in direct contrast to his sharp, piercing gaze.

Beneath the table, Sophie clenched her hands together. When Gray mentioned the SeaMount lawyer might help her, she hadn't thought about what that meant for Mr. Vole.

Vole gazed at her over the top of his glasses. "Sophie, is this what you want?"

She didn't know. Events were happening at warp speed. Her gaze bounced between Sam and her lawyer. "I want custody of my girls." She cleared her throat to remove the rasp from her voice.

Sam leaned back in his chair and regarded Vole with his dark gaze. "That's the goal Drew will help you achieve."

Sophie feared for Mr. Vole. The veins in his neck bulged and his face turned an unhealthy shade of purple.

Detective Brown pulled his chair closer to the table then flipped open a folder. He lined up several photos in front of Sophie. "In your home office we found these files on the floor. Do you recognize them?"

Sophie leaned forward to read the tabs. Her tongue stuck to the roof of her dry mouth. She nodded.

"What did they contain?"

Gray set a glass of water on the table for her. Hand shaking she lifted it to her lips and sipped before pointing to the three photos on the left. Each file bore a name of one of her daughters and the letters 'TF'.

"Tommy created them. They hold the information on the trust fund accounts he set up for Lissa, Andi and Hanna."

Sam interrupted. "The folders are empty."

She shook her head in disbelief. "Maybe the papers are in the mess on the floor."

"I don't believe so," Brown said. "When you walk through later today, you can help us verify that."

Dread curled in Sophie's already unsettled stomach.

He nudged the fourth picture closer. "What about this folder, Sophie?"

The tab bore Lissa's name and the word 'school' printed in Sophie's hand. She rubbed her palms against her legs. "Was this folder empty, too?"

"I'm afraid so."

Sophie stared at the photo. She created the folder soon after Tommy's death when she and the girls had struggled to come to grips with their new reality.

"Can't you see this is too much for her?" Mr. Vole fidgeted with his pen, clicking the point in and out.

"If Sophie wants our help, she'll answer the questions." Sam's tone brooked no argument.

Behind her, Gray moved. For one tense moment the other men focused on him.

Sophie inhaled a deep calming breath, hating every minute of the proceedings and the exposure of her personal life. But she'd do this if it had the remotest possibility of helping her keep the girls.

"After Tommy died, the girls and I went through a difficult time. Lissa was devastated. She and Tommy were close." Sophie rubbed and twisted her interlaced fingers until Gray's warm grip settled over her hands and stilled them. "Lissa planned to go out on the boat with Tommy that day. The day of the accident."

She turned her hand palm up and clung to Gray. "At the last minute a friend from school called and invited her to a children's concert in Providence. Tickets were impossible to get so she changed her plans. Tommy was disappointed but understood."

She stared at her pale hand enveloped in Gray's larger one, trying to contain the emotion building inside. "Lissa blamed herself for Tommy's death. She thought if she'd gone with him the accident wouldn't have happened." Sophie shivered. If she had lost both... A familiar sick knot settled in the pit of her stomach. "When Lissa returned to school, she dealt with her guilt and grief by misbehaving in the classroom and being mean to the other children."

"Surely the teachers understood the cause."

Sophie nodded. "The school psychiatrist worked with her. She's strong-willed." Did these men believe she'd failed as a mother? "I visited the school almost daily, but she became too disruptive. The school didn't have the resources to handle her. They thought it best to place her temporarily in a school especially for children with emotional and behavioral issues."

"Did that help her?"

"Not at first. Leaving a small private school to go to a larger one where she didn't know anyone was hard. She received counseling. Andi and Hanna, too." Sophie shifted uneasily, focused on Gray's hand wrapped around hers. "Actually, all of us. I wasn't doing very well either." The last few words were barely a whisper.

"And the file contained correspondence and records from both schools?" Sam asked.

Sophie nodded. "Who would want that information?"

"A good question. One we mean to answer. Detective Brown will accompany you home this afternoon. He and two forensic investigators will be with you to go through the house to look for anything else that may be missing."

Sam turned to Drew. "The new court date for the custody hearing is set for just over a week away?"

Mr. Vole cleared his throat in displeasure. Sam ignored him as Drew replied in the affirmative.

"Sophie, because the missing information involves your daughters, SeaMount will provide protection for your family as a precaution."

Someone meant her girls harm? How many ways could she possibly lose her daughters? Black edged Sophie's vision. The murmur of conversation became muffled as though coming from a great distance. Emotionally drained, she leaned on the table, head in her hands. *Lord, why is this happening to me?*

Gray touched her shoulder. "You okay?"

"No." She rubbed her eyes and blinked hard.

Chairs shuffled. The meeting had ended. Gray helped her up.

Mr. Vole made a beeline to her side. "Dear, you've made a grave mistake. Anything involving your father-in-law is news. We've managed to keep a lid on the custody case, but if the media discovers his company finances are under investigation, shareholders will be up in arms. Do you want to put your girls through this?"

Gray stepped between Sophie and Mr. Vole. "They'll be shielded from the press."

Crushed she'd had to reveal so much of her ordeal to a group of men who were strangers to her, Sophie pulled away. "Thank you for coming, Mr. Vole." The privacy of her room beckoned, offering escape from the cadre of overbearing men intent on doing what they considered best for her. She turned and hurried from the room.

# Chapter 18

A scissor kick corkscrewed his body around to flat on the water's surface. Gray snapped his arms forward to full extension. He pulled with his right arm, rotating his face and body up, tasting the salt in the cold water surging around him. Pulling with his lead arm, face down he started the sequence over again.

Gray sliced through the chop with full sidestrokes. Nothing existed but the water and him. He lost count of the number of times he turned and swam the same mile of coastline. Near the end of his endurance he dove once more, flipped and poured on speed using a sprinter sidestroke.

Heart pumping hard and muscles aching, Gray turned toward shore. With easy strokes he let the waves carry him closer to the white fringe of beach beneath the SeaMount bluff. Against the overcast sky, the building dominated the shoreline of summer homes and cottages.

Toes scraping the bottom, Gray dug his feet in and waded ashore. He dropped to his back on the sand hot from the noonday sun. Arms flung wide he stared at the sky and the lumpy layer of clouds scudding overhead. The muscle-grinding combat swim hadn't vanquished his dark frame of mind.

Sophie had been impossible to talk to since the meeting four days ago. Like her, he'd walked into the Club Room with no intel. He hadn't known about Moore's financial problems or the empty folders. And he certainly hadn't known Sophie's most heartrending memories would be laid bare for examination.

In his heavy-handed way, Sam was doing what he thought necessary to find whoever messed with Sophie's home *and* to win the custody battle.

Gray had told her as much, but he could see the loss of control stuck in her craw.

She neatly pointed out that *she* wasn't an employee of SeaMount and didn't want people making decisions about her life without her knowledge. His suggestion that she may be reacting a tad irrationally went over like a screen door in a submarine.

Things hadn't gotten any better when they went to her home. A distressing experience, she'd shed quiet tears through the entire ordeal refusing any comfort from him. As part of the crew assigned by Sam to help her salvage belongings and clean up, he'd been the model of decency. He'd kept his mouth shut and manned the heavy-duty workshop vacuum.

Gray jackknifed into a sitting position and surveyed the restless ocean. Gulls circled, calling out to each other. A school of small fish rippled and jumped along the surface, unaware of the danger flying overhead.

Would Sophie survive the uncertainties she faced? A carefree childhood, doting husband, cute kids and pretty home – nothing in her life had prepared her for what she now faced. Much of her perfect life had dissolved with the death of her husband. She hadn't a clue how to fight to regain what she'd lost. In anger and confusion she struck out at the people trying to help her.

Gray stood and crossed the beach to the boardwalk winding away from the water, over low sand dunes to SeaMount's manicured lawn. With Sam's help and some of the gumption she'd shown in the wilderness, Sophie would do okay. But she needed to get in on the fight.

Wide tile steps descended into the dim cool interior of the beach locker room below ground level. His sandy feet hit the bottom step at the same time a voice echoed off the hard surfaces of the spacious area.

"If my misery could be weighed and my troubles be put on the scales, they would outweigh all the sands of the sea."

Gray whirled around.

Preach sat on a bench near the lockers.

"What are you doing here?"

"Waiting for you." He tossed Gray a plastic bottle of cold water. "In case you needed your slippery hide hauled out of the water."

Gray twisted the sealed cap. "Yeah. Right." He took a swig. "What was that you were spouting?"

"The Book of Job." A wry smile touched Preach's lips. "Does it fit?"

"Sure feels that way." Gray tipped the bottle up and guzzled.

"Seems your woman is feeling the same."

Gray choked. He turned and spewed water on the

floor beneath the showers. "*My* woman?" He wanted to wipe the taunting grin off the man's face but could barely manage a breath between coughs.

"Don't hack up a lung."

The glare he trained on the other man carried no weight. Watery eyes got in the way. "What gives you the impression Sophie's mine?" How he wished it were true.

Preach cracked a knuckle. "Let's see. Could it be because you cast an evil eye at any man dumb enough to look her way?"

Gray shook his head. "You're crazy."

"The others are discussing who will be the first to get his tongue cut out for talking to her."

Gray swore and chucked his bottle at a nearby trash bin. He missed.

"Tsk, tsk. Foul language isn't allowed on the premises."

Sophie would be happy to hear that rule. "I don't know how to help her. Why has God allowed these things to happen?"

Preach strolled over to pick up Gray's bottle. "We live in a fallen world. Bad things happen." He dropped the bottle into the bin. "God has his own way of dealing with us to draw us closer to him."

Gray crossed his arms. "At times God's way really stinks."

"We may never understand, but we have to do what men like you and I find the hardest."

Gray frowned, not sure he wanted to hear this.

"Give up control and trust Him." Preach climbed the wide steps. "You might want to hustle your shower." His voice echoed in the stairwell. "Sam is looking for you."

\*\*\*

Gray stepped off the elevator near Sam's office.

Ears pink and body tense, Charlie approached. "Storm warnings, Kerr." He gestured with the file in his hand. "Sam and Sophie are toe-to-toe in there."

"Sophie?" He sped up his pace, pausing outside the door to listen. Hearing nothing he rapped on the door once and entered.

Sam stood behind his desk glaring at Sophie.

Equally perturbed, she faced him, hands on her hips.

They glanced at him then turned back to each other. Sophie spoke first. "I want to go home."

*Oh boy.* Gray closed the door and leaned against it.

"I can better protect you and the girls here."

"From who?"

"We're working on that." Sam ground out the words as though they tasted bad.

Sophie leaned forward. "What if you don't figure out who vandalized my home, Sam? I can't hide here forever."

"I'm not asking for forever." He stood straighter. "At least give me till your court appearance."

She waved her hand, bracelets jangling. "These precious few days might be our last together." Her voice wobbled. "I want to spend them at home... as a family."

"I'd have slowed the disaster clean up had I known you'd be unreasonable about this."

Uh oh. Not the way to get her cooperation.

As though reading Gray's thoughts, Sam swung

around and nailed him with a black look. "Her home is ready but I'd prefer she stay here."

Sophie's eyes snapped with challenge. She'd finally entered the fight. Didn't it just figure her ideas would be contrary to what others thought was best. Rubbing the back of his neck, Gray pushed away from the door.

"Give the idea some thought, Soph. You don't want to endanger the girls."

Lips in a tight line, she headed for the door, golden curls bouncing with each agitated step. She spared Gray a hot angry glance before flinging the door open and storming into the hall. He grabbed the handle, thwarting her attempt to slam the door behind her.

Hearing her snort of frustration, he gently closed the door and turned to Sam. "That wasn't much of a success."

Sam fell back into his leather chair and rubbed his hands over his face. "All that soft womanly beauty hides a spine of steel."

Antsy to follow her, Gray remained standing in front of the door. "Is she the reason you wanted to see me?"

"No." Sam pointed to the leather visitor's chair. "I've planned an E & E exercise for next week. You'll participate."

Sam's words hit Gray like the concussive blast of a mortar round. No warning whistle. Just *BAM* and he was eating dirt and on fire with pain. "I hoped to be here for Sophie's day in court."

"Getting the state to agree that we could do this during the summer took a great deal of planning. Not to mention what I paid for the privilege."

"Where will this take place?"

Sam pointed at a map behind his desk. "State forest in Connecticut. Postponing this exercise is out of the question."

Gray stared over Sam's shoulder at the map, noting major highways and bodies of water. Once again he was going into the wilderness. A week of war gaming wasn't a problem. The timing, however, couldn't have been worse. Preach's words from Job echoed in his mind. The fragile bubble of hope that had begun to build inside him collapsed. Here was another shovelful of misery to dump on the scale.

"Report to the loading dock Monday at oh seven hundred for a briefing. You'll leave from there immediately following." Sam leaned back from his desk. "If you still want to be under consideration for a job with this agency, you'll participate and complete this exercise."

His gut in a knot, he nodded his understanding.

"Good." Sam paused, choosing his words. "Convince Sophie to stay here. Between this training exercise and the men out of the country on business, I don't have the manpower available to give her round the clock protection at her home."

\*\*\*

Giggles floated up the open curved stairs from the lower level.

Gray's boots beat a rapid tattoo as he charged below deck hoping to find Sophie with the girls. Instead, he found Whit, Caleb and Ethan in the gym supervising a recumbent bike race. Pretending to be the announcer at the Tour de France, Caleb urged the girls to pedal faster.

Hanna's new purple princess gown tangled in the pedals. Ethan whisked her off the bike, a goofy grin near splitting his face in halves. Ethereal and insubstantial in his meaty hands, Hanna wrapped her arms around his thick neck. Her pale yellow hair wisped across his ebony skin and close-cropped hair.

Gray smiled at the sight of the big man smitten with his delicate charge.

"Hey, Princess. Nice gown."

Hanna rewarded him with a smile.

"Uncle Ethan treating you good?"

She nodded with happy approval, her hand patting the shoulder clothed in an olive drab t-shirt.

Ethan propped Hanna in the crook of his arm against his hip and held up a new tiara. "I get to carry the crown."

"Important job, man."

"Don't I know it."

Hanna squirmed to get down and Ethan released her. She ran to pluck an apple from the fruit bowl on the wide window ledge. Lissa and Andi, red-faced from exertion continued to pedal in earnest.

"Have you seen Sophie?"

Ethan motioned to the narrow hall on the other side of the stairs. "Saw her go into the spa with another woman a few minutes ago. Said something about fingernails."

"Thanks." He waved to Lissa and Andi and left the gym.

Charging past the foot of the stairs, he stopped at the mouth of the hallway. It was a portal into the unknown, softly lit by wall sconces. A sweet fragrance hung in the air. The other men had talked about the spa and Sam's need for massage therapy, the catalyst to build it. The benefits spilled over to the team with a sauna for their use as well as massage and occupational therapy, if needed.

Gray tread softly along the carpeted hall past doors with cutesy name plaques. These were cushy digs for men accustomed to working knee and elbow deep in the gut wrenching barbarity offered up by the world at large. Maybe that was the genius behind this set up. Maybe all this civility helped keep the men together emotionally as well as physically.

A soft trill of laughter halted him. Head cocked, he listened. The morning he'd found Sophie he'd noticed her manicured nails and her all-encompassing femininity, so out of place in the rugged terrain.

A quiet murmur of voices and then more laughter drifted from behind a closed door.

Gray wiped at the sweat beading on his temples. He hadn't the slightest idea what took place during a manicure. It involved hands, so she'd be fully clothed. Right?

Get a grip, Kerr. You've entered buildings infested with armed terrorist and didn't give it this much consideration. Suck it up and get in there.

Gripping the handle, he twisted it. The door opened on oiled hinges.

He stepped inside and closed it with a quiet snick. A sweeping survey of the room revealed subdued lighting, a burning candle, a potted orchid and colorful bottles of nail polish lined up on glass shelves. He honed in on the occupants, alarmed by his entrance.

An olive-skinned woman sat with her back to the door, looking at him over her shoulder. She held a small brush in one hand and Sophie's fingers in her other. An open bottle of polish and other tools of the trade sat on the small table between them.

Gray's gaze lingered on Sophie's hand before following the slope of her arm up to her neck and then her face.

Eyes round with surprise, she flung up her free hand. "Get out!"

"Agh!" The woman grabbed Sophie's wrist, lowered her hand to a foam rest and inspected each glossy nail.

Gray leaned back against the door and folded his arms across his chest. The thin dark-haired woman spoke with an accent, her words meant for Sophie but her eyes on him.

"Is this the one?"

They'd been talking about him?

The woman muttered in Italian before turning her attention back to Sophie's nails.

Lifting her chin, Sophie glared at him. "I'd like you to go." As an after thought she added, "Please."

*Not gonna happen.* He'd made it this far, no way would he retreat.

"You don't want him, I take him off your hands." The woman sent Gray a sultry look.

A waste of her time. The one he wanted sat on the other side of the table, glaring at him.

Exasperation etched on her face, Sophie wiggled her fingers. "Please hurry and finish, Maria."

"You're avoiding me." His accusation hung in the air, a harsh intrusion in the serene surroundings.

She chewed at her bottom lip, opened her mouth as if to speak but snapped it closed. Twice. Sparing a glance at the technician, Sophie took a deep breath. "Maria, finish up in two minutes and your tip doubles."

The woman paused what she was doing to consider whether she'd take the offer. She returned to her task, finishing in the specified time.

Eyes on Sophie, Gray waited for Maria to clear and sanitize the table.

Sophie thanked the woman and told her payment for her services waited at the front desk.

"You promised me extra." Dark eyes snapped back and forth between Sophie and Gray.

Gray yanked on his wallet and pulled out the first bill his fingers touched. He slapped it into Maria's open hand. Eyes wide, she bid him a hasty '*Grazie*' and hurried from the room.

Sophie remained seated. "You probably gave her a hundred-dollar bill."

"Probably." In the soft recessed lighting, her skin glowed.

"Why are you here, Gray?"

"I want to know what's going through your mind about the situation."

"Which situation? There are several."

He needed fresh air. The scented candle made his stomach queasy. "Your choice. Start with the one that keeps you up at night."

She sagged in her chair. "There's nothing you can do that Sam hasn't already done." A trace of bitterness twisted an ugly thread through her words.

He swiped a hand over his face. "He's helping you."

"I know that. And I know *you* believe you did the right thing involving him in my affairs."

*Whoa.* "Don't hold back, Soph." He tried to swallow the sour disappointment settling in the back of his throat.

Sophie waved her glossy wet fingertips in the air. "You did the right thing."

Okaaaay.

"If the girls are in danger, how would I protect them?" Her chocolate eyes gleamed with unshed tears. "Gray, who took the files? Will I lose my girls in a battle for custody, or to some...some file thief?" Misery carved lines in her face. "Those are the questions keeping me up at night." A tear slipped from the corner of her eye.

Gray moved away from the door. He pushed the small table aside and reached for her hand.

"No!"

He stopped in his tracks. His heart plummeted and landed on his diaphragm making breathing next to impossible.

Sophie held up her hands. Candlelight shimmered in the tear clinging to her chin. "My mani is still wet."

Unsure which one muddled his brain more – the stinking candle or Sophie's tears – Gray blew out the candle. Licking his thumb and forefinger, he pinched the smoking wick. "How about we take this conversation out to the deck."

"I'm not sure I want to talk to you."

Her uncertainty was like a blade to his vitals. "We're a team, Sophie. I'm no longer in command, but we're in this together."

She hesitated, then stood and walked past him to the door. "For how long, Gray?"

The woman could ask the hard questions. Her life

wasn't the only one Sam engineered. Uncertainty surrounded his situation as well. He didn't answer.

A blustery wind swayed the potted geraniums and snapped the fabric of the closed umbrellas. Gray sucked in huge draughts of air clearing his lungs and fuzzy brain.

Sophie settled in a chair. He pulled another one around and sat beside her.

"This afternoon the girls and I are to go shopping for furniture. Sam rented a van large enough to accommodate us and," she waved a hand in the general direction of the gym, "our bodyguards. I'm a prisoner."

"Until Sam has calculated all the risks, it's best stay under his protection."

The door to the deck opened and Charlie stood on the threshold. "Sophie, Drew's asking for you. He's in Sam's office."

Gray rose and followed Sophie. Charlie blocked him at the door.

"Only Sophie. Sam's orders."

Clenching his fists Gray fought the urge to throttle the man. He watched her walk away without a backward glance.

Shut out again.

The gulf between them grew wider with each passing hour.

Gray turned and braced his elbows on the top of the deck railing, bending to ease the pain in his midsection and the raw sense of loss rippling through him.

# Chapter 19

Aggie sat on the covered porch that overlooked the herb garden and green house filled with Sam's prize-winning orchids. She wore a sweater against the cool evening breeze, and rocked in her favorite chair. Taking the seat next to her, Gray jerked his chin towards the greenhouse. "So tell me, Aggie, why orchids?"

Throughout the public areas of the SeaMount building, the delicate blossoms decorated every tabletop and hidden nook. If the size of the green house was an indication, many more were available for display. Gray liked flowers, but this hobby of Sam's bordered on obsession.

The last light of evening softened Aggie's features. Her bun dipped to one side. "After he got out of the hospital those flowers gave him a reason to climb out of bed and go on living."

Having spent a great deal of time avoiding death, Gray understood the instinct to stay alive. He'd never really come up with a satisfactory reason it was a goal worth pursuing until now. "I'm looking for Sophie."

Aggie tapped her fingers on the arm of her chair. "Everyone's on the beach roasting hotdogs and marshmallows."

Gray rose and headed for the wide sweep of steps leading to the boardwalk. "Wish me luck."

Aggie called after him. "I get better results with prayer."

Smoke drifted with the breeze off the ocean. Silhouetted against the backdrop of leaping yellow and orange flames, the smurfs stood among the adults. A burning log collapsed and a plume of embers caught up by the prevailing wind sailed off into the night.

Stopping beyond the firelight, he watched Caleb help Lissa and Andi skewer marshmallows on a stick. Ethan sat close to the fire with Hanna leaning on his knee. On the other side of the flames, two men stood with their backs to the beach, their faces mirror images.

The St. John twins.

He hadn't been formally introduced, but he'd heard they'd just returned from a rank assignment and he recognized the restless tension surrounding them as they transitioned from the dangers in the field to the security of home soil. They'd spotted him as well and watched, suspicious of anyone they didn't know.

Soft feminine laughter drew Gray's attention.

Sophie sat on a log, Preach beside her smiling and roasting a hotdog.

Possessiveness propelled him out of the shadows. Controlling the urge to grab Preach by the front of his shirt and haul him off the log, he stopped in front of them. "We need to talk."

Preach had the guts to smile even wider and lean toward her. "I suggest you go talk to him. I'd like to live another day."

"That's not funny." A frown puckered Sophie's brow, but she rose without question and allowed him to guide her away from the bonfire. Whit made soft kissing noises as they passed. Her shoulders stiffened.

"Don't worry. Foul language and obscene gestures are prohibited on SeaMount grounds."

"That's a good thing." She relaxed a bit.

"I figured you'd like that rule."

Pleased to hear her soft chuckle, Gray led her to the hard packed sand at the water's edge. Ambient light caught in her golden hair. A breeze tugged at her clothes. Her beauty took his breath away. Preach's words rang loud in his mind. *Your woman.* He liked the sound of that, but the jealousy riding his back rankled.

He sucked in a deep breath to say his piece before he could chicken out. "I apologize for overreacting after the meeting with Sam and the lawyers."

She stiffened, but continued to walk with him, her sandals flipping up a spray of sand with each step.

"I know you can't wait to leave here and get back to your home and your own life."

The dark water laced with foam, rolled and rumbled ashore close to their feet. Sophie brushed hair from her face. "Even a beautiful prison is still a prison."

"Sam hasn't imprisoned you here. He's concerned about your family's welfare."

She sighed. "I appreciate all Sam has done for me. But I wish he'd show me the courtesy to discuss the decisions that affect my life and my girls."

"He's a lone wolf, Sophie. He calls the shots and gets things done. Fortunately for us, he chooses to use his money for the good of others." His mouth went paper dry. "I have something to tell you."

She stopped and turned to him.

He reached out and took her hand in his. "Sam has planned an E&E exercise. Begins Monday."

Confusion clouded her eyes. "A what?"

"Escape and evasion exercise." He rubbed his thumb across her knuckles. "I'm going back into the woods Monday."

"You're leaving? When will you return?"

"Not until after your hearing."

Her face crumpled. "But, I thought…"

Gray tugged her into his arms. She came to him willingly. "Yeah. Me too."

Her shoulders shook. A quiet sob followed a sniff. She pressed close, his chest muffling her weeping.

He burrowed his hand into her hair at her nape. He breathed in cinnamon scent that was distinctly Sophie. "Hey. You're breaking my heart here."

She sniffled. "I'm sorry I got angry with you."

"You had every right. Diplomacy isn't my strength." His reward was a breathy giggle. "Don't suppose you'll even try to make me feel better by disagreeing." In the soft light reflecting off the water and white sand, he saw her smile wobble.

Cupping her face in his hands, he ran his thumbs over her cheeks wiping away tears. An emotional rip current swept him into a sea of sensation the likes of which he'd never experienced. He was going under. Drowning in her luminous eyes and a surge of desire. "I want to kiss you."

She closed her eyes.

He kissed each eyelid, the feathery brush of her lashes tickling his lips. Trailing kisses across her cheeks he tasted her tears, as familiar as the ocean, as unique as Sophie. His lips brushed against hers and the world fell away. Nothing else existed. Only this beautiful woman and her welcoming arms. Warmth. Comfort. Home.

Cold water dashed over the tops of his boots.

Sophie squealed.

They broke apart only to come back together as she clung to him for support. Water sucked at the sand beneath his feet. He planted his boots deeper in the mud to keep his balance. His chuckle grew into a shout of laughter as a second larger wave climbed higher up the shore drawing a shriek of surprise from Sophie and drenching him to his knees. "Hold on, sweetheart."

"It's c-cold."

The wave slipped back to the sea, the foamy edge hissing in retreat.

Taking her hand, he pulled her to higher ground and a tree trunk-size piece of driftwood. They sat shoulder to shoulder.

"I want you to have this." He reached into his back pocket. "I hope it's still dry."

"What is it?"

"A map."

"Of what?" Puzzled she took it from him. "It's too dark for me to read."

"Our town. The Chamber of Commerce prints them."

She turned it over in her hands. "Why do I need a map of town?"

"Learning to find familiar streets and landmarks will help you eventually read unfamiliar maps. This isn't a hokey tourist map directing you to the nearest mini golf. It's a road map 'to scale'. You already know the material so it's easy to connect the places."

She held the map not saying a word.

Concerned he'd made a mistake giving it to her, Gray rushed on. "I don't want to worry about you getting lost again."

She leaned forward and kissed him. "Thank you. I'll study it."

His arm snaked around her waist and he squeezed her to his side. "Thanks." Harmonious snatches of singing floated on the night air. "We better go back to the fire before they send out a search party."

Flickering light illuminated the group gathered around the fire. Seated on a cooler, Whit strummed his guitar and led the singing. The songs ranged from silly camp tunes to praise and worship hymns.

Andi ran to her mother. Hanna followed and Gray swung her into his arms. In the firelight, her tiara twinkled.

Preach stood and gestured to the log. Nodding his thanks, Gray seated Sophie and then sat next to her. Lissa scooted across the sand and leaned back against her mother's legs.

Gray's insides ached. A wrenching shift of the Tectonic plates that protected his heart had left him broken, exposed... and free. He needed to figure out what the change meant. But in this moment, nothing mattered except sitting on the beach with Sophie and the smurfs.

Content, he reached out and took Sophie's hand.

\*\*\*

A tiny hand patted her cheek. Sophie scrunched her eyes hoping the little person intruding on her beauty rest would go away. She'd lain awake most of the night thinking about Gray and the kiss they'd shared. Even now remembering it, her heart leapt with a painful *ping*.

"Mommy?" The word whispered hot against her ear. A finger poked her cheek. Warm breath fanned across her face.

Giving up on the sleep, she opened one eye. A nose slid into view.

"Mommy waked up!" The volume of those three words had Sophie fighting her bedclothes and the small body anchoring them as she tried to clap her hands to her ears.

"Not so loud, Hanna. You'll wake the dead."

Hanna scooted closer. "Daddy too?"

Sophie groaned and relaxed back against the pillow. "No, baby." When would she remember Hanna took what she said literally? "That's just an expression grownups use. Daddy's in heaven with Jesus."

Andi bounced up beside Hanna. "I'm hungry. Can we go swimming after breakfast?"

"No. It's Sunday. We're going to church."

"I want to go home." Lissa climbed over Hanna and Sophie to stand on the bed leaning against the wall.

"Can we go swimming first?" Andi's gazed hopefully at Sophie.

Time to be the mom with a capital M.

"Get dressed." She looked pointedly at Andi. "Wear tee-shirts and shorts down to breakfast. I'll ask Aggie what time church starts."

Andi hurried to the adjacent room to dress. "Maybe Gray can take us swimming."

The mention of Gray sent Sophie's heart into a cartwheel. Longing for him warred with apprehension. Falling in love with a man who had a dangerous job only increased the chance of losing him. Could she ever survive another devastating loss? Could the girls?

She pushed back the covers and slid from the bed. Moving the curtains aside, she peeked out the window. Over the water, a clear blue sky held one small fluffy cloud. In the morning light the ocean sparkled like Hanna's tiara.

Close to shore seven swimmers glided through the water. Sophie might have mistaken them for harbor seals had she not known the men from SeaMount swam each morning. Keeping a low profile in the water and leaving no wake, they swam with speed and no splash, a skill that allowed them to infiltrate enemy territory undetected.

Sophie shivered. She'd overheard snippets of conversations between them when they'd been oblivious to her presence. The men of SeaMount lived with danger and the knowledge that every mission might be their last.

"Mommy, I'm ready." Andi's head popped out the neck hole of her shirt.

Sophie tugged on a sleep-frizzed braid. "Straight to the kitchen, young lady."

Andi ran for the door.

"I better find you sitting at the counter." The door closed before she finished the sentence. Shaking her head, she went to check Hanna's progress.

Lissa sat on the edge of the bed tying her sneakers, her expression troubled.

Sending Hanna out the door in Andi's wake, Sophie sat beside Lissa. She swept the bangs out of her daughter's eyes, absently thinking she needed to arrange haircuts. "What's up, Liss?" Of the three girls, she worried about Lissa the most. Tommy's death and the troubling time at school had changed her eldest daughter.

"Are you going to marry Gray?"

*Oh dear!* Sophie hadn't anticipated *this* question. "Why do you ask?"

Lissa brought her knees up and folded her arms around her legs. Sophie didn't have the heart to remind her to remove her shoes from the bedspread.

"He held your hand last night."

She should have known that wouldn't escape notice.

"Andi says you have to get married because she saw Gray hugging and kissing you on the beach."

Sophie's heart took a free-fall to the pit of her stomach. Andi had spied on them? She reached out and rubbed Lissa's back. "Gray hasn't asked me to marry him. And sharing a kiss doesn't automatically mean I have to marry the man."

"Do you love him like you loved Daddy?" Lissa's honest question deserved a truthful answer.

"Not like Daddy, Liss. Your daddy and I had a very special relationship and it was ours alone."

Lissa sighed and slid her feet to the floor. "I'm hungry." She wrapped her arms around Sophie's neck. "I love you, Mommy."

Through tears, Sophie watched Lissa leave the room. Heart aching, she slipped to her knees beside the bed. "Lord, show me what to do. Whatever your plan, give me the faith and courage to see it through."

She had to leave SeaMount. The girls were too attached to the people and the place. Who was she kidding? *She* was in love with the beautiful Victorian building and beach, not to mention the people inhabiting it, and one in particular.

Sophie rested her brow on her crossed arms and inhaled the sweet scent of cotton sheets. She had more than enough on her plate already. She didn't need the complication of a relationship, too. Especially with a man whose job took him away from home, where *away* meant a 'secretive job filled with danger'.

Sighing, she stood. Gray left tomorrow morning. She'd say goodbye then pack up the van and head home where she and the girls belonged. Perhaps the separation would help her sort out her feelings. He might very well come home realizing the last thing he needed was a ready-made family. Assuming she and the girls were still together as a family. This time next week she could be alone, the girls with Tommy's parents.

Sophie pressed a fist to her stomach as nausea threatened. *God help me through this week.*

***

The girls had eaten their way through a stack of Aggie's blueberry pancakes when Sophie arrived for breakfast. Ethan presided over the counter, doling out orange juice and cleaning sticky fingers like a pro. Whit sat with Logan and Gabe St. John at a table by the window.

Sophie met the brothers for the first time at the bonfire. Unlike the other men, they made her uncomfortable. With dark brooding eyes they watched everyone and said nothing. They had an eerie way of communicating with each other, as though they shared one brain. The ability unnerved Sophie.

A plate loaded with steaming pancakes plunked on

the counter in front of her.

"Eat up, Mama." Wearing a grin almost as wide as his broad shoulders, Ethan shoved the butter dish towards her. "Gotta keep up your strength."

Sophie contemplated the stack of pancakes listing off to the left. "All these are for me?"

"Yup." He hoisted the syrup pitcher. "They'll melt in your mouth. Butter up those babies."

Feeling the brooding gaze of the St. John twins on her back, she glanced toward the door hoping to see Gray, hoping he'd stay away. The ball of contradictions rolling around inside her only made her heart hurt and her headache.

Warm pancakes and fragrant blueberries teased Sophie senses. She picked up her butter knife and sighed in surrender.

"There you go." Ethan held the pitcher ready to flood her plate with syrup.

Pancakes wouldn't solve her problems, but they would make facing them bearable.

\*\*\*

Wearing floral sundresses, Sophie and the girls crossed the narrow village street to the small chapel. Peace settled over her as she stepped inside the cool narthex. Through open doors and windows the ocean air refreshed the dimly lit interior.

She easily picked out the men of SeaMount from among the villagers and vacationers. Oxford shirts and dress slacks couldn't conceal the raw energy that cloaked them.

Guiding the girls to a pew close to the back she was glad she'd chosen to come here instead of driving to her own church inland. Today, she preferred the brief sincere greetings of strangers to the familiar chitchat of church family.

The first soft notes from the organ drifted through the chapel as Sophie settled the girls. Following the opening hymn, she felt a familiar presence and glanced back. Gray's smile sent happy tingles racing along her spin. Disquieted by the sensation, she faced forward again. Emotions running wild and headed straight for a cliff, she took a deep breath and bowed her head with the congregation.

The voice offering up praise and thanks sounded familiar. A tiny peek from beneath her lashes confirmed Jack stood in the pulpit prepared to deliver the morning sermon. His ardent prayer confirmed why the men called him 'Preach'.

"In whom do you place your trust? A life lived in obedience to God is not a comfortable life. Noah was ridiculed and laughed at for following God's instructions." With colorful vigor Jack spoke of a life fully surrendered to God. "Our victory over life's challenges are found in joyful submission to the will of God. We may never understand God's purpose, but giving Him control is where we'll find happiness."

Weary of the burden she carried daily, Jack's words pierced Sophie heart. She lived in fear of losing the girls to Gerald and Suzanne. Sam's involvement gave her less control over her own affairs. But what if Sam's actions were part of God's plan for preserving her family? And how did Gray fit in? His skills brought her and the girls out of the wilderness. But did God's plan include something more between them?

The man occupied her thoughts with unnerving regularity. His job took him away from home and into danger making a relationship with him a less-than-ideal prospect. But her traitorous heart chose not to listen to the logical arguments whirling around in her head.

The final hymn ended and Jack gave the benediction. The moment he finished, to Sophie's mortification, Andi climbed up on the pew to reach for Gray. He hoisted her up and over the back and set her on the floor. His eyes softened to a hazy gray. "Good morning, Sophie."

The sermon had left her questioning and quiet. Alert to Lissa's watchful gaze, she attempted some semblance of a smile in return. "We missed you at breakfast."

He frowned, eyes narrowed. His gaze raked over her face.

"Can we go swimming?" Andi tugged on Gray's shirt claiming his attention.

He tweaked her ponytail. "What does your mom say?" His question set Sophie in motion.

"I say we eat lunch first." She took Hanna's hand and guided her into the aisle. "Come on, Lissa."

Gray smiled. "Guess it was good that I asked Aggie to pack us a picnic for the beach then." A happy chorus from the girls drew the attention of those around them.

"Hush, girls." Sophie herded them toward the narthex, anticipation of the picnic and time spent with Gray warring with irritation because he hadn't asked before making plans.

His hand on her elbow, she allowed him to guide her across the road and up the front steps into SeaMount. The girls took off to change into swimsuits leaving them alone in the sitting room.

"What's wrong?" Concern edged his voice.

Looking everywhere except at him, she fiddled with the handle of her purse. What was wrong? *What was right?* She didn't know anymore. She shrugged her shoulder in answer to his question and turned to follow the girls.

A hand clamped on her arm and spun her around, dislodging a wayward tear. Sophie stared at the top button of his shirt, the blazing clean white cloth a stark contrast to his muscular tan neck. A finger hooked under her chin and lifted it.

*Stupid, stupid tears.* Sophie gulped and at another nudge of his fingers glanced into his worried eyes.

"Did something happen at breakfast?"

Just like a man to figure the problem was anything but *him.*

A muscle popped in his jaw. "Did one of the men...?"

She shook her head. "No. Breakfast was fine." The next words spilled out in a breathy rush. "Except you weren't there." She clamped her lips shut not wanting to sound needy. *She was glad he hadn't been there...wasn't she?*

The confusion in Gray's eyes dissolved like early morning fog under the warm sun.

"Here I am." Aggie bustled through the front door. "Give me fifteen minutes to load your lunch in a cooler and you'll be set to go."

Thankful for the distraction, Sophie leaned over and surprised Aggie with a soft kiss on her cheek. "Thank you, Aggie." Not daring to look at Gray, she hurried away calling back to him, "We'll meet you on the boardwalk in twenty minutes."

# Chapter 20

Seated on the edge of the blanket, Sophie wiggled her feet down through the hot, sugary sand and into the cooler moist layer. A cautious seagull ventured close searching for a bit of food. "Shoo." She waved her hand at it. "Go pester someone else."

The girls and Gray had descended on the picnic basket like hungry locust. Aggie's chicken salad wraps disappeared in no time and the corn chip bag crackled with emptiness. Not even a bread and butter pickle survived the hungry hoard. At Sophie's insistence the oatmeal and raisin cookies stayed in their container to eat after swimming.

Laughter floated up from the water's edge. Andi and Lissa were teaching Gray how to dribble runny mud as decoration along the top of their sandcastles. Hanna stood inside the castle walls poking seashells and pretty rocks into the mud. Framed by the expanse of the sea and the gentle roll of the waves, it was easy to imagine them as a family.

She ran the tips of her fingers across her lips remembering Gray's kiss last night on the beach and his warm gaze in church this morning. Tomorrow she planned to go home where she belonged. Why didn't the prospect fill her with joy?

A shout and laughter brought her attention back to the shoreline where Andi chased Gray with a long whip of seaweed that trailed her through the sand. Tenderness sweet as warm taffy flowed through her. The man loved the girls. Hanna and Andi had opened their hearts to him immediately. Even Lissa's chilly tolerance had thawed to a tentative trust. Her question this morning shouldn't have come as a surprise.

Gray plunged into the water to dodge Andi.

He was leaving SeaMount tomorrow, too. Not for long and not for a dangerous place, thank you, God. But on the day she and the girls could use his support, he'd be where SeaMount sent him. Sophie wanted someone who'd be around for her and the girls. Her brain understood that need now if her heart would only get with the program.

Gray splashed ashore. The warmth flowing through Sophie had nothing to do with the sun and everything to do with the water-slick man walking toward her. She clutched a towel to keep from reaching out to trace the hollows and ridges etched across his scarred chest and back.

Stopping at the edge of the blanket, he shook the water from his short hair, spraying her with cold droplets.

"Hey!" She laughed and threw the towel at him.

He ruffed it over his head and buffed skin and rippling muscles. "You don't know what you're missing sitting here on the blanket."

"Yes I do. Turning blue and sand in my

swimsuit."

Under his frank perusal a blush heated her cheeks. The hours spent finding a modest suit that covered her and still complimented her generous curves had paid off. Between the sun and his appreciative smile, heat stroke seemed inevitable.

He must have thought better of voicing his opinion. Dropping to the blanket, he sat so close they knocked elbows. "I want some of those cookies you're holding hostage. What do I have to do to get them?" He leaned toward her.

Panic struck out of nowhere. To hold him at bay, she slapped her hand to his chest. *Oh my.* Pliant steel. Beneath her palm, his skin quivered. Tingles of awareness hit her low in her tummy as she sucked in a shaky breath. "We have an audience."

"Who?" He didn't lift his smoky, heated gaze from her face.

"The girls."

He glanced toward the water, verified her claim and leaned away, his expression a mixture of disappointment and longing.

Reaching into the cooler, Sophie pulled out the plastic container of cookies. She cleared her throat, but still her voice rasped from nerves. "There's a rumor because you kissed me again last night we have to get married."

His eyebrows shot up. She plunked the cookies on the blanket between them.

"Who said that?" Past the initial surprise, his eyes narrowed in speculation. "If that lame brain McCord ran off at the mouth..."

Sophie waved for the girls to come to the blanket.

"No, it wasn't Whit or any one of the men at SeaMount."

"Who else is there?"

Andi, Lissa and Hanna ran toward the blanket.

Gray looked at her. "Not…" he hitched his thumb in the direction of the racing youngsters.

"Oh yes. The spy in our midst has been busy."

The girls ran up to the blanket, sand spraying with each footfall. Sophie lunged to cover the cookies. "Dry off before sitting." When the three girls settled, she uncovered the sweets and let them dig in. They were quietly munching when Gray caught her eye and gave her a sly wink.

"So, I understand a covert operation took place on the beach last night." Nonchalantly he picked up another cookie and took a bite.

Andi and Lissa glanced at each other before concentrating their full attention on the cookies in their hands.

"Smurfs aren't allowed to go on secret missions without permission. Is that understood?"

Heads bent, the two oldest nodded. Oblivious, Hanna lay stretched on her tummy picking the raisins from her cookie.

"Your mother's a smart woman and wouldn't base the decision to marry a man on a couple of kisses."

*Oh dear.* Sophie took a bite of her cookie. Thoughts of marriage *had* drifted through her head more than once.

"Don't assume you understand everything you see and hear. Got it?"

The girls nodded. Sophie finished the cookie she held and took another. *I don't understand everything*

*I'm seeing and hearing either. Or feeling.* In the pit of her stomach the butterflies flapped their wings.

"Good. Finish up. There's time for one more swim before we call it a day."

Lissa and Andi jumped up and sped away. Hanna lay with her head on her crossed arms, sleeping.

Gray swiped another cookie. "I'm sorry I put you in the position to have to deal with that." His gaze darkened to warm pewter.

*I'm not.* Sophie snapped the lid on the cookie container wishing she could as easily contain the butterflies taking flight inside her. "Thank you." She smiled. "In case you haven't noticed Andi's overly protective."

He nodded and rose from the blanket, muttering. "Too much like me."

\*\*\*

"Oof." Gray tried to tuck and roll, but with hands and feet bound, his shoulder took the brunt of the fall.

Ten feet away Whit landed with a grunt. "Y'all will pay dearly for this."

Two utility belts with pouches landed in the weeds close by.

Standing in the back of the transport, backlit by the late morning sun filtering through the trees, Logan loomed above them. "You have one hour before the hunter force is let loose." With precision he threw their knives, burying the blades in moist woodland soil.

Before Logan made it back to the front seat of the modified MUTT to settle beside his brother, Gray rolled and was on his knife. Sitting up, he scooted backwards, wrapping his hand around the familiar handle. Behind him leaves crackled as Whit moved towards him.

"Hope you know how to use that thing."

Gray snorted. "Trust me not to slit your wrists?"

"I'll take my chances." Whit positioned himself at Gray's back. After some fumbling and a few choice words, the men worked together to get at the cord binding Whit's wrists.

"Got a plan?" The ropes gave beneath the blade.

"To run like fury out of these parts." Whit flexed his arms. "You got it." Another tug and his hands were free.

"Was hoping you had something more than that."

Whit cut the cord binding Gray's wrists "All I got at the moment."

They each made short work of freeing their feet.

"Then let's do it." Gray snatched up the utility belt that included the sheath for his knife, slung it like a bandolier across his chest and set off at a ground-eating jog. Fifty yards along the road they veered off to a marked trail leading south. Their immediate objective was to get away from the drop point as fast as possible.

Earlier, watching the agents on the 'hunter force' paw through his pack, the monster inside Gray had roared to life. The only thing that kept him from meting out the pounding they deserved were the bindings on his wrists and ankles. For his entire adult life his pack had been the only 'home' he knew. All part of the game, the twins in particular, took a great deal of pleasure taunting their victims as they disassembled Gray and Whit's ALICE packs, deciding what to allow for a load. The gear had dwindled to a stinking utility belt with pouches.

Well, he'd been in worse places with less. Being

the new guy in this merry band of mavericks, he'd expected torment to come his way. Sam's assigning Gray the role of the hunted gave the others an excuse to ride him hard and ramp up the emotion. Like a pack of jackals they looked for signs of weakness. Having Whit as his partner was surely part of the persecution.

The briefing at SeaMount had been...brief. To ensure zero casualties among the innocent civilians camped in the park, only weaponless close combat was to be used. Wits and strength.

"How are the others at tracking?"

"Behind Fallon's movie star face there's a blood hound." Whit's shaggy blond hair wisped out from under his boonie hat.

No good news there. "Anything I should know about the others?"

"Ethan has a sixth sense like I've never seen. If I didn't know he was a Christian, I'd suspect him being into hoodoo of some sort. The man's scary. Claims to be tight with the Holy Spirit." Whit slowed and stepped off the trail. Working his way through a stand of young pine, he headed up hill.

Gray went farther down the trail and found an old stonewall running along the base of the hill. The walls crisscrossing the woodlands were built over one hundred years earlier when the entire area was farmland. Cautious not to disturb moss or lichen, he climbed up and walked the length of it taking care not to step on a loose rock that might roll out from under him. On the backside of the hill at a spot where the wall had collapsed, he dismounted and headed uphill.

Whit sat on a boulder with a map of the state forest draped over his knee. "Here's the trail we're on."

He jabbed a finger at the top edge of the map. "Will be a good hike to get back to base camp and into the safe zone."

Taking inventory, Gray pulled out the compass he'd seen Jack slip in his pouch. Better than the stick and watch he'd used with Sophie. A band tightened around his chest making it hard to breath. Her brown eyes, bright with tears as they said good-bye this morning, flashed through his memory. With effort he pulled his attention back to the present. *One problem at a time.*

From a distance laughter and yelling drifted through the forest. "Sounds like the large pond to the east is a busy place. The activity might cover our trail." Taking out camo sticks, Gray set to work on his face, neck and the back of his hands. The jackals had allowed face paint but no way to keep hydrated. Not even an ancient WWII canteen.

Whit folded his map. "We should stay out of sight of the civilians. Nothing but a bunch of informants."

"Kids go off the trail and cut cross-country between campsites. We'll use that to our advantage." Gray blended light green cream between dark loam stripes.

Whit yanked off his hat and covered his shaggy hair with an olive drab bandana. "For the record, I miss my Stetson." He got busy with the paint.

"Quit your bellyaching." Gray pointed to a spot Whit missed. "Sophie was depending on me to go to court with her."

A slow smile spread across Whit's face. "Now there's a woman."

Gray paused mid-smear. His voice dropped to a

deadly octave. "Your thoughts better be purely innocent."

"As a newborn foal." Whit finished up, sorted through the two pouches on his utility belt and grunted in disgust. "Another twenty minutes and the others will be on the hunt...if they aren't already. I want to be long gone if they bring in the dogs."

"Dogs?" Gray swore. "Nobody said anything about dogs."

Whit shrugged. "If we're good at this, they'll get frustrated and ask Sam if they can give Caleb's canines a work out."

"He'd okay that?"

A tight smile lifted the corner of Whit's mouth. "Has before."

Gray shook his head. "I can't figure how the man ticks."

"Save yourself the headache. Don't even try." Whit slapped his boonie on top of the bandanna. "Roll with the program and watch your six."

Gray took the lead heading due east. To go into a heavily populated area was risky, but he hoped the move would buy them time.

# Chapter 21

A sharp edge of stone cut into Gray's back. A bug crawled inside his shirt giving him an itch he couldn't scratch. The buzzing and chirping of insects filled the night air. In the distance a whippoorwill gave a few short calls before settling into a steady song of *whip-poor-will whip-poor-will whip-poor-will.*

Hunkered down in an old cellar hole where a cabin had once stood, Gray listened and waited. The field stone foundation was at his back, the underbrush and dead leaves from the forest floor camouflaged his position. Ten feet away on the opposite wall, Whit was dug in.

The hunter force had followed close most of the evening. Going through the populated campground hadn't deterred them. And now, when Gray and Whit needed to be on the move under the cover of dark, they were holed up.

Heavy footsteps crunched through leaves. From beneath the foliage covering him, Gray watched a light move west.

"This is creepy, man." Davie's voice silenced the

insects.

Caleb's deeper voice murmured a response.

"Don't care if it's only three graves. Bodies are buried here."

Someone stumbled.

"And that crazy bird is freakin' me out."

Uneasy, Gray scanned the area above and behind Whit's position. Why'd Sam allow the kid to tag along with the big boys and why wasn't Caleb muzzling him?

Something heavy thumped. "Ow!" Davie spit out a few salty words followed by a groan. "That hurt."

Leaves rustled on the foundation's rim to Gray's left. Dirt and debris sifted into his position.

Caleb.

A beam of light played across the cellar hole, probing the scrubby bushes and trees that hid the rock walls. The light sweep closer to Whit's hiding place.

*Stay still, man. Keep your cool. Blend. Blend. Blend.* If Caleb tagged Whit, Gray would have no choice but to take the man down. He didn't want to play that hand this early in the game.

The light moved past Whit, doubled back for one more sweep and moved on. He tracked it coming his way and tensed. Before it hit his brush pile, the light veered back to Whit's cover.

Gray's heart picked up pace. Whit had been made. Caleb may not know for sure, but he saw something he questioned.

As swift as a snake striking, Gray grabbed Caleb's ankle and surged up to lock his arm behind the other man's knees then brought him down into the hole.

Caleb hit the ground with a grunt. He lashed out with his foot and clipped Gray's hip. Then Whit was on him and Caleb relaxed, unconscious.

Gray scrambled back to the rock foundation. Where was Davie? The kid would have heard the struggle. He signaled Whit. They needed to bug out before the kid thought to call in reinforcements.

Keeping low, they went up and over the rim of the foundation and faded into the woods.

\*\*\*

The smell of fresh paint in the house had always lifted Sophie's spirits.

Not this time.

Seated at the kitchen table, she rubbed the palms of her hands up and down her arms. So many personal mementos were lost in the vandalism her house. It no longer had the familiar comfort of home. Even her tattered quilt would have been a comfort. But no one at SeaMount seemed to recall taking it out of the van.

The map Gray gave her the night of the bonfire was spread open on the table.

Her heart panged remembering his departure two days ago. The task of putting her home back together hadn't distracted her from the loneliness or the worry about tomorrow with its possibility of monumental change to her life.

Andi entered the kitchen dressed for bed and dragging Hanna's new dolly, Sweetie Pie, by one hand. A gift from Ethan, the rag doll was the same height as Hanna. Delegated the status of alter ego by Hanna and scapegoat by the two older girls, the doll took the abuse with a happy smile on her muslin face.

"What's this?" Andi tucked floppy Sweetie Pie in a kitchen chair and climbed up beside her mother.

Pushing worries aside, Sophie smoothed her hands

over the creases in the paper. "It's a map of our town. See this star? I stuck it there to mark our house on our street."

"Cool." Andi placed her finger on the star. "Where's Gray's big house?"

"Hmm. Good question." Sophie referred to the index, found the letter along the top of the map and the number on the side. Moving both fingers to the point where the lines intersected, she read the street. "Bluff Avenue. Right there. Hand me a star." Sophie affixed the sticker. "Now let's try to follow the roads from here to there." With her fingertip, she traced the road to SeaMount.

"Can I try?" With a few corrections, Andi's tiny finger traced the same route. "When will we see Gray again?"

Sophie rubbed a hand across her brow trying to keep irritation at bay. She'd answered this same question at least a hundred times in the past two days. "I'm not sure, Andi. Remember he left with the other men for training."

"But his house is there. Can we go visit Aggie?" Brown eyes fringed with spiky dark lashes pleaded for an answer.

A sharp knock on the front door interrupted them.

The hour was much too late for company. Had something happened to Gray? Leaving Andi at the table, she hurried to the door.

"Mr. Vole!"

Her lawyer stood on the step, briefcase in hand. "Good evening, Sophie." His gaze skittered the length of her. He smoothed a pale hand across his comb-over and pushed on the bridge of his eyeglasses. "May I come in?"

She stepped back. "What's happened?" Sam and Michael had reviewed the custody case with her on Monday before she left SeaMount.

"An issue has come to light." He settled his briefcase on the coffee table and turned to take her hand. His thumb stroked the inside of her wrist. "It's concerns your time in Maine... at the camp."

Sophie jerked her hand away. "That horrible experience." She sank to the couch. "I didn't know it had become a sporting camp. I'd planned a family weekend."

He sat beside her and snapped the latches on his briefcase. "Not knowing more before you left could be viewed as irresponsible."

She rubbed her palms against her slacks. "I had the brochure."

Mr. Vole pulled a manila file from the tidy interior of his case. "I received this today." He pulled an 8 x 10 photograph out of the folder and held it up.

In the photo, Sophie stood on the steps of the lodge hair tousled, no makeup, and bundled head to toe in a blanket.

*Taking pictures of the wildlife* echoed in Sophie's mind. "Where did you get this?"

"It doesn't matter how I acquired this photo, dear. What matters is how compromising this looks for you."

Her heart stopped for a second before pounding painfully against the wall of her chest. "That's a horrid thing to say! The shower in our cabin broke. I needed help. My clothes were damp so I covered up with a blanket." The pitch of her voice grew shriller with each word. "Andi went with me."

Shaking his head, Mr. Vole tucked the photo back into his case. "This doesn't look good."

What he implied made her feel dirty. "Mr. Vole, you know me well enough to know I wouldn't jeopardize my children."

"The photo suggests otherwise." He reached out and trailed his finger across the back of her hand. "With the proper compensation I'll make the picture go away."

Shock immobilized Sophie. She stared at this man she trusted. He was spinning a sordid fairytale out of nothing more than a photograph. She wanted to speak but her tongue was stuck to the roof of her dry mouth.

Mr. Vole leaned close. "There's nothing the SeaMount lawyer can do about this... evidence. No one needs to know."

His hot breath on her cheek proved to be the key that unlocked her frozen brain. "What's *wrong* with you? You're my lawyer. This is blackmail!"

"Don't play games with me, Sophie."

An inappropriate urge to laugh rose up in her. Games? He was the one playing a deceitful game. She rose from the couch and walked to the front door. Her chest heaved with the effort to keep the near hysteria under control. "Please. Leave. Now."

"Dear, we all want what's best for the girls." He smiled and stepped out the door. "Call me if you change your mind. Otherwise, tomorrow may be a disaster."

Sophie slammed the door and slumped against it. Shock reverberated through her. Disbelief warred with a rising outrage. She'd *trusted* him. She was paying him to *win* the custody case. Reeling with shock, she turned away from the door. Wobbly legs carried her to the kitchen.

Gray questioned Vole's loyalty. Did Michael believe in her innocence? She had to call him. She'd have to tell him the unsavory details of her attorney's visit. Her cheeks burned with embarrassment. A soft thump snapped her attention back to her surroundings.

Wide-eyed and pale, Andi remained kneeling in the chair at the kitchen table. "Will we have to live with Grandmother and Grandfather?"

*Oh God, please, not that.* She hugged Andi close. "Shh, sweetie. Everything will be okay." *God, please let everything be okay.*

\*\*\*

Sophie checked the clock on her nightstand for what felt like the hundredth time in the last fifteen minutes. Nightmares had plagued her throughout the night. Discussing Mr. Vole's visit and unethical behavior with Michael hadn't been a recipe for peaceful sleep. Her apology for calling so late had been brushed aside. He'd assured her she'd done the right thing.

Shock continued to reverberate through her over Mr. Vole's treachery. How had she missed his true nature? Nausea threatened as she recounted the many times, before and after Tommy's death, she'd sat with the man and conducted business. How had he come into possession of the photograph? *Thank you Lord, for Gray's insistence to involve Sam and the SeaMount lawyer.* Though still dark outdoors, a cardinal began to sing and whistle his way through his morning repertoire.

Giving up on anymore sleep, she threw off her bed covers and swung her feet to the floor. Time to face the day. A verse from the book of Jeremiah came to mind. *'I know the plans I have for you, declares the Lord, plans to prosper you and not harm you, plans to give you hope and a future.'*

Lord, I want desperately to keep my children. Please let your plan be that they stay with me. That's the future I want.

She'd lost Tommy. She couldn't bear losing the girls, too. Praying for God's will to be done was beyond her ability. Her faith, frayed around the edges, was too fragile to withstand an examination of God's unfathomable ways. She wanted today to end in one way and one way only. Her girls at home, tucked up in their beds for the night. The urge to look in on each of them quickened her steps.

Hanna snuggled beneath a teddy bear bedspread surrounded by the new stuffed animals she insisted share her bed. Would it be Suzanne who accompanied Hanna to school on her first day? Sophie's throat ached with unshed tears.

Lissa lay knotted up in her bed covers. More sensitive than either of the other two girls, Lissa's tough façade was riddled with cracks. She would always miss her daddy. Could she survive losing her mother and home, too?

Sophie paused at Andi's door. The protector, now a lump nestled deep within blankets and comforter, had heard Mr. Vole's ugly accusations. Even if she didn't understand his malicious insinuations, she'd seen Sophie's reaction and been frightened. She'd cried herself to sleep in Sophie's arms.

The urge to take a closer peek at Andi carried her on tiptoe to the bedside. She lifted the edge of the blanket.

Eyes open wide, smile frozen in place, Sweetie Pie doll stared up at her.

Confusion speared through Sophie. She pulled the covers back and ran her hands over the bed and through the jumble of stuffed animals. "Andi?" She liked to get her own breakfast. Maybe....

Sophie hurried from the room.

Her voice rang hollow through the empty kitchen and living room. "Andi?" There was no answer to her call. Anxiety rising, she returned to Andi's bedroom to check under the bed and in the closet.

A thump came from Lissa's room.

Sophie met her oldest daughter in the hall. "Liss, is Andi in your room?" Even as she asked the question, she pushed past Lissa and entered her bedroom.

She peeked in the closet and under the bed. Hiding wasn't Andi's way. Her middle daughter thrived being in the center of whatever was happening. Controlling the alarm clamoring for release she searched Hanna's room, waking her youngest daughter.

"Have either of you seen Andi?" The question hung in the air as Sophie hurried back to the kitchen and the door to the basement.

The hem of her nightgown flapped around her ankles as she raced barefoot down the stairs clinging to the banister, not wanting to tumble in her haste.

"Andi? Where are you?" A quick circuit of the room and adjoining garage proved futile. Sick with fear, she opened the walkout basement door and peered out into gray light of early morning. "Andi?" Listening for an answer, she flicked on the floodlight. A shower had passed through overnight. The grass glistened and the air was heavy with the scent of damp earth.

No one answered her call. Panic ballooned inside her. She closed the door and raced back to the stairs. Lissa and Hanna stood at the top, eyes wide.

"Get dressed." Fear gave her voice a harsh edge. She stumbled on a carpeted step, caught herself and kept moving.

The girls raced to their rooms.

Grabbing the cordless phone on her way past, Sophie's feet automatically carried her back to the last place she'd been with her daughter – Andi's bedroom. She pressed the numbers for SeaMount, and then tossed the colorful bedding as if that would reveal Andi's whereabouts.

Sweetie Pie sailed across the room and hit the wall with a soft thump.

A folded piece of paper fell to the floor. Sophie dove for it, her breath coming in short gasps.

"SeaMount."

"Hello?" Her hands shook. She fumbled with the paper.

"This is SeaMount."

"This is Sophie." Red crayon letters wobbled their way across the plain sheet of paper.

"Good morning, Mrs. Moore. Charlie here. How can I help you?"

Mommy
I do not want to live with granfather. I want to live with gray.
I love you.
Andi

Sophie choked on tears as an unearthly cry rolled from her raw throat. The other end of the phone line clattered.

Lissa and Hanna burst through the door.

"Sophie?" Sam's gruff voice cut through her blind terror.

"Andi's gone! I can't find her anywhere. There's a note..." A sob tore from her aching chest.

"I'll be right there." The line went dead.

She doubled over and sank to the rug clutching the phone and Andi's note. Unable to think coherently, even the ability to pray eluded her.

Hanna crept close and leaned against her mother, crying because her mother cried. Lissa tentatively wrapped her arms around Sophie's neck.

Clinging to Lissa, Sophie wept. Wanting Gray with her, she waited for Sam.

# Chapter 22

"Think they've gotten word to expect us?" Gray gnawed on a piece of jerky and contemplated the distance between their position and the log cabin shrouded in murky predawn light. His shirt, wet from a passing rain shower, clung to his skin.

"Yup." Whit waved off a persistent deer fly then drank water from a bottle he'd pilfered out of an unsuspecting camper's cooler. "But I can't see these boys putting on a pig roast to welcome us back."

"Supposed to be a safe zone. Think they have something else in mind?"

"The gruesome twosome has sat here for three long days wishing they could be in the field."

Gray finished up what passed for breakfast. "You saying they could turn this escape and evasion exercise into capture and interrogation?" He rubbed a hand across his mouth. "Been there done that. I want this over."

"Sophie's in good hands. Drew's the best."

"I want to see for myself." The yearning for Sophie and the smurfs plagued him like a bad case of the flu. "But I have to do this right or I can't even be pool boy at SeaMount."

Whit nodded. "Sam's strict about the rules. Guess with the bunch of boneheads he has working for him, he has no choice."

A puff of smoke drifted from the cabin chimney. Both men tensed, alert to the change.

"What do you say we do some recon?" Gray's gaze ricocheted off the small weathered building back to Whit. "Maybe we could take the cabin."

"Capture Gabe and Logan before they nab us?"

Gray glanced at the brightening sky where a cover of low clouds had begun to roll in. "Hold the place for the last twenty-four hours."

A slow smile spread across Whit's face. He studied the cabin and the surrounding area. "I like the way you think, Kerr."

They worked their way to the side of the cabin hidden behind woody shrubs. Vines crawled up the rough exterior logs. Crouched beneath a window that was raised two inches, Gray and Whit paused to listen.

A pan clattered. Running water hissed. A radio squawked and in brief bursts Caleb's tinny voice updated the men in base camp.

The hunter force remained split into teams. Caleb continued to hurt from his scuffle with Whit and Gray.

Chairs scraped across the floor and the aroma of bacon and eggs wafted past Gray making his mouth water. Eating utensils clinked. Voices drifted through the window opening.

"We're supposed to stay here?"

"I haven't raised Preach on the radio yet. One of us may have to go beat the bushes for him. But, yeah, the rest of us are stuck here."

Uncertain, Gray thought it was Logan speaking.

"Guess all of us can't bug out and leave Kerr and McCord wandering in the woods hiding from non-existent hunters. Any attempt to call them in would be viewed as a trick."

A questioning look passed between Gray and Whit.

"In their shoes, I'd come to the same conclusion. How far can a little girl run, anyway? "Gray jerked with surprise. Whit's hand closed around his arm in an iron grip. Appalled he'd reacted he braced to hear more.

"Whatever she heard last night frightened her pretty good to send her running from home in the middle of the night. Hope they find her before the storm hits us."

"She took a map of the town Kerr gave her mother. They assume she's headed for SeaMount."

Gray's heart splintered in his chest. One of the girls ran off? Who? Why? Hanna wouldn't leave her mother. Lissa possessed the attitude but not the fortitude.

That left Andi.

He rubbed his hand across his face.

Andi would take the risk. From the moment she jumped out of the van that first morning in the wilderness, she'd been willing to do whatever necessary to survive. Something had frightened her. She needed him and he wasn't there.

His stomach roiled with anxiety. He wished he had eloquent words like Preach, but all he managed was a simple thought. *Lord, protect her.*

Whit tapped him and signaled retreat. Following

him back to the top of the hill, Gray struggled to get a grip on his worry before it rendered him useless. *Focus, Kerr.*

Whit spun around. "What do you want to do?"

Here it was. The ultimate choice. Sophie or SeaMount. His stomach churned as he stood staring at the cabin, wrangling his options. Sophie would be in a panic. Andi's disappearance made a bad day worse. *God, where are you in all this?*

Sam's displeasure with his past performance knotted his gut. Blow this opportunity and kiss the job with SeaMount goodbye. Thoughts of what could happen to Andi alone on the road flashed through his mind and raised goose flesh on his arms.

"Our orders are to report to base camp." He snapped his gaze back to Whit. "What if we report to home base?"

"SeaMount?"

Gray nodded.

Whit's roguish smile gave him hope. "Worth a try."

Gray looked at the cabin for a long moment then turned. His decision made, he walked in the opposite direction.

***

Sophie stood at the large living room window. Rain pattered on the front step and porch railing as the neighborhood awoke to the new morning.

Raincoat flapping around his knees, old Mr. Crummel hurried out of his house to the pickup truck sitting in his driveway. The police cars and mobile command unit slowed him for a moment before he hurried on his way. Speculation about the neighborhood would surely accompany his early morning coffee at the local Honey Dew donut shop.

Sophie glanced at the clock. Only fifteen minutes had passed since her last check of the time. "I feel useless staying here doing nothing."

Earlier she gave the police a photo then had gone through Andi's closet to try to figure out what she'd be wearing. In the search, she'd found Andi's pajamas stuffed in a half empty Lego container and her backpack missing from its hook.

The policewoman assigned to her came and stood beside her. "The chief wants you where he can reach you for immediate transport if necessary, Mrs. Moore."

Tears spilled along her cheeks. She wiped them with an already damp facial tissue. "I know."

Transport. A ride in the police car. To the hospital? To the morgue? To Andi. She pulled in a shaky breath. *Don't get ahead of the situation, Sophie.*

Lissa and Hanna snuggled on the couch watching a Veggie Tales video.

On the front porch, Michael spoke into his phone. He and Sam had been in huddled conversation before Sam received a phone call and left.

The center of operations, a mobile command unit, hummed with activity. Another K9 unit from a neighboring town had arrived twenty minutes ago. A flurry of activity around the van caught Sophie's attention.

A detective broke away from the knot of men in yellow slickers and trotted up the brick walk carrying a brown paper bag. Michael followed him through the front door.

"Mrs. Moore. Can you identify this for us?" He

opened the paper bag and pulled out a sealed plastic bag holding a child's red sneaker.

Dread closed Sophie's throat in a painful chokehold. Her words were a whispered rasp. "Is a heart drawn on the inside with a marker?"

He nodded.

She licked her dry lips and wiped away tears. "I yelled at her for drawing in her shoe. What did it matter? So stupid..." Her voice broke. She had to know. "Where did you find it?"

The detective hesitated before he spoke. "On the edge of the salt marsh."

The salt marsh, with its sticky mud and tidal flooding, was no place for a child alone during the day never mind in the dark of night. Had Andi tried to cross at low tide and been trapped by the rising water?

Michael squeezed her hand then followed the detective back outside.

Yesterday she'd believed nothing could be worse than losing the custody battle for her girls. This morning God chose to remind her of the complete separation of death. She had survived losing Tommy. Could she keep body and soul together if Andi followed him?

Needing privacy, she slipped into her bedroom, closed the door and sank to her knees beside the bed.

*Lord, let them find Andi alive.* Her breath shuddered. *And I want the privilege of raising all three of my girls.* She sniffed and wiped her nose. Her universe centered on home and family. Did she have the strength to give all she held dear – her girls, her home, everything in her life – to God? Did she trust Him enough to surrender all that she loved to His keeping?

*Lord, what you ask is hard to do.*

In the hours since her discovery, the anxiety and turmoil of the past few weeks had grown into a burden greater than she could bear alone. Pushing the anxiety aside, trying to forget, running off to Maine, had not given her relief.

Cries wrenched from deep within Sophie's tight, aching chest. Fear and doubt poured out with contrite tears.

Lord, I'm not strong enough to hold my life together. I can't control the circumstances or the outcome. Only You can do that. She swallowed back a sob. I surrender every thing and every one to You, Father. Watch over Andi. Wherever she is, let her feel your presence. Only an all-knowing God with a sovereign hand could protect those she loved.

Gray making daisy wreaths with the girls, flashed through her memory, stealing her breath. *Give me wisdom in this relationship, Lord. Show me your will.*

Outside, the wind grew in strength buffeting the rain-smattered window. Indoors, curled up beside her bed, the storm of emotion gripping Sophie eased. In the center of the heartache peace, fragile as a new flower, unfurled.

\*\*\*

His fingers ached to fall off.

Gray looked down then thought better of it. Two inches from his nose, the rock ledge smelled of metallic minerals. He searched for a toehold with his boot, then pulled himself up and reached for the next finger hold. Breath whistled between his teeth as he inched his way up the rain slick cliff.

Below, Whit grunted and cursed. "Whose idea

was this?"

Gray strained to find another finger hold. "Yours." Panting, he stopped to rest.

"Wasn't one of my best."

The bay of hounds grew closer, setting the men back in motion.

"I'm leaving a blood trail with my fingers." Gray wiped them on his damp shirt.

"If those hounds can follow us up this cliff, I'll go willingly into captivity."

Breathing hard Gray climbed faster. "Speak for yourself, cowboy."

"Horseman."

With a groan, Gray heaved up and over the rim. Whit followed and they ghosted into the scraggy pines. Stopping to catch their breath, they watched the dogs bound from the dense trees.

"How do you suppose they found us so fast?" Whit mused between chugs of water.

"Wouldn't have anything to do with you sweet talking those two women into letting us borrow their canoe?"

"They promised not to say a word."

Gray snorted and left Whit to follow him.

According to their map, they weren't far from the border of the state forest. Technically, they weren't to leave state land. But the moment they changed where they'd report in, the border rule bit the dust.

A breeze rustled the leaves of the small trees and woodland undergrowth. Making their way down the slope, Whit grabbed Gray's arm. "Did you hear that?" He surged ahead not giving Gray time to answer. "Horses."

Cutting through a windrow of trees, they entered a pasture where several horses grazed. On the other side of the field a small house with peeling paint and a questionable roof sat next to a gleaming new two story red barn.

On the move, Whit studied the set up. "When was the last time you rode a horse, Kerr?"

"Afghanistan." Gray pulled out his bandana. "Wipe the face paint off before you frighten someone."

"Worked for those other two gals."

"Yeah, well..." His thoughts were better left unsaid.

A woman wearing muck boots and carrying a pitchfork stepped into view in the open barn door. She was short and muscular, her gray hair sticking out in all directions around her lined face.

"Well, I'll be." Whit smiled "It *is* her." His gait morphed from soldier ready to cowboy swagger.

Eyeing the pitchfork, Gray hoped the woman was as happy to see Whit, as he was to see her.

"Hey, beautiful!"

She responded by grasping the fork in both hands.

Whit whipped off his boonie and bandana. "The gymkhana. Last October."

A tentative look of recognition crossed her face. "McCord? That you?"

"Whooo weee! Shor' is." Whit took the pitchfork from the woman's hands and danced her in a tight circle.

"Mz. Rhetta, I'd like you to meet Gray Kerr. Gray, this lovely lady near beat my pants off running the bleeding heart barrel race." He gently chucked her under the chin. "I still say the timekeeper had a thing

257

for you."

She blushed and waved him away.

"Didn't know this place finally sold. Coming across the pasture there, thought I spotted your hoss."

The woman lapped up Whit's cowboy cajolery like it was ice cream melting on a hot summer day. Gray shook his head. He was thinking the way Whit was talking.

"What're you doing here dressed like Rambo?"

"Well now, there's a story. Remember I told you I'm paramilitary?"

Mz. Rhetta frowned. "My son works for the state. Said a group was using the park for training."

Gray studied their back trail. The bay of the hounds came from a distance. "They're coming."

The woman's gaze flicked back and forth between Whit and Gray. "Who's coming?"

"Here's the thing. In this training, we're escapees evading capture. If we're going to get away, we'll need something faster than our own two feet."

"How far you got to go?"

"About five, six miles to Horsin' Around Rescue. We can leave the horses there and trailer them back tomorrow."

"Come on." She pointed at Gray. "I'll saddle a ride for Butch. You're saddling your own, Sundance."

"You're breaking my heart here, Mz. Rhetta." Whit followed her into the barn.

Gray stood in the shadow of the barn doors listening to Whit. The man's mouth moved as fast as his hands.

"When the others show up with those hound dogs, you raise a holy ruckus for bringing them on your property and upsetting the stock."

"You want me to buy you some time, McCord?"

"Why Mz. Rhetta, you're as smart as you are purty."

The woman *giggled*.

"Delay them any way you can. I don't care if you give 'em both barrels or honey-talk the lot of them." Whit walked towards the door leading two bay geldings.

On his heels, Mz. Rhetta once again armed herself with the pitchfork. "You got it."

"I owe you, beautiful."

"I'll be sure to collect."

# Chapter 23

Sophie fluffed the bow at the back of Hanna's floral dress. "No, sweetie. For the last time, you can't wear your princess gown."

Hanna whined and pulled at the bow her mother had just straightened.

When the police van drove away to relocate closer to the marsh, Sophie had begged to go with them. She'd lost that battle. Soon after, Michael insisted they head for the courthouse earlier than originally planned. Her imagination ran wild with reasons for the change. None of them were good.

"Mommy, we can't go without Andi." Lissa shrugged into her bright pink rain slicker and frowned at Charlie who waited near the front door.

He checked his watch again. "Time to leave."

Sophie snapped closed the front of Hanna's red ladybug raincoat, collected her purse and umbrella then herded the protesting Hanna and Lissa out the door. *Minus one child. The judge will have a field day with me.*

The ride took forever. The moment the courthouse

came into view, Sophie's heart lurched and suddenly the ride had been too short.

***

Whit veered off the narrow country road, crossed a ditch mucky with runoff and rode beside a stone wall topped with one strand of barbed wire. "We're almost there."

A narrow gate secured a break in the lichen-covered stones. Plagued with anxiety for Sophie and the smurfs, Gray guided his horse through the gate Whit held.

They cantered across a narrow meadow where two horses lifted their heads to watch. Beyond the field an enormous metal building sat low among the trees. Several corrals connected to the side of the building. Each held a horse or two, some animals in better shape than others.

Whit gave a short piercing whistle and dismounted. "End of the line, Kerr."

Muscles protesting, Gray slid from his horse.

A tall, rawboned man exited a small shed at a run. "Boss? Didn't expect you for another three, four days."

"No time to explain, Ten. Take care of these boys will you? I'll call later. Need the keys to the truck."

Ten fished in his pocket and handed over a ring of keys then snagged the reins of each horse.

"Appreciate it."

Running feet thudded nearby.

Gray turned to see Davie coming toward them at full tilt. He glanced at Whit. The man was full of surprises. Gray didn't like surprises.

Eyeballing Davie, the horses sidestepped nervously. With cat-like grace Whit intercepted the boy. "What've I told you about running near the stock?"

Ten murmured and soothed the tired animals before leading them to the barn leaving Whit to give Davie a dressing down.

Making it quick and to the point, Whit didn't waste any breath tiptoeing around the teen's feelings before ordering him back to work then making a run for the truck.

Glad to be out of the now steady rain, Gray sank back into the soft comfort of the double cab truck. The vehicle had the *Horsin' Around Rescue* logo emblazoned in gold on the door and was loaded with every option money could buy. "This is your operation?"

Whit slammed his door and swept the dripping boonie off his head. "A little side thing I do."

Gray snorted. The last few days had convinced him this man didn't do anything 'little'. "And Davie?"

"Hoping to rehabilitate one juvie along with the horses."

\*\*\*

Wind tugged at the umbrella Charlie held as Sophie helped Hanna out of her car seat. The gray, wet weather wreathed the courthouse with an ominous aura.

Sophie shuddered and blinked back tears. So much depended on today. Had she already lost one daughter? The ache in her heart grew with each hour Andi remained lost. *Where are you, Andi?* Longing for Gray added to her heartache. No matter how many arguments she created, the yearning didn't stop.

Heart heavy, she guided Lissa and Hanna through the carved wooden doors of the courthouse. Inside the foyer of the historic building, a necessity of modern life greeted them. A uniformed officer stood beyond the metal detectors framing the interior entrance. Another officer stood behind a narrow table wearing latex gloves.

"Good morning." He smiled and gestured toward the table. "Handbag and umbrella on the table, please. Step through one at a time."

Sophie did as the man asked, reaching out for Hanna to keep her from walking through the metal detectors at Lissa's side. Past security, she and the girls followed Charlie.

Brass-toned signs attached to the granite block walls directed them to an open stairway. The wide wooden banister, dark with age, wound upward. Surrounded by the historic grandeur of stone, crown molding and chandeliers, Lissa and Hanna spoke in hushed voices.

"In here, ladies." Charlie opened a door into a small conference room.

Anger jolted through Sophie.

Mr. Vole sat at the table with Michael.

Lissa and Hanna squealed and ran to the opposite end of the room straight into Aggie's outstretched arms. The tiny woman embraced them and flashed an encouraging smile at Sophie.

Michael rose from his seat. He looked every inch the lawyer in his gray suit and burgundy tie. "Thank you for coming early, Sophie. Aggie will take the girls across the street to the library."

After last night, Sophie wanted nothing to do with Mr. Vole. Unable to speak past the fury clogging her throat, she nodded her acceptance.

Mr. Vole offered her a solicitous smile. "I'm sure you're worried about Andi." He turned back to Michael. "Your message said new information has come to light you'd like to review?"

Michael seated Sophie then took his place. He shuffled papers. "Tell me about your years of service in the legal department of Blue Moor Brands."

The lawyer tugged at his starched collar. "I believe I told you. I worked for Gerald Moore for years."

"You began as a junior advisor and worked your way up to senior corporate counsel."

"Yes, but what does this have to do with the custody case?"

Michael smiled.

Goosebumps shivered along Sophie's arms. Above the angelic smile, Michael's hard gaze glittered.

\*\*\*

Gray bailed out before the wheels of the truck stopped rolling. He ran through the rain across the asphalt to SeaMount's service entrance. This could be the last time he'd enter through the back door.

At the top of the stairs, Preach poked his head around corner. "Where's the fir... What are you doing here?"

"Looking for Sam."

"In the Club Room." He spotted Whit. "You, too?"

Gray steamed past. Whit's boots pounded along behind.

The door to the room stood ajar. With one sharp knock, Gray pushed it open, charged through and halted. Whit plowed into his back with a grunt.

Sam stood in front of the windows looking out. Beyond the panes buffeted by wind and rain, the gray churning ocean displayed nature's raw power.

Digging into his distant past, Gray straightened to attention. "Reporting as ordered."

"Reporting here was not the objective, Kerr." Sam turned and pinned Gray with a hard glare.

Undaunted he stood his ground. "Did Andi run off?"

"How did you hear about that?"

Unsure what answer would save his smelly hide and move him on his way, Gray opted for the truth. "We overheard Logan and Gabe talking in the cabin."

"Excuse me." Preach shouldered past Whit and Gray. "Sam, I'm leaving."

His eyes narrow and targeting Gray, Sam nodded. "Take Kerr with you."

Was he being dismissed? He hadn't come this far to be further delayed. "Let me help find Andi."

"Follow orders for once, Kerr. Go with Jack." The precision with which Sam enunciated each word telegraphed his anger.

Under his breath Preach murmured, "You'll want to come with me."

When he turned and left, Gray followed. Behind him Sam growled. "McCord, stay."

Gray caught up to Preach in the hallway. "Where are we going?"

"To the courthouse."

When Preach got behind the wheel of the black SUV and immediately opened the windows, Gray didn't take offense, having had no access to soap and hot water for the better part of a week. The splatter of cold rain on his face helped him focus. He glanced at the clock on the dash. "Why? Sophie's court appearance isn't until this afternoon."

"Security detail."

"Courthouses have their own security. Is she in danger?"

Preach hesitated. "Michael asked for more coverage."

"Heard Gabe and Logan say you'd been called in."

Hands tightening on the steering wheel, Preach shot Gray a narrow-eyed look. "You were that close to the cabin?"

Gray nodded and switched the conversation back to his immediate concern. "I want to search for Andi."

"Officers from three police departments and the state are out looking for Andi. That includes three K-9 units."

"She took off to find me. They have a mobile command center? Take me there. Please." Gray ran a hand over his face then around to the back of his neck. *Lord, please let Andi be alive.*

Preach glanced at him then back at the road. He made a sharp right turn, cut through a residential area away from town and the courthouse and back towards the seashore. "Both of us could be hunting for work by the end of the day."

Gray let out the breath he'd held. "Thanks."

Set up on the road running the edge of the salt marsh, the Mobile Command Post hummed with activity. Gray stepped from the SUV and waved Preach on his way. Recognizing Detective Brown in the knot of men and dogs shielded by a blue canopy, he approached hoping to be briefed.

The detective stood before a large map of the area. His sharp gaze traveled the length of Gray. "Thought Sam's men were engaged in training."

"Just got in."

Brown turned back to the map. "I'm here checking things out before heading to the courthouse to meet Drew."

Determined to eek out any information available, Gray ran a practiced eye over the map. "Sophie's there now. Seems early to me."

Brown's lack of response didn't sit well. Gray roughed his hand through his hair. Something was going down at the courthouse.

Overhead, the canopy flapped in a gust of wind. A spray of cold rain peppered the men. Brown turned up the collar on his trench coat. "The commander pulled everyone on foot off the marsh. This nor'easter blew in on a spring tide."

Fear for Andi knifed through Gray's solar plexus.

"He's sending out the Rescue One boat with a K-9 team and divers." The detective pointed at the perimeter of the salt marsh. "Volunteers are canvassing the neighborhood bordering the marsh." His hand-held radio squelched. "You spent almost a week in the wilderness with the Moore family. Tell me what you can about this little girl."

Andi's face, fierce with concentration as she learned to build a campfire, flashed through his mind. "Determined." He glanced toward the salt marsh. "If she hasn't run into trouble with the tide or gotten hurt, she'll fight to get through."

"Her mother positively ID'd a shoe we found."

Gray's throat constricted and the inside of his chest splintered in a million different directions. His voice rasped. "Where'd you find it?"

# Chapter 24

Mr. Vole waxed eloquent on his time at Blue Moor Brands. The man's pompous attitude grated on Sophie's already frayed nerves. Unsure what Michael hoped to accomplish with this information, she nevertheless trusted his judgment and listened.

The conference room door opened on silent hinges and Detective Brown stepped in. Mr. Vole paused mid-sentence, sending a questioning look to the SeaMount lawyer.

The detective nodded to Sophie then found a seat at the table.

Michael smiled. "As senior counsel, you were privy to the negotiations and funding for all acquisitions."

"Absolutely."

"Research shows several of the acquired firms closed. What happened?"

"Bad economic times." Mr. Vole shook his head. "It's all in the annual report."

Michael slid a glossy booklet across the table. "The share holders see only robust growth in this current annual report. In truth, Blue Moor Brands is in arrears on property tax in three states and drowning in debt. What do you know about that, Mr. Vole?"

\*\*\*

"I'm going that way." The volunteer firefighter looked at Gray from beneath the frayed bill of his baseball cap. "Come on." He ran through the rain to a pickup truck outfitted with light bar and strobes.

Gray followed, careful not to disturb the man's turnout gear as he climbed into the cab. "I appreciate this." His gaze searched beyond the rain sheeting the windshield of the pickup and the slapping wipers trying to keep up with the deluge. He wanted to see where they'd found Andi's shoe. That was the place to begin.

On either side of the road the high tide covered all but the green tips of cordgrass. An occasional dark knob of shrub rose out of the choppy water that surged higher than normal, reaching deep into the high marsh.

Praying Andi hadn't gotten stuck in the soft, sticky mud of the flats, Gray listened to the crackling communication on the fire radio. He understood the need to protect the volunteers and first responders, but time was running out. The rescue mission needed to move forward now to avoid a possible recovery mission when the tide receded. Reading street signs, he caught an occasional glimpse of volunteers, paired up and searching for Andi. Behind the cottages lay the salt pond and marsh.

If she'd tried to cut across the marsh.... He fisted his hands. *God, don't let anything happen to her.* Odd how in a crisis he didn't worry about finding the right words to say to God.

Slipper Shell Lane. The sign marked the street

where the searchers found Andi's sneaker.

"Let me out here."

"You sure? I can take you closer. You're gonna get wet."

*More than you know.* "I'm good. Thanks for the ride." Just a regular nice guy, no way did Gray want the man caught up in what he was about to do. He stepped out of the cab, rain beating on his shoulders. Water sluiced over his cheeks to run beneath his collar. Back hunched, he walked the narrow street lined with beach cottages.

A short distance away, a black and white blocked the street. Yellow crime scene tape cordoned off an area to the side of the road. The search radiated out from this point.

Two uniformed officers hunched together, their yellow slickers shiny with rain. They eyed him with suspicion. "This area is off limits."

Everything in him wanted to barge through the ridiculously thin barrier. The need to examine every inch of ground burned in his gut. But he wasn't in command. He wasn't even part of the team.

Exactly the way he preferred to go in this time.

Shoulders bent, hands in his pockets, Gray's gaze momentarily met the direct glare of the officers before skittering to the grassy roadside and the small marker. "I know the little girl that's lost. Had to come see." He let his voice trail off.

"If you want to help with the search, go report in at the Mobil Command Unit."

*Been there. Done that. Sorta.* "Oh. Okay. Thanks." Lingering for a moment, as if unsure about leaving, he rubbed the water from his face, exhaled and smiled sheepishly at the hard-eyed police.

Turning back the way he came in, Gray stayed on the grassy berm of the narrow lane. He kept moving until he didn't feel the burn of watchful eyes between his shoulder blades.

He glanced back. A pair of volunteers spoke with the officers. Stepping off the road, he ducked between a high hedge and garden shed. Back against rough weathered shingles, he inhaled and closed his eyes. He focused on the tang of salt mixed with rainwater and the beat of rain on the shed roof.

In the distance, a voice called out. *"Andi?"*

\*\*\*

Mr. Vole mopped at the perspiration on his brow and upper lip. "Mr. Moore's business practices are above reproach."

Sophie clenched her hands together beneath the table. Someone within Gerald's company had shared the truth behind the glossy pictures and columns of numbers printed in the annual report.

Mr. Vole stood up. "You aren't wise to believe the lies of a disgruntled employee."

"Not disgruntled. Afraid." Michael set his pen down. "Afraid they'll take the brunt of the blame when the façade crumbles."

"Accounting isn't my forte."

For the first time Brown spoke. "No, but the law *is* your expertise." He drew a photo from the folder he carried and slid it toward Mr. Vole. "You know blackmail is against the law."

Sophie gasped. On the desk before her lay a mug shot of the man who'd taken her picture at the sport camp. Her stomach turned queasy remembering last night and the immoral behavior Mr. Vole implied.

Face ashen, Mr. Vole sank back into his chair. He stared at the photo before lifting his eyes to Sophie.

Her heart sped up at the hatred reflected in his gaze.

The detective tapped the photo. "He's in custody."

\*\*\*

On his left, the iron-gray water frothed with white caps hiding the mudflats beneath roiling water. Gray half-walked, half-swam through the flooded low marsh. Cordgrass tugged at his water-filled boots and sawed at his hands. Careful not to stumble into a mosquito ditch, he kept his eyes trained on the high marsh where tall reeds waved in the wind and rain.

In Maine, he'd told Andi to head for higher ground if the river water rose. Would she remember? Did she get into the upper marsh before the tide overtook the flats? Might not have done her any good. Even the upper marsh was under water today. In this extreme high tide, fingers of brackish water reached into the uplands.

Beneath the water's surface a school of tiny mummichogs swirled past. Ignoring the cold seeping into his muscles Gray pressed on, scanning the dense mass of reeds towering above him, searching for sign of Andi passing that way.

The wind carried the chug of an outboard motor across the water. The rescue boat nosed through the chop, navigating the far edge of the marsh.

He paused at a break in the wall of reeds. Some were bent, others broken off completely. Something or someone had forced their way through. Searching out solid ground underfoot, he propelled his way through the break, studying the damaged foliage.

The water became shallower as he moved toward the upland, following the narrow trail before him. Local kids could have played here or a dog or curious deer may have wandered through before the flooding. He pressed on, coming out of the water where the reeds thinned giving way to small hillocks of rush. The cold wind, fierce and chilling, blew across a salt hay meadow dotted with marsh elder and bayberry.

The waterlogged ground squished beneath Gray's boot. The trail melded into the tufts and cowlicks of the tall grass. He glanced back wondering if Andi could be neck-deep in water, or worse. But an unknown force urged him forward and his searching gaze followed. "Andi?" The buffeting wind and pelting rain absorbed his shout. He drew back his lips and whistled, sharp and clear. If she heard him, could she answer? Would he hear her if she did? He stopped and whistled again.

The whipping wind carried a small cry, like that of a catbird.

Surrounded by nature's white noise of wind and rain, Gray couldn't isolate the source of the sound. He issued another piercing whistle; again an answering cry followed. His heart jackhammered into his throat. To his right, low bayberry bushes skirted a thicket of marsh elder. Beyond the knoll and meadow, the backs of several summer cottages peeked out from behind a windrow of trees.

Gray jogged through the clumps of grass, gaze sweeping the area. "Andi?" On the ground among the low bayberries, a flash of blue caught his attention.

Drawing close, the blue was nothing more than a lid from someone's garbage can. He bent double to breathe. Rain thumped his back as he whispered "God, help me find her."

From deep in the clump of elders another cry went up.

Taking no heed of the branches clawing at his clothing, Gray pushed through the close growing bushes.

"Gray!"

Bits of purple flashed in the brush. He scrambled closer.

Andi!

She crawled on hands and knees through the close interwoven shrubs. He reached out and pulled her into his arms. She clung to him trying to talk between the sobs convulsing her thin torso. "I...knew...you'd come...f-for me." She hiccupped and wrapped her arms around his neck.

"I got you, honey." His throat jammed with emotion. What made him head toward *this* particular grove of marsh elder? The urge to move forward – had that been the Holy Spirit's doing?

He peeled her arms from around his neck and took inventory. The smell of mud flats at low tide clung to her. Globs of mud stuck in her hair. Scratches scored her cheeks. "Your foot." Lacerations, smeared with blood, cut deep into the sole of her shoeless foot.

Andi's lips, blue with cold, wobbled. "S-something scared me."

"Ran out of your shoe?"

She shivered violently. "D-dark. Couldn't find it."

Gray lifted her. "Let's get you out of here."

Pushing his way out of the thicket, Gray protected Andi from the worst of the branches. Crossing the meadow, he fought the battering wind and cold steady rain as he headed toward the line of trees and cottages. A shout carried on the wind soon followed by the scream of a siren. A volunteer hastened out to meet him, her fearful face breaking into a grin when she saw Andi was alive and responsive.

An EMT hustled toward them. "I'll take her."

Gray shouldered past him carrying Andi to the back of the ambulance. He sat inside the open door. Someone draped a warm dry blanket across his shoulders and tucked another around Andi still snug in his arms. He refused to relinquish her.

The EMT did his best to work around him.

"Why'd you run, Andi?"

Her eyes filled with tears. "I want to live with you."

Gray rested his chin on the top of her head, his insides soft as jelly. "Don't you want to live with Mommy?"

Andi nodded. The grit in her hair scraped his chin. "But Mr. Vole said today would be a disaster."

Gray stiffened. "When did he say that?"

"Last night when he came to our house. He showed Mommy a picture and said he could make it go away."

Rage flared to life in Gray's gut.

She shoved hair out of her face. "What did that mean?"

"I'm not sure." Better not mean what he was guessing. "What did your mom do?"

"She called Michael."

*Thank you, God.* "Were you spying again, Andi?"

Andi shook her head. "He came while Mommy

showed me the map you gave her. I didn't listen on purpose." She frowned. "Is that spying?"

Gray hugged her close then loosened his grip when the EMT cleared his throat in annoyance. "You shouldn't have run away."

"How do you play blackmail?"

He nearly choked on his tongue. "What?"

"Mommy told Mr. Vole it was blackmail and he told her not to play games."

The man wouldn't live past today. "I'll talk to your mom." His voice rasped with fury. "I'll ask her what he meant." *And try to remember I'm one of the good guys now.*

# Chapter 25

The rap on the door startled Sophie.

Jack entered and stepped aside to allow Gerald and Suzanne Moore to enter the room.

Sophie stiffened. Fear and anger roiled inside her. *Forgive me God, but I'm struggling not to hate them.* Clutching her purse so tight her fingers ached, she willed herself to stay calm.

Jack stepped out of the room and closed the door.

"Why are we here?" Ever the man in charge, Gerald Moore looked around the room. "Vole." He extended his hand dismissing Sophie without a word. "Care to explain why we were contacted by someone from SeaMount about my granddaughters?"

Michael stood and introduced himself and Detective Brown. "I contacted you. Please, won't you sit?"

"I haven't much time."

"Then right to the point. I have a request. Please withdraw your suit for custody of the Moore girls."

Surprise brought Moore up short. He guffawed. "No. Are we done here?"

"No." Cool in the face of Moore's disdain, Michael continued. "As Sophie's lawyer..."

Moore directed an icy glare at Vole.

"...I've concluded the accusation of negligence is without merit. Your sole purpose for such a claim is to gain access to the money your son set aside for his daughters."

Gerald wanted the money? Sophie dabbed at the corner of her eyes. What part did Suzanne play in all this? She looked at her mother-in-law from beneath her lashes, but tears blurred her vision.

Moore waved a dismissive hand. "Nonsense. Why would I do that?"

"Your firm is on the brink of fiscal collapse."

Apart from Suzanne's stifled gasp, the room remained deathly quiet.

Sophie trembled with anxiety.

His face a mottled red, Moore's gaze landed on Sophie. Hostility emanated from him. "What lies have you spread?" He shook his head. His smile a mere show of teeth. "It doesn't matter. Andi ran away. No judge will ignore that."

Sophie's stomach lurched. Her hand flew to her mouth. She willed herself not to throw up in front of this roomful of people.

Unperturbed, Michael pointed at the photo on the table. "Your minion, George Frost, traveled to Maine with instructions to discover anything he could, even if he had to invent it, to damage Sophie Moore's reputation."

Moore blustered. "I don't know what you're talking about."

Detective Brown stood and faced Moore. "We

have Frost in custody. He's more than willing to share what he knows. He admits to participating in the unlawful entry of Sophie Moore's home and the vandalizing of her property," the detective's gaze swung across the table, "with the aid of Vole."

Mr. Vole's complexion turned deathly white. The swift turn of the conversation left Sophie reeling.

Moore spun on his heel. "I'm done here." Before he could reach the door, it swung open with an abrupt bang.

Gray stepped into the room with Andi in his arms.

Sophie cried out. Jumping to her feet, she scrambled around the table. "Andi!" Tears of joy and sobs of relief mingled with whispered words of love as she lifted Andi from Gray's arms. "Oh, sweetie." Gazing at her daughter's dirty scratched face, she didn't know whether to laugh or cry. She lifted her face to Gray. "I'm so glad you're here."

He stroked her cheek with his finger. "I couldn't be any place else."

Sophie clutched Andi tight and turned to Michael. After only this moment having Andi returned to her, would she lose her again?

Quick footfalls echoed in the corridor. Jack opened the door to admit two uniformed policemen into the already crowded room.

Beside her, Gray stiffened. His fists clenched at his sides. His warm expression hardened into a fierce mask.

Bravado gone, Moore stood unmoving and pale. Mr. Vole sat in his chair, visibly shaking.

"I promised the EMT a doctor would check out Andi." Gray looked from Michael to the detective.

"May Sophie go with her?"

Detective Brown smiled and nodded.

"I believe we're about done here." Michael stepped away from the table. "Hanna and Lissa are at the library with Aggie."

Sophie wanted to hear the words. "The girls are mine?" She looked at Andi. "No one will take them?"

Michael smiled at Sophie and looked at Moore standing stone-faced beside his weeping wife. "I'd say the custody suit has been withdrawn."

Heart filled to overflowing, Sophie's gaze bounced between Andi and Gray. Giddy with joy she said the first thing that came to mind. "You're both filthy." Silly with relief, she hugged Andi closer and squeezed her eyes shut. *Thank you, God. Thank you.*

\*\*\*

"Preach will drive you to the hospital." Gray herded Sophie out the door. "I have some business to attend to." He stepped back into the room. A desperate war raged inside him narrowing his field of vision to the double-dealing rodent who'd violated Sophie's trust. He wanted to tear Vole limb from limb. Moore, he'd happily take out quickly, but Vole deserved to suffer.

A firm grip stopped Gray's advance on the two men being taken into custody by the uniformed officers and Detective Brown.

"Kerr. Stop and think." Michael eased up. "They aren't worth it."

Fists clenched, he stared at them. "They hurt Sophie."

"Let it go, Kerr. 'It is mine to avenge, I will repay, says the Lord'."

"I want to help Him."

Michael shook his head. "Leave the outcome to God and the judicial system."

The two men were escorted out of the room. Suzanne followed, sobbing into a handkerchief.

Michael's hand tightened. "You do something stupid, you won't be around for Sophie and the girls."

Gray listened to their footsteps fade. His muscles hurt from tension. He closed his eyes willing the monster back into its dark corner. How long would he wrestle with the brute? Did he deserve to work for SeaMount?

"All of us battle some flaw or temptation, Gray. Being human doesn't disqualify us from serving."

He opened his eyes. Had he spoken aloud? "Sophie deserves better."

"Why don't you let her be the judge of that?"

Because I'm scared she'll run the other way if I show this part of me.

Michael gathered up his papers and slipped them into his briefcase. "I have some loose ends to tie up here. Why not ride back to SeaMount with me and clean up some before you go to Sophie's place."

\*\*\*

The cool ocean water sluiced over his skin as muscles and tendons propelled him forward. Gray dove and swam deep. His stomach scraped the sandy bottom. The sting matched the soreness in his heart. Would he have won his internal battle at the courthouse if Michael hadn't reasoned with him? He pulled and kicked until his lungs burned, forcing him to the surface.

On his left, the water swirled. In the low light of

the evening sun, he recognized the slicked-back shock of light hair.

Whit swam with him.

A cocky flash of pearly whites issued a challenge Gray couldn't ignore. He ramped up his speed and the race was on. He'd hit two markers before he registered a second man swimming to his right. For an instant, the sun cast Preach's profile in chiseled relief.

Gray gave no quarter, pushing his endurance, testing that of the other two men. He let his mind drift to Sophie only to skitter away like a frightened crab. He feared the darkness in him would taint the memory of her gentle beauty.

Hands grabbed his ankles. Weight bore down on his back. As he went under, Gray twisted and thrust a brutal elbow to his assailant's ribs. The water churned with his counter attack before he fully realized it was the idiots he swam with that had ambushed him and were doing their best to drown him.

He fought them back to the surface and pulled Whit into a headlock. Gasping for air, they wrestled and broke apart.

Preach moved to flank him, but Gray would have none of it. Treading water he returned their disgruntled glares. "Sore losers."

Whit wiped the hair from his eyes. "You're not human, Kerr."

"Half fish." Preach turned and struck out for shore. Gray and Whit followed.

Above the wrackline where the turning tide had deposited marine flotsam on the sand, they collapsed to catch their breath while staring up at the darkening sky.

Whit heaved a sigh. "Thought you'd be with

Sophie whooping it up."

Gray closed his eyes and swallowed around the lump in his throat. "She's probably glad to have time alone with the girls."

"Michael told us what happened." Preach rubbed his bruised ribs and sat up.

Refusing to be drawn into a conversation he didn't want to have, Gray said nothing. Preach didn't take the hint. "We all have demons we fight."

Whit snorted. "Speak for yourself."

Preach threw a clod of mud at him.

"Hey!" Whit fended off the wet projectile. "I spent the last four days with him while you and the rest of the jackals hunted us like bunnies."

Keeping his eyes shut, Gray smirked at the mental picture.

"And we would've caught you if you'd stuck to the game plan." Preach cast an ominous scowl in Whit's direction.

"We made plans that didn't include you."

"We noticed."

"When?"

"When the horse woman proclaimed the dogs needed water and treats and wouldn't take no for an answer." Preach threw a pebble into the foaming waves. "Logan caught up with me about that time. Told me to report in at SeaMount."

Whit chuckled. "Mz. Rhetta's one determined woman."

Gray opened one eye. Whit's direct gaze was trained on him.

"You're a fool if you don't take your sorry self to Sophie's place to celebrate." Whit jabbed the piece of driftwood he played with into the sand. "I'll go over and celebrate with her if you don't."

Gray swore and jackknifed to a sitting position.

Whit grinned. "Cursing ain't allowed here."

Staring out over the glittering ocean, Gray voiced what troubled him. "I could have easily killed both those men today."

Preach leaned back on his elbows with a groan. "Justice needs to be meted out."

"Somebody I love gets threatened," Whit tossed the driftwood into the waves lapping at the shore, "I'd have the same urge."

Gray's heart pounded triple time. What if Sophie didn't want a rough-around-the-edges soldier? "According to Sam, I'm on my second warning. Says I don't follow orders." A mild stating of the facts. Sam's reprimand still rang in his ears. "I'm going with Caleb to South America. Even if I play by the rules this time and stay with SeaMount, Sophie deserves to have a man who comes home every night."

Whit wrapped his arms around his raised knees. "I'd figure out something to hold onto a woman who looked at me the way Sophie looks at you."

Sick of talking about his own woes Gray jabbed Whit in the ribs. "That what you were doing with Mz. Rhetta?"

Preach sat up straight. "The horse woman?"

"No." Whit scowled. "She's twice my age."

Gray snorted. "You were two-stepping in the middle of the barnyard with her and her trusty pitchfork."

Preach guffawed earning a stinging clout to his bicep. Countering the strike, he dove at Whit and the jesting spun into an all out wrestling match.

Taking the chance to get out of Dodge, Gray jumped up and beat feet for the locker room.

# Chapter 26

Gray tugged on the collar of his leather jacket and loosened his grip on the flowers he held. *What if she hates the flowers?* He cast an uneasy glance at the box resting at his feet. *Too late to worry about what he'd done.* Taking a deep breath, he rang the doorbell.

A flurry of movement preceded the door swinging open. Lissa spotted the flowers and yelled, "Mooom."

A bang in the kitchen followed by hurried footsteps set his heart racing.

"For heaven's sake, Lissa, don't yell –" Sophie stopped. "Gray?"

He reached down to snag the box by the twine wrapped around it and stepped across the threshold. "Am I too late to help you celebrate?"

Eyes on the flowers and box, Sophie shook her head. "No."

Dressed in pajamas, Andi and Hanna ran into the room and skidded up to him on socked feet.

"Gray!" Andi flung her arms around his waist.

He lifted the flowers to keep them from getting crushed and dropped the box on the couch. "Got off all

287

the mud, I see."

She giggled and grasped his belt.

He held out the flowers to Sophie. "These are for you."

Taking the daisies, she sniffed and thumbed the corner of her eye.

*She hates them. They remind her of things she'd rather forget.* "If you don't like them you can throw them out. I thought..." He ran out of air and quit talking.

Her soft gaze was shiny with tears. "They're beautiful." Her smile was a balm to his aching heart. "Where did you pick them?"

"The side of the road." Heat worked its way up his neck.

She smiled. "They remind me of Maine and the obstacles we've overcome. Together."

Gray breathed easier. He'd thought the same thing when he picked them.

"What's in the box?" Lissa stood beside the couch fiddling with the twine.

Andi leaned on the overstuffed arm and patted the lid. "Is it a present?"

He cleared his throat, hoping he hadn't truly messed up this time. "It's for your mom."

Sophie stepped back, curiosity mingled with uncertainty as she eyed the huge white-lidded box. "Today isn't my birthday."

"It's not a birthday present."

"But – "

"Just open it." She might be angry with him for what he'd done. The not-knowing was killing him.

Sophie fingered a daisy. "I'll put these in water."

"Hustle it." Delay tactics. He'd allow her this one.

\*\*\*

Sophie hurried to the kitchen and took a cut glass vase from the cupboard. What the flowers lacked in florist perfection they made up for tenfold with special meaning.

Against her better judgment she'd fallen in love with Gray. The desire to know the heart of the man hidden beneath the tough exterior grew stronger each time they were together. Setting the daisies in the center of the dinner table, she returned to the living room.

Gray stood at the end of the couch where she'd left him, tapping the side of his thigh with his hand. The girls crowded around the box, testing its weight, trying to guess the contents.

"Let your mother sit." Gray's face wore an expressionless mask.

What had he done? Was he afraid she wouldn't like his gift? Sophie sat and lifted the box to her lap. She pulled the end of the cotton twine unraveling the bow and with the girls' help, pulled the string free.

She lifted the lid.

Sophie's breath caught. A patchwork of finely stitched dark maroon, navy and beige fabric lay nestled in white tissue paper.

With trembling hands she pulled her mother's quilt from the box. Tears backed up in her throat and made speech impossible as she unfolded the first layer. Matching fabric and tiny stitches repaired the once shredded corner.

Gray cleared his throat. "I had it professionally restored and cleaned. It's not perfect like before but..." He gestured with his hand.

"Oh, Gray. It's wonderful."

"...maybe... It is?" A hint of a smile played across his lips as if he were afraid to believe her.

"Yes. It's more than wonderful." A tear escaped. She tried to smile, but trembling lips didn't allow her to bend her mouth the right way.

The couch cushion next to her sank and his arms wrapped around her. "I didn't mean to make you cry."

"They're happy tears." Had she left her precious quilt at home during the weekend trip, it would have been destroyed beyond repair. Catching her breath, she straightened away from him. "Help me unfold it, girls. I want to see every inch."

Held aloft by her daughters and Gray, Sophie drank in the restored beauty of the mariner's compass, each tiny patch a testament to their time in the wilderness. Odd how she could look back on those long, difficult days and heart-stopping events and not feel a bit of anger or horror.

"Thank you, Gray." Sophie ran a hand across one tip of the compass where her mother's old work melded with the new. "This is the nicest thing anyone has ever done for me."

He visibly relaxed for the first time since coming through the door. "I know how much the quilt means to you." Helping her refold it, he glanced toward the kitchen. "Do I smell cake?"

"As a matter of fact, you do. A celebration calls for cake and ice cream." Sophie tucked the last corner into the box. "Come have some with us."

\*\*\*

The counter wiped clean and the last dish in the washer, Sophie peeked into the living room.

Gray sat on the couch with the girls watching a DVD of fairytales. He looked so right with Hanna on his lap and the other two snuggled close on either side of him. Her heart warmed at the sight. *Lord, what am I to do about him?*

"Okay, ladies. Time for bed."

Gray wrapped his hand around Andi's arm as she scooted off the couch. "You won't ever take off again, right?"

She nodded.

"Good. I'll trust you on that. Give me a hug."

Sophie marveled at the moisture in Gray's eyes.

Settling the girls for the night took longer than usual. All of them, including Sophie, wanted extra hugs and kisses. She had asked God for the day to end like this – with her girls in their own beds. *Thank you, Lord.*

Gray stood in the living room studying a DVD case. "Didn't know about all the violence in fairytales. Two kids get stuffed in an oven!"

"If the girls hadn't gone to bed, you'd have witnessed a wolf eating a little boy no bigger than a thumb."

An awkward silence followed.

She longed to walk up to him, wrap her arms around him and lean into his strength.

He tossed the case aside. "I like what you did with the house."

"Thanks." To keep her hands from reaching for him she fluffed a throw pillow on the couch. "Sam made the clean up and redecorating as painless as possible."

Gray roughed his hand over his hair. "I hear a 'but' in there."

She hesitated. "I don't want to sound ungrateful."

"But?"

"It doesn't feel like home anymore. Not because of the new furniture. That's all lovely. But someone broke in and..." Her voice wobbled. "I trusted..." And then her arms *were* wrapped around Gray. She leaned against him embraced in his warmth.

Beneath her hair his hand massaged her nape. "They stole your sense of safety, Sophie." His lips rested soft against her ear.

"Yes." The cotton of his shirt caressed her cheek. His heart beat strong beneath her ear. She tried not to cry but couldn't hold back the tears. The day's emotional extremes had taken their toll.

"Let it out, sweetheart. You've had one...*bad*...day."

In the deluge of tears a tiny giggle hiccupped from her lips. "Y-You almost swore."

He pulled her tighter against him. "Yeah. It's a bad habit I have. But I know a fine woman who's helping me break it."

The storm of tears soon passed leaving Sophie exhausted and content to stay within the circle of Gray's arms. "You were to come home tomorrow."

"When I found out Andi had gone missing, I figured out a way to finish the trial sooner."

"I thought Mr. Vole wanted to help me." She shuddered and Gray hugged her closer. "Why didn't I see the reality?"

He leaned back and ran his hand up her arm. "You're honest and trusting. You had no reason to suspect him of anything underhanded."

Her skin tingled where he touched. "But you did.

Right away."

"A talent I've honed over the years."

She hurt for him and wished his life experiences hadn't made him so wary, though his suspicious nature had served her well this time. "Thank you."

He sighed. His breath ruffled her hair. "Andi's home and the girls are yours, forever." He pressed his lips against her temple.

Her nerves hummed with the attraction sparking between them.

He cleared his throat and shifted his weight. "Sam has given me my next assignment."

The blissful haze of contentment evaporated under the scrutiny of his troubled expression. "Where are you going?"

"South America with Caleb. We fly out late tomorrow."

Dismayed, her breath left her in a gust. "You're officially employed by SeaMount?"

"I'll know once I'm back from this mission."

Sophie rested against him and closed her eyes. Was she brave enough to let herself truly love this man? *Lord, what do you want for us?*

"Soph?"

"Mmm?"

"I won't be gone long." Beneath her cheek his chest expanded. "Can you wait for me to get back?"

Her eyes popped open. "Wait?"

"Yeah." His arms tightened around her. "So we can figure out this thing between us?"

Cheek against his incredibly hard muscles, she squeezed her eyes shut and opened them again. "This 'thing'?"

He brushed his mouth across her hair. "I never expected I'd be lucky enough to find someone like you and I don't want to lose you before...before..."

She lifted her head and cupped her hands to his face. "Do you believe the minute your plane takes off, I'm going to go out and find someone to take your place?" She wasn't sure what exactly his 'place' in her life was at the moment, but that wasn't the point.

"Some of the men..."

"What men? SeaMount men?"

He nodded. "They think you're pretty special."

"And you? Do you think I'm special?"

Gray groaned and without any warning claimed her lips with his own. She clung to him. He tasted of peppermint. His beard scratched her chin. Their breath merged in shared passion.

He lifted his head, breathing as though he'd run a hard race. "You're more than special." His chest expanded with a deep breath. "We've known each other for what is really only a short time..."

Voice raspy with emotion, she ran her fingertips across his cheek. "But it feels like I've known you forever."

His warm pewter gaze drifted over her face. "I've never felt like this about anyone before."

Her heart fluttered with nervous elation, the thrill of his declaration tempered with the fear of navigating uncharted waters. "This 'thing' between us...it scares me."

"Me, too."

"You? You're never afraid."

"Oh yeah I am. I was sick with fear just this morning."

Her whispered "Me too" ignited another fierce kiss that wasn't about the press of body against body but the melding of souls. Something intangible shifted. Beneath a flood of longing, the barriers around Sophie's heart buckled. Her mind scrambled to wedge them back in place.

He stroked his hand down her back and pulled her closer. She surrendered the fight and opened the gates to her heart.

\*\*\*

Gray broke off the kiss and willed his heart to stop pounding so hard he feared it'd burst through the wall of his chest. He'd never known anyone as giving and full of love as Sophie. Why didn't he admit it? He loved the woman. "I should go while my intentions are still honorable."

She stared at the first button on his shirt. "Alright."

"Hey. You okay?" He ran his thumb along her jaw.

"Yes."

"You're a horrible liar." With his finger under her chin, he nudged her to look at him. The urge to kiss her trembling bottom lip speared through him. Instead, he ran his thumb along the edge. "What are you thinking?"

She stepped back. "You haven't even left and I miss you. I'm not sure I can handle this part of a relationship with you."

"Being a part of SeaMount is important to me, Sophie." She stood within an arm's length but loneliness swept through him. "I've seen how easily a man can be sucked into doing evil all in the name of good." He roughed his hand over his hair. "The monster inside reminded me of that today."

She frowned. "The monster?"

*Here it was then.* "I'm a warrior, Sophie. Trained to kill in more ways than you can imagine. Knowing what Vole..." Gray shrugged uncomfortably. "Revenge might have appeased some of my rage."

"Revenge is best left to God, Gray."

"Which is why I want to be certain I'm using my skills for good. God led me to SeaMount. And you."

She stepped close and placed a feathery kiss on his lips. "You're a good man, Gray."

Yeah, that's what he was hoping.

# Chapter 27

Gray dumped his gear in the corner of his room and made a beeline for the shower. Four weeks of stifling heat, humidity and foreign soil needed washing away before he drove to Sophie's. She didn't expect him home for another three days.

The event he and Caleb worked had wrapped up early when a key Arab delegate took offense and walked out, his pristine white *thobe* in the proverbial twist.

Out of habit he checked the walls and floor of the shower for crawling occupants before he stepped under the stream of water.

While away he'd lived for the moments he'd found to call Sophie. The conversations opened windows to her soul he might have missed if they hadn't been forced to talk.

He came back sure of one thing. He loved Sophie Moore. If he had to give up SeaMount to have a life with her, he was ready. "I surrender the job to you, Lord." Now those were amazing words coming from his lips.

Whipping a towel across his neck and back, he drank in the fresh scent. Not a whiff of tropical mold or mildew. He dressed and looked out the window at the ocean below.

On the beach, the fabric of a colorful umbrella flapped gently in the breeze. Children splashed and played in the shallows. One tyke reminded him of Andi. Her wet braids flapped with each jump of a wave. She held hands with a tiny pale haired—

Gray's heart stopped.

He dove for his pack and yanked out his tactical binoculars. *Turn around. Turn around.*

Scanning the beach, he found a third older girl. Adjusting the focus, he zeroed in on the woman beneath the umbrella. Oh, yeah.

He lowered the binoculars. *Oooh, yeah!*

\*\*\*

"Eeee!"

A cold bottle of water slid across Sophie's warm back.

She tried to scramble away, but a strong arm pinned her face down on the blanket. A low chuckle vibrated in her ear.

"I'm not letting you go, sweetheart."

"Gray!" Breathless with joy, she pounded her fist against the only part of him she could reach – his forearm. "Let me up."

"Nope." He nuzzled her neck.

The air erupted with high-pitched squeals, skinny arms, sandy knees and giggling as the three girls threw themselves into a pig pile on top of Sophie and Gray.

Squished at the bottom, Sophie's laughter ended with a groan.

Gray's deep voice tickled her ear. "Isn't this the way we met?"

Her face, mashed against the blanket, muffled her words. "You're outnumbered, tough guy."

"And I couldn't be happier. Ow! Hey!" He jerked away to dodge another flying body part. "Excuse me. I have something to take care off." He pushed up off the blanket.

Sophie rolled over to watch.

Hanna dangled from Gray's neck and Andi clung to his back. Lissa tumbled off his legs into the sand as he raced for the water. Andi giggled and flopped with each jarring step. He plowed waist deep into the water and dunked under with both girls.

They surfaced screeching and splashing.

Grabbing them around the waist, one under each arm, he waded back to shore where Lissa stood laughing at her sisters. Dumping his giggling load on the sand, Gray jogged to the blanket, shook off and sat next to her. "Now where were we?"

Water beaded in his hair, ran down his face and off his chin. Sunlight sparkled in the rivulets of moisture on his neck. Giving up the fight to keep her hands to herself, Sophie reached out and smoothed the palm of her hand across his jaw. "Welcome home."

He grasped her wrist and turned his face into her hand. The brush of his lips on her palm sent tingles coursing through her. All the lonely hours, waiting for him to call, praying for his safe return, faded away. She could see the Lord's hand in their time apart. "I missed you."

He lifted his head. His eyes, warm with desire, roved over her face. Leaning closer he touched her lips with his in a soft kiss.

"I missed you, too," he whispered before he claimed her lips with a hard insistence that stole her breath away.

They broke it off when the choice became come up for air or black out.

Gasping, a breathless giggle escaped her. She buried her face in the curve of his neck and breathed in the masculine scent of him.

His lips found her ear lobe and nibbled, his voice velvet soft in her ear. "I love you, Sophie Moore."

Her heart leapt in her breast. He'd presented her the greatest gift he had to give – his heart. She slid her arms around him. "And I love you, Gray Kerr."

He peppered kisses across her brow and cheek. "I've been thinking. If you'd be happier, I can give up SeaMount."

She pressed her fingers to his lips stopping his words. "But you've worked hard to become one of them."

"I'm officially theirs now. They can call me any time. If you can't live with that, I'm willing to find a different job."

She shushed him. "Right now I don't want to think about anything other than you're home and here with me." She rested her hand on his chest. "Kiss me."

She didn't need to ask him twice. With the first caress of his lips, her thoughts scattered to the four winds.

Ear-piercing screams and drops of icy water cooled the passion simmering between them. Andi stood close by taunting a dripping wet Lissa with the now empty plastic pail. Screeching, they raced back to the water for refills.

Gray recaptured her attention. "How about dinner tonight?"

Sophie tried to pull together a coherent answer. "The girls...a babysitter..."

His knowing smile warmed her further. "The girls can come, too." With his thumb, he brushed sand from her cheek. "I want to be sure all four of you love me."

"You do?" Her lungs didn't want to work.

"Yeah. When I ask you to marry me, I need to know the girls want it too."

"Oohhh."

"So, where do you want to go?" His fingers toyed with her hair.

She couldn't think beyond the words, 'when I ask you to marry me'. They'd have a long engagement, maybe a year. Or, she could plan a simple wedding for three months from today.

He frowned. "Sophie, you *do* want to go to dinner, right?"

His question jerked her back to the decision at hand. She nodded. "Yes, but I can't think where."

He turned toward the water and let out an ear-splitting whistle. The girls came on the run, spraying sand and water in their wake.

"Where do you want to go for dinner?"

The three looked at each other then shouted in unison. "Frankie's."

Needing guidance, he glanced at Sophie.

"It's a diner downtown. The décor is a Fifties theme. Best burgers in town."

"Okay then. Frankie's diner it is."

The girls let out a whoop.

"Go collect your sand pails while your mother and I pick up the rest of the stuff." He stood and held a hand out to Sophie.

She didn't hesitate to slip her hand in his.

\*\*\*

Gray understood why the girls loved Frankie's Diner. The color pink dominated the décor. Not even the black booths and trim could subdue the bright neon walls. Vintage vinyl records hung amidst photos and posters of celebrities from the 50's.

Lissa spattered ketchup on the table as well as her burger. Andi built a log cabin with her fries. Most of Hanna's meal clung to her shirt. All their faces wore contented smiles, including Sophie's.

He wiped his hands on a napkin. This was what Joe Q. Public felt like on a family outing. Normal. He could do this. "Are you going to church tomorrow morning?"

Sophie licked chocolate milkshake from her lips and nodded. "Sunday school and church. Can you come with us?"

Other than the chapel across from SeaMount, he'd never been to church. Or rather, he'd never gone inside another church while a worship service was in session. He'd slept in a bombed out church once in Nicaragua, but that had nothing to do with worship.

"I'd like that." His cell phone vibrated.

Hand in mid-air, Sophie paused, her eyes wide and questioning.

He pulled the phone from his pocket. His heart sank. He flipped it open. "Yeah?"

Sam's voice grated through the earpiece. "I need you back here now. We have a situation."

Gray rubbed his eyes. When was there *not* a situation? "Give me twenty minutes."

"Make it ten."

He snapped the phone closed. "SeaMount. I've got to go."

Sophie's expression told him she knew by morning he'd be gone to parts unknown, far from the country church where she worshiped. She reached out and grasped his hand. "It's okay."

Her attempt to be brave only increased his frustration.

The ride back to SeaMount was quiet. Sophie drove her van into the rear parking lot and up to the service entrance. She turned the ignition to OFF. "Everybody out." She turned to him. "We're going to give you a proper goodbye."

He wanted to kiss the brave smile right off her lips.

"I'm sorry, Sophie. I'd hoped this wouldn't happen so soon after getting back." He glanced toward the entrance. "Not even twelve hours."

She ducked her head and reached for the door handle.

Hanna held both hands high and he hoisted her into his arms. "Bye, Princess. You be good for your mama." Reluctantly, he handed her off to Sophie.

Andi flung her arms around his neck. "I don't want you to go."

His throat constricted leaving him unable to offer his pixie any solace other than a bear hug.

He turned to find Lissa standing next to him. Her restrained hug and whispered, "Come back fast," cast an unexpected beacon of hope into a still dark corner of his heart.

Gathering Sophie into his arms, he buried his face in the slope of her neck and inhaled. Cinnamon and Sophie.

She trembled in his arms.

Lord, why do I have to leave now? "I love you."

Sophie gave him a half-hearted shove. "Go. People are depending on you and your skills. We're safe and happy and will be waiting for you to come home."

He lingered, helping her load the kids back in the van. In the process he took every opportunity to touch Sophie and steal kisses.

Then he stood alone and watched until the taillights of her van disappeared over the rise in the road.

*** 

She would not cry. Crying did nothing but give her a juicy red nose and bloodshot eyes. Sophie sniffed and set out Andi's dress for church the following day.

Gray insisted working for SeaMount was his calling. From her own ordeal she'd learned there were times when people needed heroes and the men of SeaMount weren't afraid to be God's tool in the dark and dangerous corners of the world.

Dressed in pajamas, Andi ran into the room and jumped on the bed with a satisfactory bounce.

"How'd you do?" Sophie tipped her daughter's chin and inspected the teeth bared in a Cheshire cat grin. Pronounced clean, Andi found her hairbrush and knelt on the bed her back to her mom. With long strokes, she brushed Andi's hair.

"Mommy?"

"Hmm?"

"Are you going to marry Gray?"

Sophie's hands stopped. "Why do you ask?"

"You kissed him on the beach and when you said goodbye."

*Oh dear!* "Would you mind?"

Andi started to shake her head and thought better of it. "I'd like that."

Lissa padded into the room followed by Hanna. "Like what?"

"Mommy marrying Gray. And get out of my room. I didn't invite you."

"Andi." Sophie's reprimand earned a disgusted little huff.

Lissa cast a sly glance at her sister before climbing on the bed and helping Hanna up. "When?"

Sophie sighed. "You're jumping to conclusions, girls. I can't just decide to marry him. He has to ask me to marry him." From what he'd said at the beach, he was contemplating marriage. But, thinking about it and actually taking the steps to do it were two very different things.

Lissa leaned back on the pillow. "I don't want to forget Daddy."

Sophie's heart twisted. "Neither do I, baby. We won't. I promise." She handed Andi the brush and braided her hair.

Finished, Andi turned to her mother and declared with all the wisdom of a seven-year-old, "Maybe if you kiss him again, he'll ask you."

Prickly heat raced up Sophie's neck and cheeks. She climbed up on the bed and tickled Andi. "What if he doesn't want to kiss me again, Miss Smarty Pants?"

Giggles and silliness filled the room. Lissa and Hanna joined the tickle fest, poking and prodding any body they could reach.

Many breathless minutes later Sophie ordered the girls to bed, thankful she'd found a way to distract them from pursuing the kissing conversation.

"Good night, Andi." They rubbed noses and Sophie pecked both her cheeks.

Her hand was on the light switch when Andi's muffled voice stopped her.

"Mommy, Gray will kiss you again. He looks at you all lovey-dovey."

"Good night, Andi." Sophie turned out the light. *Lovey-dovey indeed!*

# Chapter 28

Gray wheeled his jeep into the church parking lot hoping and praying he arrived before the service ended.

Still in town after a sleepless night at SeaMount, he counted it a blessing he wasn't in Columbia. Sophie's fears had teeth. His line of work came with high risks and she'd already lost one husband.

Strains of organ music floated from the open windows of the church as Gray sprinted across the parking lot and up the steps. An elderly usher met him at the door, bulletins in one hand, the other outstretched in greeting. "Good morning! Welcome to God's house."

Gray grasped the thin hand. "Good morning." He glanced into the sanctuary where the congregation stood prepared to sing a hymn. "Is Sophie Moore here?"

The usher led Gray to the side aisle and pointed. "Half way down. Service is almost over."

Andi hung out of the end of the pew, her braids replaced by a long swinging ponytail tied up with a ribbon. He laid a gentle hand on her shoulder and looked over her head at Sophie's beautiful face lit up with surprise.

Andi flung her arms around him.

Lifting her into his arms, his gaze remained on Sophie. Moving into the pew, he set Andi down at the end. Lissa and Hanna stood between him and Sophie.

She held out the open hymnal.

Sharing a hymnal with Sophie. He wanted many more Sundays like this – together in church, surrounded by her daughters.

If all went as he hoped, they'd be his daughters, too.

He stumbled over the words he sang. He wanted to adopt them. Would they want him as their father? The thought made singing impossible.

The song completed, the pastor closed the service with prayer.

Gray didn't hear a word of it. Focused on his own prayer that the smurfs would love him as much as he loved them, he caught only the 'amen' at the end of the benediction.

Sophie snapped the hymnal shut and sank to the pew. "You're here." She waved her hands, flustered. "I seem to say that often."

Gray wanted to grab her and hug her tight but settled for taking her hand. "They didn't need us."

The smurfs chattered nonstop until Sophie hushed them. "Let's go to the playground." She glanced at Gray and he nodded, following them to the small playground behind the church parking lot.

Andi ran straight for the swings. Lissa and Hanna, dressed in their Sunday best, knelt in the sandbox. Sophie sat on the picnic table bench with her back against the table top, situated to watch both the swings and the sandbox.

Gray sat next to her. His entire future hinged on the next few minutes. "Things resolved themselves so the mission was scrubbed."

"I'm glad." A blush turned her smooth skin a pretty shade of pink.

"While on standby, I talked to Sam about my job and a future at SeaMount."

She reached out and grasped his arm. "Gray, this job means everything to you."

He sucked in a deep breath trying to stretch the band tightening around his chest. "Not as much as you mean to me."

Her hand squeezed his arm. He cleared his throat uncertain how to proceed. "I know this is fast, but what we've experienced tends to compress time." A nervous gust of laughter escaped his lips. "We work well together, Soph. We're a team."

Sophie frowned. "Are you trying to recruit me for SeaMount?"

"No!" He was making a mess of this. *Lord, a little help here? Please?* "You know I love you."

"And I love you." Her whispered response had him reaching for her, tasting her warm welcoming lips.

Giggles broke through the haze of love.

Sophie's arms around him were joined by a smaller pair with patting hands and a chorus of 'Mommy. Mommy.'

Gray pulled back.

Andi knelt on the table top, an arm slung around the neck of each adult. "Are we getting married?"

He guffawed, shocked by the pixie's audacity. He

began to laugh and couldn't stop. The blessed release of tension left him with tears streaming from his eyes.

Sophie rubbed his back. "Don't keel over on me, Gray."

Andi's gaze ricocheted back and forth between the adults. "Well?"

Regaining his composure he said, "I love your mother and she loves me."

Not to be outdone, Andi flung her other arm around him. "I love you, too."

"You do?" He wrapped an arm around her.

She tossed her ponytail back with her hand. "I do."

"That's real good. Because I love you." He tweaked her nose then smiled at Lissa and Hanna. "And I love you and you, too."

The girls reached for him and shared a hug.

"*Now* can we get married?" Persistent to the end, Andi frowned at her mother.

"If Gray wants to marry us."

He frowned. "Yes, I want to marry you. But this isn't how I expected a proposal of marriage to play out."

"What did you expect?" Sophie elbowed Andi aside and lifted her arms to encircle his neck.

"I figured a romantic evening with dinner and candlelight."

She kissed his cheek. "Instead, you're on the playground with an audience."

"Yeah." He looked around at the girls. "You're sure you want me as your new dad?"

Sophie reached up and placed her finger against his lips. "Listen to them, Gray. They want you to be their daddy as much as I want you for my husband. Even with the job you have. It's what God has called you to do. I accept that and will love you all the more when you're home."

"Actually, about the job." He cleared his throat. "I've taken on the training position. I'll be home more than I'm gone. Sam says I'll be less trouble for him if I work from the home base."

Her lovely face glowed. "You're sure you'll be happy?

Gray wrapped his arms around her. "I have you and my very own smurfs. How can I be anything but happy?"

# Epilogue

Gray stood at the front of the church looking out at the men who were like brothers. Eight months ago he hadn't known any of them. Now he couldn't imagine life without them. After all the hardship and dirt they dealt with on the job, the men were happy to have a celebration to enjoy.

The music started and his best man, Preach, elbowed him. Everyone stood and turned toward the church narthex.

Dressed in fluffy pale green gowns and crowned with daisy chain wreaths, the girls lined up to process down the aisle.

Lissa, thrilled to be the center of attention, measured each step as practiced the night before at rehearsal. Andi followed at a sedate trot, the ribbon on her flowers untied and flopping. She arrived at the altar on Lissa's heels, earning a frown from her sister. Hanna dawdled, distracted from either side of the aisle by doting 'uncles'. When she finally arrived at the front, Lissa showed her where to stand.

He loved them so much it hurt – in a good way.

Acting as Sophie's witness, Aggie marched down the aisle as though on parade. Tiny daisies ringed her ever-present bun. With each step her black comfort shoes peeked from beneath her dark green dress.

The bridal march swelled and Sophie stepped into view, radiant in an ivory gown carrying an airy bouquet of wildflowers.

Gray's heart expanded to the point of bursting. The sanctuary filled with people faded away and there was only Sophie, beaming with love, walking towards him. She reached the altar and he helped her up the step to stand at his side.

He said his vows aware the words he and Sophie spoke bound them together before God in a holy union. He loved this woman more than he ever thought he was capable of loving another person.

The minister turned to the girls. Gray held his breath. Sophie didn't know about this part of the ceremony.

"Do you Lissa, Andi and Hanna Moore, take this man to be your father, to love and honor for always?"

The unexpected question left the girls momentarily speechless.

Andi and Lissa glanced at each other.

Sophie's eyes sparkled with unshed tears.

"Yes." Andi dodged around her mother and wormed her hand beneath his dark suit jacket to grip his belt.

Taking Hanna's hand, Lissa stepped to Gray's side. "Yes for me and Hanna, too."

Happy tears made moist tracks on Sophie's cheeks. Tears Gray wanted to kiss away as his own heart turned to molten liquid in his chest.

In His infinite wisdom, God had blessed Gray, not with just the love of one good woman, but with the love of one good woman and three precious daughters.

"You may kiss the bride."

And to Andi's delight, he did.

# ABOUT THE AUTHOR

Anita lives in Rhode Island with her husband, son and a spoiled Belgian Malinois. When she's not writing, she enjoys reading, gardening, needlework, sewing and making cards. She hopes to one day get all her photos into scrapbooks.

Anita enjoys hearing from her readers. You can email her, akgreene@mac.com, or visit her website, http://anitakgreene.wordpress.com, or follow her on Facebook (Anita K Greene Author).

Made in the USA
Charleston, SC
10 September 2013